Spellbinding Tales
of Terror and Romance
Signet Double Gothics:

House of Dark Illusions

&

The Secret of the Chateau

House of
Dark Illusions

AND

The Secret of
the Chateau

by Caroline Farr

(/)
A SIGNET BOOK
NEW AMERICAN LIBRARY
TIMES MIRROR

IN ASSOCIATON WTH HOROWITZ PUBLICATIONS

House of Dark Illusions © Copyright 1973 by
Horwitz Publications, a division of Horwitz Group Books
Pty Ltd. (Hong Kong Branch), Hong Kong B.C.C.

The Secret of the Chateau © Copyright 1967 by
Horwitz Publications, a division of Horwitz Group Books
Pty Ltd. (Hong Kong Branch), Hong Kong B.C.C.

Originally appeared in paperback as separate volumes
published by The New American Library.

SIGNET TRADEMARK REG. U.S. PAT. OFF. AND FOREIGN COUNTRIES
REGISTERED TRADEMARK—MARCA REGISTRADA
HECHO EN CHICAGO, U.S.A.

SIGNET, SIGNET CLASSICS, MENTOR, PLUME AND MERIDIAN BOOKS
are published by The New American Library, Inc.,
1301 Avenue of the Americas, New York, New York 10019

First Printing (Double Gothic Edition), September, 1977

1 2 3 4 5 6 7 8 9

PRINTED IN THE UNITED STATES OF AMERICA

House of Dark Illusions

Chapter One

I was a confused and worried girl when the letter came from my aunt, Lissi Ferrari, inviting me to my dead mother's family home in Nova Scotia following the unexpected death of my father. If I had not been so disoriented, I might have had second thoughts about going to the Ferrari house. But then, the years, added to my own distress, had caused me to forget so many things.

My aunt's letter arrived by special delivery just as my father's attorney and friend, John Carson, was explaining to me that my father, who had been a professor of philosophy at a Boston college, had made provision of less than two thousand dollars in bonds, a small savings account, and the contents of our apartment on Boston's North Shore.

John Carson did not have to spell it out for me. It meant, for one thing, I would be unable to graduate. I would also have to find a smaller and cheaper apartment as well as a job if I were to conserve the small inheritance for as long as possible.

These considerations were very much on my mind when the letter arrived.

Even the envelope was unusual. There was a heavy black border around it that immediately caught my attention. It was very unusual, I thought, to see something like that in this day and age. Ostentatious? Yes, I guessed it was. Then I noticed the Canadian stamp and the Sussex Wold postmark. My curiosity quickened at once. The letter could only be from my mother's people in Nova Scotia. I was puzzled, because they were the people most unlikely to mourn my father. In fact, they had hated him even before my mother's death. I had been six years old at the time. They had always hated him. He had told me so.

"It's from my aunt in Nova Scotia," I explained to John Carson. "My mother's sister."

He looked as puzzled as I felt. He was smiling uncertainly. "I know, of course, that your father and your mother's family never did get along. Still, I think you did the right thing to inform them of your father's death."

"But I didn't." I frowned down at the black-bordered letter in my hand. "I didn't write to them."

"No?" His eyebrows lifted slightly. "Who would have told them?"

"I don't know. There are no other family ties in Boston. Or friends, as far as I know."

"There's probably a logical explanation," he said.

"Probably." I couldn't imagine what it might have been, though. As far as I was aware, the Ferraris were a closed community in themselves, with no need, or any desire, for contact with the outside world. From the little I had heard about them, I gathered that it was a rather strange, isolated family. My father had once told me that they spoke only French among themselves.

I tore open the envelope and unfolded the sheet of heavy notepaper and began to read the neat, well-formed handwriting. Fortunately, the letter was written in English. I read it aloud.

My Dear Megan,

We have learned of your father's death. He told you of the bitterness between us—but do you know this was no reflection of the way we Ferraris felt, and still feel, about you? For you, who are blood of our blood as your mother was, we can have only the same deep affection that we had for her.

We became bitter toward your father

7

because he took *you* away from us against her wish when your mother died. That, we could not forgive. But with his death, that bitterness is ended. It never did apply to you. Our only wish was to have you with us to love and cherish as your mother wished. Your father denied her that right, and us the pleasure it could have given. Despite his malice, over the years we have seen you many times. We know that physically you grow more like our beloved Bernadette each day. But are you like her spiritually? Bernadette had a rare natural gift from her mother, one that few people possess. We wonder if you have inherited it from her, as she did from your grandmother.

Your father has left you alone and almost destitute. We Ferraris are still a wealthy and powerful family, and a part of whatever we possess is yours. You are saddened by your father's death, and you have no other blood relatives who might help you. Because of these things, we beg of you to right the wrong your father did when he took you away from us.

Come home, dear Megan, as your mother wished. We wish you to have her jewelry and private papers. Money, affection, and sympathy and understanding await you here.

Lissi Ferrari

John Carson had watched me silently as I read the letter out to him. His brown eyes had studied my face closely. He was an attractive-looking man with thick black hair that was graying interestingly at the temples. He had gone to college with my father, and they had remained friends ever since. I knew he wasn't married.

"There is something else in the envelope, Megan," he reminded me.

I shook the remaining contents out onto the table. There were airline tickets linking Boston with Halifax, Nova Scotia, and a check that had fallen face down on the table. He picked it up, glanced at it, and handed it to me.

"Spending money for the journey," he said, and added: "Your Aunt Lissi appears to be generous. I wonder if the amount is a coincidence, Megan."

I shook my head as I glanced at the check. The amount, over Lissi Ferrari's signature, was for two thousand dollars drawn upon a bank in Halifax, Nova Scotia. It must have been a coincidence, I thought. There was no other answer. Two thousand dollars was the total amount of my father's estate.

"Yes," I said. "A coincidence."

"Maybe." He sounded dubious. "And there's still no explanation of how they learned of your father's death."

"No, there isn't." I glanced down at the letter again. "She doesn't say."

"And there's another thing," he said thoughtfully. "She mentioned something about having seen you many times over the years. Is that right?"

I shook my head. "No. Impossible. Perhaps she means in the mind's eye."

"Yet she says you are looking more and more like your mother. You are, you know."

There was only one photograph of my mother in the apartment. It had been taken in Quebec when she and my father were on their honeymoon. She had been only a couple of years older than I was now.

Now, looking at the photograph again, I could see there *was* a definite resemblance. There was the same raven hair; and the eyes, I knew, were violet, as mine were. Her figure was a little fuller, more mature than mine, although I estimated us to be about the same height. Still, I was only nineteen. There was plenty of time for my figure to fill out more.

"Your father and I often talked about the Ferrari family," John Carson said thoughtfully. "Your aunt was quite right—they *are* a powerful family. I guess your father told you quite a lot about them."

He hadn't—or not much, anyway, beyond the fact that he was wholeheartedly hated by the Ferraris; but I had no intention of letting John Carson know that, so I just nodded.

He went on. "It has just occurred to me that they've had somebody down here, keeping an eye on you. It's possible. It wouldn't be so difficult."

"Possibly," I murmured. "But it seems a lot of trouble. . . ."

"As I said, they're a powerful family. And wealthy." He tapped the letter with his forefinger. "They *do* seem to know a lot about you." He laid the letter down on the table. "What will you do?" he asked. "Will you accept the invitation?"

"Do *you* think I should?" I countered.

He shrugged. "It's not really for me to say," he said with a chuckle. "I guess you have to make up your own mind about that."

I smiled at him. "Yes, I guess so. I would still like to hear your opinion, though."

"Well ..." He thought for a moment. "Well, it *could* be an experience, I guess. Frankly, I don't see any reason against it. You could learn quite a lot, I'm sure."

"I wonder *why* they invited me," I murmured, more to myself than to him. "It *does* seem odd. I mean, it's been so long."

"Your aunt seems to be a very proud woman," he said. "Unbending. Unforgiving. She nursed a hatred against your father for so many years. She is obviously a woman who feels very deeply."

"It seems she does," I said. "It's thirteen years now since my mother died. That's a long time for anyone to hold a grudge."

When I came to think of it, the Ferraris were about the only relatives I had left in the world. My grandparents, who had looked after me for a period while I was a child, had died about a year before. They had died within a week of each other. I remembered them well enough, but I was darned if I could remember anything about my aunt, Lissi Ferrari, beyond the fact that she had a very pale face, and that she had seemed perpetually angry as she supervised the servants who looked after the big house. That was about all.

John Carson was studying the air tickets. "I see they're for Thursday," he said. "The day after tomorrow."

"Oh? So soon?"

"It could be a wise idea, Megan," he said soberly. "You need to get away, even if it's only for a while. I'll handle all the arrangements at this end, so you won't have that worry. I'll bank the proceeds from the disposal of your father's assets, so that will be waiting for you when you decide to return. Also, if you let me know when you intend coming back, I'll arrange to have an apartment ready for you. That shouldn't be too difficult."

It seemed he had already decided I would accept my aunt's invitation to go to Nova Scotia. I guess I had, too, by that time. He was right. I needed to get away for a while. I needed a new environment, new interests that would help cushion the shock and misery caused by my father's sudden death.

After John Carson had gone, and I was alone again, the sense of loss swept over me with greater force than ever before. It remained with me while I made my preparations, packed my things, and said good-bye to my friends. It stayed with me until the aircraft taxied down the runway at Logan Airport, and gathering momentum, became airborne.

Below, the Gulf of Maine looked oily and flat and gray as we left the white buildings and green trees of Boston behind. It wasn't until then that I remembered the envelope which had been handed to me at the airport by a messenger from John Carson's office. I took the envelope from my bag and opened it.

John Carson's note had been hastily scribbled. It read:

My Dear Megan,

My secretary reminded me this morning that I had the enclosed document, left with me some years ago by your father. As it is purely personal, being something your mother wrote and signed, and to which your father added (to me at least) some rather incomprehensible comment, I did not give it much importance.

As you are returning to the Ferrari house it occurred to me that you should have it. Perhaps you can understand the reason for its existence better than I can.

I am also happy to inform you that your father's assets brought rather more than I expected, the sum total being $2,298.50. This will be placed to your account, pending further advice from you.

John Carson

I unfolded the enclosed document. It had been handwritten on stiff legal paper, and the ink used was so faded that it had acquired an unreal, almost ghostly look. The handwriting itself was spidery, with each word finished off with ostentatious curlicues and flourishes. I was seeing my mother's handwriting for the first time, I realized as I glanced down at her signature.

The document began with a biblical quotation: *"There shall not be found among you the faithful anyone that useth divination, or an enchanter, or a wizard or necromancer. For all these things are an abomination unto the Lord."*

The document continued:

So is the prescription laid down in the Christian Bible in Deuteronomy 18:10–12. Yet throughout the centuries there have been many who claimed or were attributed with these "abominations." And for every one of these, whether cheat or faker, dupes of their own superstitious beliefs, or members of that rare and privileged minority to whom such power and vision are granted unsought and often unwanted—there are always many thousands of distraught people crying for the right in séance to hear the voices and see again the faces of their beloved dead. People who demand to share the vision of the medium, without knowing or caring whether the vision is real or unreal. People who care nothing that by their importunity they spur the medium toward her ultimate possession and destruction by forces far beyond their understanding.

So, we are told, King Saul importuned the Witch of Endor, to communicate through her with the dead Samuel. The Greeks built temples to such mediums and called them oracles and revered them. Roman emperors sought their advice in the conquest of the known world of their time. Julius Caesar raised his cloak to cover his eyes as he accepted the death his assassins gave him, and which was inevitable because it had been foretold.

In medievalism we read of the young and sensitive girl, or the pious recluse who saw visions of Christ and was granted the power of healing. For some this proved a power for which their contemporaries destroyed them, even though after death some were granted sainthood by the clergy. Others saw different visions, heard a different voice, so were burned alive as witches or warlocks. *For the medium in séance cannot control the powers she unleashes.* It is never the medium who controls the séance, no matter how experienced she may be. It is the séance that controls her.

Strange and inexplicable things happen at such times—things beyond any human understanding. Things incomprehensible to even the scientific mind. For in some people (perhaps in all people, for who can know this with certainty?) lies a dreadful power that science, in merely brushing against the fringe of it, has termed extrasensory perception.

The term is badly chosen, implying awareness and understanding where there is none.

It is true that first we must perceive, and that this perception is extrasensory. But the opening of our extrasensory eyes to see the unknown reveals a two-way street. The horror the medium sees is as nothing to the horror *that sees her*. She sees, but she is seen, perhaps desired by the unknown that sees her. She is certainly possessed and ultimately destroyed.

Who can possibly know and understand these things, save the possessed? Who else can bear the insufferable agony, or know the ultimate terror and the awful mental torture of possession, save the possessed?

Least of all can they understand or care who demand this sacrifice from another human being.

At the end was my mother's signature—"Bernadette Ferrari."

After her signature, something had been written, but then erased. I thought perhaps it may have been a date. Still wondering about the purpose of the document, whether it was in fact intended as a letter, or an essay of some sort, I turned to my father's notes. Perhaps, I thought, they might provide me with an explanation.

Suddenly I felt cold. I glanced around, thinking perhaps that the air-conditioning might be faulty, but I detected no signs of discomfort in any of the other passengers. The elderly man in the seat beside me was fast asleep. His face was flushed slightly, and he looked so comfortable that I decided I must have been imagining the chill. Just looking at my neighbor made me feel warmer.

By now we had left the coast far behind us. There was only the sea below.

My father's notes had been scribbled on lined sheets of foolscap. I began to read them.

"In more modern times, Bernadette," my father had written, "such séances are fraudulent—and conducted solely for the profit of the medium."

"Inexplicable?" he had written a little farther down.

Things beyond human understanding happening at séances? No. Hocus-pocus! Extrasensory perception? What's wrong there? It means perception of something beyond, or outside the reach of normal sensory perception. And it was coined by the people claiming to have such powers—*not* by the scientists investigating their claims.

But where so-called psychic perceptivity is concerned, how can one establish fact? Take me. I'm predisposed against such things. I always have been. I can't believe. But Bernadette could. Everybody is predisposed for or against ESP by beliefs already instinctively shaped by either never having encountered anything like it, or having been involved with something they couldn't explain for which in self-defense they adopted supernatural explanation.

There I go again. Biased. Dogmatic.

It would be better logic to assume that those with the strongest convictions, which include people like myself, trained in one professional field or another, make the least trustworthy witnesses when it comes to psychic phenomena. Thus a scientist can be completely honest and objective in observing and classifying almost any fact that he can establish by verifiable and familiar laws—except where, as with ESP, he has preconceived convictions.

How many scientists could research psychic phenomena with an objective mind? Damned few! It would be the study of a phantom thing, bound to none of the physical laws as I see them. Uncanny, without substance or reality, so therefore confusing even to the inquiring mind. Full of the imagining of centuries of human superstition, the prescriptions and exorcisms and fears of the ignorant. Add the distorted human frailties of greed, of trickery, of self-interest and bigotry, of desire and hatred. Equals a rare confusion—for even a conscientious researcher with a totally objective mind. *If* one so dedicated could be found.

The danger in the use of such a pure scientist in researching psychic phenomena would appear to develop as he became more deeply involved.

Supposition: Suppose that among all the guile, the trickery of fake mediums, the cheating, and the lies, the scientist suddenly discovered himself facing the unexplainable, the uncanny happening for which neither his training nor experience could find any answer?

What then, Bernadette?

It is then that he, too, would find the agony and the terror. . . .

I stared at the last line. It was not the same handwriting. Again, I was looking at the flourishes and curlicues at the end of each word.

The words slanted sharply down toward the bottom-right-hand corner of the page, with the last word, "terror," ending in a heavy straight line where the pen had plowed almost right through the paper.

In the left-hand corner my father had written. It was almost a quotation. "This happened July 15, 1967. I had not the strength to prevent it. Adam Marshall. Ph.D."

I was puzzled. He had not the strength to prevent . . . what? Certainly not that last line. He had written his notes in 1967. My mother had already been dead for eight years. That line, that last line, had not been in my father's handwriting, but in my mother's. The ink with which the words had been written was just as faded as in the first document I had read. It was obviously something she had written at the same time.

I shook my head and replaced the papers back in the envelope. Ahead I could see Halifax harbor, one of the finest on the eastern coast, and behind it the buildings and streets of the city rising tier upon tier to the great, star-shaped citadel on the heights behind it.

The aircraft's instruction panel flickered and came to life. It was time to fasten our safety belts prior to landing at the airport a few miles northeast of Halifax.

As we began the approach I wondered if

Aunt Lissi might know the circumstances in which my mother had written those words, and why my father had waited for nine years after her death before compiling his notes.

Chapter Two

The narrow road hugged the edge of the cliff, winding past fenced fields on the eastern side, where blueberries were fruiting and long-wooled sheep, feeding among the vines, lifted their foolish faces to stare at us. A gray colt, startled by our approach, whinnied and fled across the field to its mother.

The chauffeur's name was Maxwell. I had learned that much at the airport, where he had met me. He was a dark-skinned Nova Scotian, thickset, thirtyish, and not at all communicative. I gathered he had been with the Ferrari family for a long time. I asked him now if he remembered my mother.

His dark eyes briefly met mine in the rear-vision mirror. "Yes."

I sensed his reluctance, but this didn't deter me. "What do you remember about her, Maxwell?" I asked.

"They said she was . . . beautiful. I remember that."

I frowned. "But you said you knew her? Didn't *you* think she was beautiful?"

"I was sixteen when your mother died, Miss Marshall," he said, meeting my eyes in the mirror once again. "She had been sick for a long time. I can remember your mother only dimly. I was still a boy when I last saw her."

"I always believed my mother died suddenly," I murmured. "Of a heart attack."

"Your father told you that?" Now his dark eyes were examining me carefully.

"Probably. I've forgotten. But I know I've always believed she died suddenly."

"I've seen her stone in the family cemetery often," he said. "She was twenty-four when she died, the inscription says. But she didn't die suddenly. She was . . . ill for a long time."

The road was now red gravel. A mist clouded the angry sea at the foot of the cliff. Momentarily, as the road curved, I glimpsed, through the shifting mist which was rising from the sea, four tall towers.

Maxwell said laconically, "Even in summer we get fog. We're almost there, which is just as well. You saw the towers, of course. You should recognize them. You used to watch the tide from up there, didn't you?"

I could vaguely remember. "Yes, I did." I

looked at him. "You do remember me, then, Maxwell?"

"I'd see you up there looking down. Mostly from the windows of the northwest tower. That was just before your mother died. They nursed your mother in the other tower, on the north side. Sometimes I'd see her up there, too, or her nurses. They would be watching the tide, too. I remember those nurses. Big women, they were, from Quebec. No one liked them."

The great house began to emerge through the thickening fog. It perched on the hook of high ground that thrust out across this arm of the Bay of Fundy to form the Minas Channel, a funnel through which the world's highest tides roared twice in every twenty-four hours. When the moon exerted its maximum pull, the tides below the Ferrari house rose as much as fifty-three feet, to pour boiling, tumultuous water into the Minas Basin.

It was typical, I thought, that the first Ferrari to settle into this wild place should build his house above a whirlpool.

Maxwell had slowed the car to a crawl as a gust of wind forced a cloud of sea fog to boil up the side of the cliff and across the road before us. He muttered something beneath his breath and switched on the fog lights, which nevertheless failed to penetrate the white pall ahead for more than a few vague feet.

"We only had the sea fogs in the evening when you lived here, Miss Marshall," Maxwell said apologetically. "Now they come in from the sea at any time, as you can see. I mean, it's only noon. Miss Lissi said I was to get you back in time for lunch at twelve-thirty, and you'll want to freshen up, no doubt."

"I'm not in any hurry to get there," I said truthfully. I was beginning to feel more and more apprehensive as we crept through that writhing sea fog toward the house. It was an odd, cold sort of fear I felt. I couldn't explain it.

"Well, I know every inch of this road," Maxwell said more cheerfully. "There's no need to worry."

As I thought of the great house with its four towers, and wondered at that vague, chilling menace which seemed to reach out to me, I remembered something else. "There was a man," I said. "He gave me flowers. His name was Maxwell, too."

He smiled. "My father. I'm a junior. He's the head gardener. You had a thing about yellow roses, so he'd find a choice bud and nurse it especially for you. None of us dared touch it." He shook his head. "That was before your mother became ill. Things were so different then."

"Different? How?"

He shrugged. "People change. Your grandfather was alive then. People came and went, friends of your grandfather and grandmother, or of your mother and father. When Miss Lissi would come back from Europe to spend her vacations here, her friends would come too, and the house would be full. There was always something happening. But now ..." His voice tapered off into silence.

"What happened, Maxwell?" I prompted. "Why has it all changed?"

"Now there's only Miss Lissi," he said. "And she doesn't bother with her friends. She just ... stays home. Tradesmen don't come to the house. Even the mail has to be fetched from Sussex Wold, ten miles away on Copequid Bay. Except for something urgent that has to be done in connection with the estate, and she has to go to Halifax, Miss Lissi leaves anything to be done on the outside to me."

Ahead of us, the fog was beginning to disperse before a brisk breeze. I could see the house more clearly now, with the sun shining on it beyond the shredding fog. I could feel the breeze, made cold and clammy by the defeated vapor on my face.

I distantly recognized the great iron gates

between the twin columns of hewn stone, beyond which the red-gravel, stone-bordered drive wound up to the stone pile of the great house.

It was a square house, three floors high, with its flat roof hidden behind stone battlements slitted with sinister loopholes. The four square towers at each corner contained modern picture windows, behind which I could see fluttering white curtains.

We were turning toward wide stone steps at the main entrance. I looked admiringly out at the rose gardens set in vividly green lawns.

It was certainly a gracious setting. It occurred to me unexpectedly that I didn't blame Aunt Lissi for not wanting to leave the house. I thought I might feel that way myself, if it belonged to me. It had a dignity and a beauty that I hadn't known in a house before, set as it was in its setting of fine, sweeping lawns and gardens above the sea, from which the fog was now in full retreat.

The only reservation I might have had about living there was the sheer size of the house. If Aunt Lissi lived here alone except for a few servants, it was likely she was a very lonely woman.

After we had pulled up at the foot of the steps, Maxwell came around the car to open the door for me. I noticed a uniformed maid standing by the front door, looking curiously down at us.

"I'll have your bags sent up to your room, Miss Marshall," Maxwell told me.

I thanked him and walked up the steps to where the maid was waiting.

"Miss Ferrari is waiting in the reception room for you, Miss Marshall," she said in French. "Please follow me."

I followed the maid along a wide passage; through glassed double doors I could see the cluttered interiors of great high-ceilinged rooms. The furniture and fittings of these rooms looked ancient. The first of these rooms was apparently a music room, for it contained only musical instruments and chairs. There was a gleaming grand piano and, in a glass-fronted cabinet, several stringed instruments in their cases. The chairs had spindly, old-fashioned legs and were upholstered in gold-colored fabrics.

Through the second door on the same side I saw a magnificent cedar table and heavy chairs. The walls were lined with bookshelves. There looked to be thousands of books in the room. There was a typewriter at one end of the table, a sheet of blank white paper rising emptily from the roller.

The maid opened a door to our left.

"Miss Marshall is here, Miss Ferrari," she said importantly.

"Bring her in, Denise." The voice put me in mind of the rustle of dry leaves. It was a lifeless voice.

The reception room was huge. In fact, the apartment my father and I had shared in Boston would have fit quite comfortably into one corner of it. Or so it seemed to me at the time. The floor was heavily carpeted, except at the far end, where, on the highly polished boards, stood another grand piano. There were also other musical instruments beneath covers. The furniture, clustered in groups, seemed to be in contrasting settings, so that in one place there was more of the spindly French period furniture I had noticed in the music room; in others, heavier and more comfortable colonial couches and chairs. I looked around for some sign of my aunt. Then, suddenly, I noticed a slight movement in a high-backed chair facing one of the big windows that framed a scene of rose beds and smooth green lawn.

"I am here, child," the dry voice said impatiently. "Where I have been waiting for you for the past half-hour."

She stood up and turned to face me.

Taller than I, she was a slim woman with a good figure. The Ferrari family resemblance was in her face and the full, curving lips. It was her eyes, I decided, that set her apart from my mother and me. They were a very dark brown, so deep in color that in this room, with her back to the windows, they appeared an obsidian black. I couldn't see their pupils. Her black hair was powdered with gray at the temples.

"I am glad you decided to come to us," she said. Placing her hands on my shoulders, she kissed me very lightly on both cheeks. Her lips felt cold and smooth and dry.

Releasing my shoulders, she turned back to her chair.

"Come here, where I can see you, Megan," she ordered more cheerfully.

"I'm sorry I kept you waiting."

"Your plane was late. I suppose the fog made landing difficult." She settled back in her chair, and expressionlessly studied my face.

"The fog was on the road," I told her. "We drove slowly."

She shook her head. "Maxwell can be overcautious. The road is perfectly safe. Even in fog." She moved in her chair and smiled up at me. "When I look at you, I see your mother just before . . . your father married her. The resemblance is striking. In fact, I find it hard to believe that this is now, and not then. That I am not still a girl of eighteen talking to my sister."

I don't know why her words should have triggered another vague, crawling sense of apprehension—fear even—but they did, nevertheless.

"I'll have Denise take you to your room," she said. "I've had your old room prepared for you. Your mother's old room is next to it, and there's a connecting door, as you will probably remember. Nothing has been changed. Nothing." She smiled slowly. "There's the same huge old four-poster bed you slept in. Oh, yes, you had plenty of room in which to move. You were certainly comfortable. I . . ." She broke off. Denise was standing at the door.

I was a little mystified at first; then I noticed the bell push on the arm of Aunt Lissi's chair.

"Has someone been looking after my niece's things, Denise?"

"Yes, Miss Ferrari. Frances has been putting them away."

"Then you may take Miss Marshall to her room. Then, when she is ready, bring her down for lunch."

"Yes, Miss Ferrari."

Just before I followed Denise out into the passage, where she said she would wait for me, I remembered something I had almost forgotten. "Aunt Lissi, you said in your letter that I was growing more like my mother every day. There was something in it, too, about seeing me often in Boston. I've been wondering about that ever since. I mean, about *how* you knew I was so like my mother."

"Through friends of mine, who saw you there quite frequently. They told me a great many things about you."

"Who were they? Perhaps I know them."

She smiled. "No, you don't know them, Megan. But you will, I promise you. I expect you to meet them very soon."

I thought I saw a sudden wariness in my aunt's dark eyes, which was almost immediately gone again.

"Did they know my mother?" I asked.

"They knew your mother very well," she replied. "Very well indeed. But no doubt they'll tell you about that when you meet, as I'm sure you will. Now, really, you must go with Denise. Our lunch will be ready before you are."

On our way up the steep flight of stairs, Denise told me that my room was on the top floor beneath the northwest tower. I remembered that this was the tower from which Maxwell, as a boy, had watched me staring down at the sea. As we climbed, I caught glimpses through the windows of the sea and the cliffs beyond the protective stone walls of the house. Some fishing boats were chugging toward the narrows that led into the Minas Basin. I could see the Bass River shore across the basin.

Denise opened a door at the end of the passage and handed me the key. "This is your room," she announced. "It has its own bathroom. Everything has been made ready for you."

"Thank you, Denise."

The same impressive view, with its background of pine forests on the far shore, that I had glimpsed on the way up the stairs could be seen through the windows of my room. They overlooked the surrounding stone wall and the mighty cliff all the way down to where the sea lashed furiously against its base.

A girl was carefully hanging my clothes in a huge wardrobe. As I entered the room, she turned to smile at me. She might have been Denise's sister. I looked with interest at the four-poster in which I had once slept, and at the highly polished red-cedar dressing table with its large oval mirror and tapestry-covered stool. The room was vaguely familiar. I found myself looking too, for the connecting door. It was where I knew it would be.

"You can go, Frances," Denise said to the other girl. "Frances is my cousin, Miss Marshall," she explained to me. "Your bell is beside the bed. If you need anything . . ." She broke off, then cried indignantly, "*Zut!* There's that confounded board in here again! I'll just put it back where it belongs."

She picked up a square board from the table beside my bed. I glanced at it. "Board?"

"Someone keeps bringing it in here. It belongs in the other room."

"Show me."

It was a square of heavy wood marked with rows of black letters and numbers across one half of its white surface, while the other half was divided into three spaces—the one on the left marked with the word "No" across its center, the space on the right with the word "Yes"; while the middle space was left blank. It looked like some kind of game. The surface upon which the symbols were inlaid looked to be ivory. "What is it? A fancy Ouija board?"

She glared at it. "I don't know. Perhaps it is a game. I don't know. There was another part, but it seems to have got lost. It was a gadget with two or three little castors and a sort of socket in it."

When I had freshened up a little, we went downstairs together.

Lissi Ferrari was waiting for me by the dining-room window, staring out at the grounds. Once again I was impressed by her tall, graceful figure.

I was introduced to Madame Larre, a tall, thin woman with an austere face and faded brown eyes, who officiated as my aunt's housekeeper and who supervised the preparation and serving of all meals. Madame Larre remarked that I very much resembled my mother, and hoped I would like my lunch. I certainly did. The veal kidneys with cubes of ham cooked in cognac-and-mushroom sauce were superb. I told Madame Larre as much, and for the first time, she smiled. For dessert there was *tarte au sucre*, a rich morsel of pastry made, I learned, from maple sugar, eggs, and cream. My aunt ate sparingly, and sipped the light white wines that had been served with each dish.

After lunch I retired to my room, where, I had told Lissi Ferrari, I might rest for an hour or so before coming back down again. It would be ample time, I said, to allow my lunch to settle.

As I entered my room, I glanced automatically at the four-poster. What I saw there didn't quite register until I looked again. My bed that had earlier looked so immaculate now looked as though someone had slept in it. One of the two pillows was missing, and the covers had been thrown right across to the far side.

I moved around to the far side of the bed and pulled the hanging covers back up onto it. Then I stooped to pick up the pillow that had also been thrown to that side. I had it in my hand when I noticed the board lying beneath it, with the letters and numbers uppermost. It was the same board Denise had complained about earlier. I picked it up. It was heavier than I had somehow expected it to be. I glanced at the door to the next room instinctively. It was open.

Tossing the pillow onto the bed, I walked across to the door. "Is anyone in there?" I called.

When there was no answer, I pushed the door wider and looked into the other room.

There was a warmth inside that room that was like a welcome for me, particularly when I saw the big bed with its four posts and canopy. My mother and father had slept in that bed. My mother had sat on the brocaded stool before the great oval mirror of the dressing table. I placed the board on the dressing table and sat on the stool in front of it. My reflection stared solemnly back at me. I looked back down at the board.

My earlier guess that the surface of the board was of ivory proved, I found on closer examination, to be correct. The inlaid letters and numbers looked to be onyx. I turned the board over and examined the back. I could make out some faint, indecipherable handwriting in one corner. It looked to be a signature of some sort. I carried the board across to the windows to examine it in brighter light. It *was* a signature, or part of one. I stared at it, frowning in concentration. B-e-r-n-a-d. It ended there; the rest had been worn away. Bernadette? Of course. The board had been my mother's. The signature must have been made a long time ago, I thought, because there were none of the curlicues or flourishes I had seen in her later writing. It was very basic, almost childish writing.

I carried the board back to my room and placed it on the table beside my bed. Then, kicking off my shoes, I stretched out on the bed. It was like floating on a cloud, lying there with a feather mattress beneath me. It was so comfortable that I was asleep within a matter of minutes.

Chapter Three

"Do you find it lonely here, Megan?" My aunt lowered her coffeecup. Her dark eyes probed mine intently.

I smiled and shook my head. "It's a little too soon to tell," I said. "I slept for most of the afternoon, so I haven't had a chance to look around."

She nodded. "Of course. You were tired after your journey. I hope you weren't disturbed in any way."

"No, not at all."

"It's just that I remember how afraid you were of the high tides when you were small. We had a particularly big one while you slept. It was tumultuous in the caves below the cliffs, so of course we heard it all too clearly up here."

I was a little surprised. I wasn't normally a heavy sleeper. I hadn't heard a thing.

"Then it didn't wake you?"

"No." Yet as I said it, I realized that since waking, I had lain on the bed for some moments, it seemed, listening for something. I knew now for what it was that I had been instinctively listening. It was for the coming in of the tide, a sound which, so long ago, had terrified me.

"I'm glad you weren't disturbed, Megan," Lissi said.

We were sitting in the library, surrounded by the ceiling-high shelves of leather-bound books that seemed to belong to another age. Madame Larre had brought in a tray of liqueurs and coffee, which she had left on the table between us before leaving us alone again.

At the far end of the room was a portrait of my mother done in oils. The artist had captured a personality that even to me seemed very much like my own when I am in a serious mood. I couldn't take my eyes from it.

My aunt noticed my interest. She said, "She was twenty when that was painted. That was a year before she married your father, against the wish of our family. Bernadette was happy then. She had everything a girl could wish."

"Except my father," I said involuntarily.

For the first time, my aunt's mask slipped a little. "She could have done without him. All he brought her was disaster."

"And me?" I suggested coldly. I was angry myself.

"I didn't mean that, Megan," she said quickly. "We never resented your birth. We loved you from the moment you were born, because you were Bernadette's child."

I was also my father's child, I almost retorted, but decided against it. I sipped my liqueur instead. I glanced again at my mother's portrait, and as if I were drawing reassurance from it, the tension drained out of me, and I was relaxed once more.

"In your letter," I said, quickly changing the subject, "you talked about a natural gift my mother had inherited from my grandmother. You wondered if it had been passed on to me as well. Do you remember writing that?"

Lissi nodded. "Yes, I do," she said slowly. She hesitated for a long moment; then, "Your mother had what is known as extrasensory perception. She could see and hear things beyond normal perception."

I stared at her. "Really?"

"Yes—really. More than that, she could make others see the things she saw, hear the things she heard. I have seen this happen many times in a way that even your father, for all his knowledge and his doubting, could never refute."

I remembered the envelope that had been

handed to me at the airport in Boston. "You're saying that . . . my mother was a . . . a spiritualistic medium?"

"I am saying more than that, Megan," she said quietly. "Have you heard of psychokinesis?"

"No." I don't know if it was the effect of the liqueur or not, but I was beginning to feel strangely insubstantial. I felt as if I were almost ready to float through the library and away.

"Psychokinesis is the process of influencing through mental means the movement of physical objects," my aunt was saying in the same low voice. "Bernadette had that power, as indeed had our mother. I've known heavy objects to move, drawers to fall out and spill whatever was inside, and small objects move from one room to another. Nobody touched them. That is, nobody any of the people present could see."

I shivered involuntarily. "It's unbelievable."

"No, Megan," she said seriously. "If one believes, all things are possible. But then, you've never been allowed by your father to attend a séance, have you?"

"I haven't been to a séance," I calmly told her. "I've never really given them much thought."

"A pity," she said. "You might have been surprised if you had."

"Surprised? You think I ... have my mother's ... gift?"

"I don't know yet. It's too soon. But if you don't share at least in part the extrasensory perception your mother had, yours will be the first generation of this family that hasn't had a woman with the power of communication with those who have gone before us."

I felt the flesh on the back of my neck crawl. "You mean with ... the *dead*?"

"That's why séances are usually held, Megan," she said dryly.

"Yes, of course," I murmured uncomfortably. "But wouldn't such a power be dangerous to the medium?"

"Your father told you that?"

I shook my head. My mother had said it, not my father. "It seems to me that anyone who unleashes powers beyond human understanding or control looses something unhealthy and dangerous. Such a person asks for trouble. What does it do to the medium, the in-between? You should be able to tell me that."

Frowning a little, she shook her head. "Only one of us in each generation is granted this power, Megan," she said. "That is the way it has always been. One in a generation. Because it was given to my sister, Bernadette, it could never be mine. Bernadette never spoke of it much to me. It was something that . . . kept her apart from the rest of us. Then she married. But this is a very old family, so it has been well-recorded. You may read it. I will fetch the book."

She stood up and walked across to the bookshelves. Watching her, I had the impression she still resented that the so-called "gift" had been passed down to my mother and not herself. She extracted a book from one of the shelves. Its leather binding was scuffed and worn from usage.

"You do not read Old French, of course," she said, turning back to me. "Or Latin, I suppose. But that doesn't matter. It's better if you read only the recent pages. You should find your grandmother's comments most interesting. Poor Bernadette did not add very much to it at all. Some of the earlier pages are now quite impossible to read, even by a student of Old French. The early pages were written on parchment. No doubt there were others before Maria Ferrari wrote the first entry, because I remember my mother reading it to Bernadette and me when we were girls, and she pointed out that Maria mentions that the gift has been passed down from *her* mother."

She was holding the volume out to me. I

took it from her, and resting it carefully on my knees, opened it.

On the first page, only the signature and the date remained: *Maria Ferrari. 1641 Anno Domini.* The writing was faded and yellow with age. Looking at it, I knew it would soon disappear, as the rest of the writing on the page had done, and then nothing more of Maria Ferrari would remain. But there was enough of her handwriting there to have me staring at it, and for the cold, creepy feeling to start up once more at the back of my neck. It was my mother's handwriting—the writing I had read on the document that had been signed by my mother.

I quickly flipped over a few pages and found a new date, a new name: *Yvonne Ferrari. 1718 Anno Domini.* This signature was clearer, and again, as in my mother's handwriting, there were the same curlicues and flourishes.

"Have you noticed the handwriting?" my aunt asked.

"It looks the same."

She nodded. "It is something that happens when the power comes," she said thoughtfully. "Your grandmother said this happened to her. I know it happened to your mother. It came when she began to see the visions."

"Visions?" I stared at her.

"Bernadette's perception of the world

beyond this was far greater than that of any of the other women of our family—or those who recorded in this book. She had a power that carried her farther than any of the others. She saw places and things that had been denied them. But you will understand these things better when you read."

"Yet she wrote nothing here herself." Apart from my mother's name and date of birth at the top, nothing else had been written on the page that had been reserved for her.

"Your mother died too soon, Megan," she told me gently. "It was a great pity. She could have told us so very much."

Recalling what the chauffeur, Maxwell, had told me about my mother's death, and how it had differed from my father's version, I demanded, "How did my mother die?"

She studied my face. "Surely your father told you."

"He said she died suddenly. That's all I know. She was so young."

Lissi's dark eyes were probing mine. "Nobody is too young to die," she said quietly. "It happened as your father told you. He left as soon as it was over, taking you with him." She smiled suddenly, and reaching over to me, closed the book. But she didn't take it. "We've talked enough of such things for one night," she said. "Now there is something else I want to tell you. I brought two cousins of yours here from Europe a few months before your father died. They are twins—girls—and are at college in Halifax. They will be coming here for the weekend. So they should provide you with agreeable company nearer to your own age."

That, at least, sounded promising. "I didn't know I had any other relatives," I remarked.

"Another branch of the family." She hesitated. "I'll be frank with you, Megan; I thought we'd never see you here at this house, so I thought—I hoped—there might be someone in that branch of the family who had your mother's gift. I brought them here to live where she lived." She shrugged and smiled. "It didn't work out. They could never have Bernadette's concentration or courage. They are just ordinary young girls, with nothing to distinguish them. They will soon be returning to Europe."

Still smiling, she stood up. "I am inviting some friends for dinner tomorrow night. These are the ones I told you about—your mother's friends. I'm sure you will be interested to meet them, as I know they are interested to meet you. They can give you a clearer perspective of this house and your mother's people."

About ten minutes later, with the leather-bound chronicle of family events under my arm, I was climbing the staircase to my room.

Chapter Four

The covers of the bed had been turned back, and the desk lamp was casting a subdued light into the room. After changing into my night-clothes, I carried the book across to the deep chair by the windows. The room was warm. Beyond the windows, the gray fog swirled. Runnels of salt-whitened water streamed down the outsides of the windowpanes. Opening the book, I settled back in the chair and began to read what my grandmother had written.

Irene Ferrari! Born 1903. The power came to me soon after my twenty-second birthday in May 1925, when I was three months pregnant with my first child. It began as I sat at my window watching the tide come in. I began to feel light-headed, as I remember it. An odd, dreamy feeling, not at all like the syncope my doctor had warned me I might experience during early pregnancy, with its feeling of sickness, its cold sweats, and the fright that accompanies fainting. This feeling, I knew, had something of exaltation and ecstasy. I seemed to leave my room by the window, even though at this time it still had iron bars from the early days of constant skirmishes with the Indians. I felt as if I were soaring through the air, swooping over the sea like an eagle.

I took fright, and tried to fight this feeling that possessed me, but it was too strong. Instead, as though to punish me, I was sent soaring back to my room. There I found my room occupied. There was a woman in my bed with her hair all awry and her eyes staring. Sweat was pouring from her, and she kept crying out in pain and fear. I wanted to help her, to go to her, but the power prevented me, held me still. And gradually I began to realize that there was something familiar about the woman on the bed. This woman straining in the agony of childbirth was me, while I stood apart, a wraith, watching, unable to help the young and unknown doctor who struggled to turn the child in my womb so that it could be born.

When at last it was over, and the

woman that was the physical me had borne her child, a son, I watched this strange doctor try vainly to bring it to life. I watched him finally tire of trying and return to help me. I heard him instruct the nurse to inform my husband that our first child, a son, was stillborn. And watching, hearing what was said, I seemed to know that the fetus I carried was doomed never to exist beyond my body. I took my story in fear to our family doctor in Sussex Wold, who told me I had merely been dreaming as I dozed in my chair, and that he meant no other hands than his to deliver our baby.

I accepted what he said, but I could not forget the dream as the slow months passed until my time came upon me. And on the night when I became uneasy and felt the first rending pain that set my husband calling the doctor, it was a strange voice that answered the telephone. A younger voice. A voice that told my husband he was a doctor from Truro who had been called to Dr. Wilson, our family doctor, who had just passed away. He said he would come in Doctor Wilson's stead, and that he would bring his young wife who was a trained nurse with him.

I was terrified when my husband told me these things. I had never spoken of the dream to him before, not wanting to worry him, and him so proud at the thought of our child. But I told him now. He tried to reassure me, but I could not be reassured. When the young doctor came, it was the doctor and the nurse I had seen in my vision that day six months before. And it happened as I had seen. I knew the agony of a transverse birth, the agony of the stillbirth of the only son I would ever bear.

This was the manner in which the power came to me. Yet except for the son I lost, unlike the way it appears to have been with others before me, the power seemed to me a beneficent thing. Seven years passed before I had another child, my darling Bernadette, and later Lissi, my third-born. Our family prospered, I dare say as never before. Of the horrible things others had seen and known before me, there was none. Perhaps because there was a closed door beyond which I could not pass, though from pique and curiosity I tried more than once.

These were the years between the wars, and I was able to help many to see and hear their lost ones. Many blessed me for

it, and I counted myself blessed, not cursed
—except only for the loss of my only son.

Irene Ferrari. 1969 Anno Domini.

Someone tapped lightly on the door. I started. Then, placing the book on the carpet beside the chair, I stood up. The tapping persisted. I moved across to the door and opened it. There was no one there. Nor was there anyone in the passage. I looked up and down it, but there was no one there. No light showed beneath the door of my aunt's room, and I guessed she was still downstairs.

I closed the door and turned back into the room. I could still hear the tapping, and it wasn't until then that I realized that the sound was coming from behind the door connecting the two rooms. I moved quickly across to it, and standing beside it, listened more closely to the soft, irregular tapping on the other side.

"Denise, is that you?" I called softly.

The knocking stopped at once, but there was no reply. Carefully I opened the door and peered into the other room. I could see nothing. I was about to close the door again, when, suddenly, the sound started again. I tensed.

"Who's there?"

The tapping stopped at once. I looked around to see where it might have come from, but without success. I waited for it to start again, and presently it did, in the same faint but busy manner. Now I could hear that it was coming from the eighteenth-century walnut bureau in the far corner. I was certain of it. I moved silently across to it.

There was something in one of the six bureau drawers. I wondered idly if a mouse had been trapped in there. The tapping continued. As I came closer to its source, I decided it was coming from the top-left-hand drawer of the bureau. Standing to one side of the drawer so I would be out of the way of the mouse, or whatever it was trapped in the drawer, if, in its panic, it decided to leap out at me, I pulled the drawer. Nothing happened. The drawer was locked.

Perhaps, I thought, the key was in the top part of the bureau. I remembered that it opened out to form a desk. At the back of the desk was a maze of small pigeonholes into which my mother had thrust all manner of miscellaneous objects.

The hinged flap that formed the desk moved, which meant it wasn't locked. Yet when I pulled it, it refused to budge. There was nothing my fingers could grasp in order to loosen it. With some annoyance I looked around. Beside the open fireplace I saw a pair of fire irons.

I eased the tip of the fire iron into the crack of the bureau flap and levered. The flap fell with a clatter that startled me, and, I was sure, the mouse trapped in the drawer. The bunch of keys was in front of me. The pigeonholes were all empty.

The third key I tried reluctantly turned the lock. It felt as though the wood, swollen with damp, had gripped the tongue of the lock and was holding it fast. It did not occur to me now to stand aside. I wrenched the key impatiently. I felt the lock turn, freeing the tongue.

The drawer burst from the bureau. It hurled itself at me as though fired from a gun, striking me with such force that I was thrown backward. With a startled cry, I fell heavily on the carpet. The drawer fell on top of me. For a long moment I just lay there as though paralyzed, unable to move or even think. My heart thudded violently. My breathing was loud and harsh in my ears. The drawer was across my thighs. As far as I knew, I still held whatever had attacked me with such ruthless strength.

I gasped and kicked it away from me. At the same time, I scrambled hurriedly to my feet.

The drawer lay upside down on the floor. As I looked down at it, my mind began to clear, and I reasoned that whatever it was that had been trapped in the drawer and had hurled it at me with such force was not likely to be contained now. There was a sharp pain in my arms and across my ribs where the drawer had struck me.

I remembered the fire iron I had dropped near the bureau. I picked it up. If the thing, whatever it was, was still beneath the drawer, it wouldn't find me unprepared this time. Armed with the iron, I apprehensively approached the upturned drawer, which was lying near my mother's great four-poster bed. I reached out and struck the side of it with the iron, driving the drawer along the carpet until it stopped against the wall near the head of the bed. It made a subdued rattling noise as it moved.

I don't know what I expected to happen, but whatever it was, it didn't happen. The upturned drawer lay motionless and silent. Nevertheless, I still wasn't taking any chances. I carefully slid the tip of the iron beneath the drawer, and holding my breath, flipped it over with a quick movement.

There was something beneath the drawer. It lay on its side against the wall, but it did not look dangerous. It was just a little wooden platform about two inches square with a hole in the center and tiny rollers beneath it. It looked more like a toy. I became aware that it was becoming cold in the room. I shivered. I was still tightly gripping the fire iron as I stared down at the strange-looking wooden gadget.

I edged closer to the wooden gadget. The nearer I came to the bed, the colder the room seemed to become.

"What on earth are you doing with that iron, child?"

Lissi's voice startled me. The iron dropped to the floor with a ringing clatter. I swung around to face her.

"What's the matter, Megan?" Lissi's expression was concerned. "You look as though you've seen a ghost."

"It's cold in here," I murmured.

"Cold?" A new interest flickered across her face.

"Yes. Don't you feel it?"

"No." She shook her head. "I was on the way to my room when I heard something fall," she explained, walking across to the fallen drawer. I watched her bend to pick it up, then freeze as she spotted the wooden gadget.

"The planchette!" she cried. "You found it, Megan!"

"Is that what it is? A planchette?"

"This was your mother's." Lissi picked up the object. "That's funny. How did it get here?"

"I don't know."

"Your father threw it from the tower," she said, thoughtfully examining it. "He threw it into the sea. That was the night before he took you away from us."

"When my mother died?"

"Yes," she said. "I just saw the board in your room, but I never expected to see the planchette again."

"It was locked in the drawer of the bureau." In a few words, I told her what had happened. I felt a little easier in my own mind by the time I had finished. By then, too, I had convinced myself that it had simply been a matter of my pulling the drawer too hard so that it had leaped out at me the way it had.

My aunt was still staring down at the object in her hand. "Do you know what a planchette is?" she asked, holding it out to me.

I could see now that its castors and legs had been carved from ivory, as had the surface of the board in my room. The platform I had thought was wooden was, in fact, the same black gemstone from which the inlaid letters and figures on the board had been carved. I took it from her.

"Let's go back to my room," I suggested. "It's still cold in here."

"Yes, of course," she said. "I'll just put the drawer back first."

When she replaced the drawer, fitting it onto its runners, and pushing it in, I was a little surprised to see how easily it moved.

"It doesn't seem to be tight, does it?" she observed.

"Perhaps I opened the runners wider when I fell."

"Perhaps."

Back in my own room, she closed the connecting door, then turned to me. "Are you still cold, Megan?"

"Yes, but it's much warmer in here. Can't you feel the difference?"

"Did it feel like a damp cold?" she asked.

"Yes. I mean . . . so close to the sea."

"Of course."

Then, changing the subject, I said, "You were about to tell me about the planchette."

"A planchette is a rather primitive telepathic instrument that in the hands of a genuine medium can produce spirit writing at a séance. It can either write directly upon paper, or point to certain letters in answer to questions put to it."

"How?" I asked.

She carried the planchette over to the table beside my bed and placed it on the board. "Do you have a pencil?"

"Somewhere. . . ." I found a pen in my handbag and handed it to her.

"The pen fits through the hole in the planchette, giving it a third leg." She demonstrated. "It stands upright now. See? At a séance the person asking the question, if sensitive, places a finger lightly on the planchette, barely touching it, and the planchette moves."

The planchette didn't move. I pointed this out to her.

She laughed. "I told you, Megan. Your mother had the gift, not I." She gestured to the planchette. "Try it; I'm certain now that it will write for you."

But I was reluctant to try. I didn't like the idea at all of toying with something I didn't understand. I shook my head.

She smiled. "Are you afraid, Megan? Your father also feared the things he couldn't understand." Her eyes, as they held mind, were almost hypnotic in their intensity. "But your mother feared nothing."

"I'm a little tired," I said evasively.

"Of course you are, child. I'm sorry. But you asked, and the answer is there if you look for it."

I stared at the planchette. "My mother used to do this?"

"Your mother did not need a Ouija board. To her, this was just a toy our mother gave her as a child. It was something for her to play with. Hers was a wider, deeper perception than childish scribbling, or answering questions with simple affirmatives or negatives. The power that came to her was of divination. She did not have to seek it. It came to her. I thought she did not want it, even though she *was* a Ferrari. But in part that was your father's fault. He could neither understand nor believe. None of us blamed Bernadette."

Coming to me, she placed her hands on my shoulders and lightly kissed my cheek.

"Good night, Megan," she said, then added soberly, "You are so very much like Bernadette."

"Good night, Lissi," I murmured.

At the door, she turned and smiled at me. "Have you read the book?" she asked.

"Only what my grandmother wrote."

She nodded. "Do you remember your grandmother, Megan? She was wise and kind and beautiful. A wonderful woman. To her it was a beneficent gift. It brought her nothing but good. She used it to help and comfort those around her. It could be the same for you."

"She lost her only son," I reminded her. "And my mother died young. Was that a part of the price she had to pay for the gift?"

For a moment I thought she was about to make an angry retort, but all she did was bow her head as she closed the door. I heard the lock click, then her footsteps as she walked along the passage to her own room.

I resisted an impulse to follow and apologize for what I had said. Instead I went to my bag and took out the envelope John Carson had delivered to me at the airport. Sitting on the edge of the bed, I reread what my mother had written. And as I read, I began to experience the first hint of understanding, now that I knew a little more about my mother's so-called gift. I knew that the document was my mother's contribution to the family history of extrasensory perception. I read again the opening words. "There shall not be found among you the faithful anyone that useth divination, or an enchanter, or a wizard or necromancer. For all these things are an abomination unto the Lord." I wondered what it meant, and sensed, somehow, that they were not words Lissi would have appreciated.

Or: "People who care nothing that by their importunity they spur the medium toward her ultimate possession and destruction by forces far beyond their understanding." That could have been written especially for Lissi. With a new ripple of apprehension, I suddenly remembered that *I* now seemed to be the one she spurred uncaring toward the unknown horrors my mother *must* have encountered to feel the need to write that warning for others.

I lay in the large bed, trying to sleep, but it wasn't easy. I was still too tense. In order to induce sleep, I took deep breaths and closed my eyes, forcing my body to relax by using a trick my father had once taught me, and which, so far, hadn't failed me. This involved relaxing all the muscles of the body, one by one, beginning from the top of the head and working down from there. It required an effort of concentration to force these muscles to release the tension and go flaccid.

Slowly, as I concentrated, I felt my apprehension flow away from me. The big old house was silent. The sea and the sigh of the wind beyond the windows of my room had eased. I attributed the quietness of the sea to the flat of the ebbtide, that soon would change to pour into the Minas Channel in an increasing tumult of eddies and tide rips that, as the tide rose, would pound and swirl below my window.

A little puff of breath burst from my closed lips, waking me as I drifted into sleep. I had by now reached the muscles of my left forearm. Then, just as I was drifting off again, I heard a faint rubbing sound in the room. I stiffened. All my concentration vanished in an instant. The sound was very close to the bed.

Slowly, carefully, I turned my head on the pillows toward the source of the sound. Again, I thought it might be a mouse. Then, as I turned my head, I suddenly saw it—a faint movement in the darkness less than a foot from my face. It was coming from the Ouija board on the table, beside the bed. Across the top of the board, where I had left it, I could dimly make out the document my mother had written.

The soft rubbing persisted. It sounded as if it were working its way right across the page. Not taking my eyes from the table, I reached out for the pillow on the other side of the bed, then, taking hold of it, and as a continuation of the same movement, swung around and brought it down on the paper and the thing that was moving across it, as hard as I could.

I must have hit it at an angle. The table fell heavily to the floor, carrying the board with it. Something skidded halfway across the room—something wooden, which with a sharp cracking sound struck an obstacle of some sort and stopped. The mouse, if that was what had been making the sound, would be gone. I sat up and switched on the lamp.

The small table had fallen on its side, with the Ouija board still lying face down a short distance from it. The only other thing I could see was the pillow lying still farther away. I couldn't see my mother's document.

Clambering out of bed, I stood the table upright, then picked up the pillow. Beneath the chair I found the planchette, which was what, I now realized, I had heard sliding across the floor. The pen my aunt had fit into the hole, which had been left there, was shattered.

I was on my way back to the bed when I noticed a corner of paper protruding from beneath it. I retrieved it quickly and brought it across to the reading lamp to examine it more closely and see what damage, if any, had been done to it. I spread it out on the Ouija board.

The paper was unmarked. I had expected it to be marked, as I had been almost certain that a mouse had been nibbling at it. I was beginning to feel cold again, as I had done earlier in the adjoining room. I folded the thick paper, intending to put it back in the envelope. Suddenly, as I was folding it, I noticed the writing on the back, where there had been no writing before. It was my mother's handwriting.

As I stared at the written words, I found myself becoming more and more frightened. The short hairs on the back of my neck began to prickle. There was no doubt at all in my mind that it was my mother's handwriting, just as there was no doubt that the words had been written with a ball-point pen of the type my aunt had fit into the hole of the planchette. The writing looked fresh. Aware that my heart was pumping furiously, I read the words: "Bern . . . Berna . . . Bernadette, Meg . . . Megan . . . don . . . do . . . not . . . let . . . you . . . your . . . yourself . . . listen to . . . the . . . tem . . . tempter. . . ."

I stared disbelievingly at the message. "Megan, do not let yourself listen to the tempter." It ended in almost a straight line that speared away from the last letter. I remembered that the words she had added to my father's notes had ended in the same abrupt, almost violent manner. I turned back to my father's notes.

He had asked, "Suppose that ... the scientist suddenly discovered himself facing the unexplainable, the uncanny happening for which neither his training nor experience can find any answer? What then, Bernadette?"

My mother had written, "It is then that he, too, would find the agony and the terror. ..." And it ended with a straight line plowing a black furrow through the page.

Beneath, my father had commented, "This happened July 15, 1967. *I had not the strength to prevent it.*"

He had not the strength to prevent it! I was reading a different meaning into that line of his now than I had in the aircraft. A horrifying meaning. Could what she had written be the answer to his question, not as I had thought at first something she had written years before? It seemed so. Yet how could this be possible? In 1967 she had already been dead for eight years.

Unless she had forced his hand against his will, and in her handwriting, to write that answer in the notes he had made eight years after her death. As she might have guided the planchette to write her warning to me.

I stared at the written words. I didn't *want* to believe what I saw. I *couldn't* believe it. Because if I did, it seemed to me, I must also believe that my own mother had the unholy power to return from the grave, to warn me, as she had warned my father, against fearful dangers that only she understood. But I couldn't believe that. It was against everything I had been brought up to believe.

As I studied again the words that had been written on the back of my mother's original document, a strange thing began to happen to me. My hand, as though compelled by a will stronger than my own, began to reach toward my mother's written name that began the warning she had written. It was as though a much stronger mind than my own were forcing my fingers to touch the blue-black ink. Though I tried to pull my quivering hand away, I couldn't: it was an irresistible urge.

Horrified, I saw my index finger touch my mother's name and begin to rub it gently. I watched the ink begin to smear beneath the ball of my rotating fingertip. I snatched it away from the paper, and throwing myself back into the bed, lay there, shivering, with the blankets pulled right up to my chin.

Suddenly, for the first time, I became aware of pain in the fingers and palm of my right hand. My right hand felt quite frozen. The fingers were so paralyzed by cold that I could neither bend nor straighten them. As the cold began to flow out of my hand to fill the room, it created a dank breeze that touched my face.

And then, below my windows, I heard the rush and swirl of eddying, racing water.

One of the great tides from the Bay of Fundy was forcing its way through the Minas Channel.

Chapter Five

Somehow, I had managed to fall into a deep, dreamless sleep. Looking back, I don't see how this could have been possible; yet it was. I had slept soundly.

My first impulse when I awoke was to tell Lissi what had happened during the night. I looked around the room. Everything was as it had been. The Ouija board and planchette were on the table.

The drawer into which I had thrust my mother's testimony before going to sleep was partly open. I glanced inside it. The folded paper was still there. My father's note had been turned back, and what had been written on the back of my mother's testimony lay uppermost, in plain sight.

Then, as I allowed the significance of last night's events to sink in, bringing with it a renewed sense of apprehension and sheer alienation, I decided not to tell Lissi what had happened. Not if I could help it. I felt more strongly than ever that what my mother had written referred directly to Lissi, even though her name was never actually mentioned. The trouble was that Lissi believed so implicitly in the beneficence of the *power* she worshiped, whereas my mother seemed to fear and hate it. That was why my mother blamed Lissi for whatever unpleasant things had happened to her. I believed she had reason to feel that way, considering my own experience.

I had just finished showering and was returning to the bedroom when Denise arrived with coffee and crisp, hot rolls smothered in fresh farm butter. I realized then that I was ravenous, and breakfast would not be served downstairs for another hour.

Denise was telling me about the guests who were expected for the weekend. She sounded quite excited. Apparently, guests were a rare commodity at the Ferrari house. "You'll like Nadine and Anita, Miss Marshall," she told me as she poured my coffee. "They're full of life. They're identical twins, you know. It's incredible how alike they are. Apparently they even think alike. Nadine was telling me during their last vacation that when one gets a fright or something like that, the other one feels it too, even though they may be miles apart."

"Really?"

"Oh, yes, there's a very close bond between them. That's Dr. Schiller's opinion, too. He's been making notes on their experiences ever since they came here. He's going to write a paper on them for a medical journal."

I sipped the coffee. It was hot. "Who is Dr. Schiller?" I asked.

"A friend of Miss Lissi's. She knew him when she was at college in Quebec. He owns a private hospital on the Minas Basin road, about halfway to Sussex Wold. A peculiar place—high stone walls, iron gates, guards. It's a mental hospital. People come there from all over the world. Anyway, you'll meet him today when he and the others come for dinner."

"Who else are we expecting today, Denise?"

"Madame Larre didn't say, but I should imagine Miss Cavendish will be here. She always comes. Madame Grasse, if she's feeling well enough. I'm sure she'd be under pressure to come."

I studied her face. "You say that as though these gatherings are a regular thing."

"Not anymore," she said. "They were once. But with Madame Grasse's health failing, they're not so regular anymore. Of course, it's a big strain on her. She is the only one in the group with sensitivity. None of the others can do it. They've all tried."

I frowned at her over the rim of the coffeecup. "You're talking in riddles, Denise. Do what?"

Suddenly she looked anxious. "You mean . . . you don't know *why* they're coming here today?"

"My aunt said she was inviting some friends of my mother's for dinner tonight—that's all."

Although Denise said nothing, her expression suggested she wouldn't have mentioned it if she had known that. She shrugged. "I talk too much," she said ruefully. "I was sure Miss Lissi would have told you. Madame Larre told us, so it's no secret. They come here to hold séances. Madame Grasse is a medium. About two years ago during one of these séances, she had a stroke in the library. She's partly paralyzed now."

My curiosity was fully aroused. "Do you think they really communicate with . . . with the dead?"

She avoided my eyes. "I don't know," she murmured uncomfortably. "They believe your mother will communicate with you."

Remembering last night, I suddenly felt weak. "My . . . mother?"

"Compared with your mother, Madame Grasse is nothing," Denise said. "Madame Larre says there never was a medium like your mother. The things that happened when she was here were unbelievable. Uncanny. The

71

whole house went crazy. Heavy furniture moved, drawers flew open . . ."

"Drawers . . . flew open?" I stared at her.

"Once Madame Larre told me that the cutlery drawer in the dining room shot right across the room, spilling knives, forks, and spoons all over the floor. Heavy furniture moved, books fell off the library shelves, people heard voices, saw people who weren't there. All sorts of things happened that nobody downstairs could explain. I remember when I was a little girl in Sussex Wold people said that the Ferrari house was haunted. The tradesmen stopped calling here. They still won't deliver anything if they can help it. Maxwell has to fetch everything we need from town."

I had finished the coffee and the first roll. Denise poured me a second cup. I said, with a light but uneasy laugh, "You'll frighten me away from here if you keep talking like that."

She smiled. "Oh, that all happened a long, long time ago," she said cheerfully. "When your mother was alive. Nothing like that ever happens here now."

A short time later, as I came downstairs for breakfast, I noticed that there seemed more activity in the house than usual. Frances was polishing the banister, and a girl I hadn't seen before was going into the library with a variety of equipment. Outside, I could see Maxwell polishing the already gleaming Daimler, while near the surrounding wall, beneath the oaks and maples, a white-haired man was steering a power mower over a smooth green carpet of grass. I wondered if he was the chauffeur's father, the man who had once so jealously guarded yellow roses for me.

My aunt was waiting for me. "I hope you slept well, Megan," she said, unfolding her napkin. "Please sit down and have your breakfast. Your cousins are coming from school today, and we have other guests. I have already told you about your mother's friends. I think you'll like them."

I sat down hurriedly. "I'm sorry if I've kept you waiting," I said.

Lissi sipped her tomato juice. "Megan, do you know someone from Boston named Fulton? Denis Fulton? He says he knows you."

I looked my surprise. "Denis Fulton? No ... no, I don't think so."

"He telephoned this morning and said it was most urgent that he talk to you. Apparently he is staying with relatives in Halifax. He said he is opening an office in Halifax for a John Carson. Do you know anyone of that name?"

"Yes, of course," I said. "My father's attorney."

"I see." She was looking at me closely. "Anyway, I told him he could come to see you today on whatever business he has been sent to transact with you. I did feel it necessary to warn him, however, that you might not be available to see him immediately when he arrives."

"What do you mean . . . unavailable?"

"I told you we are having guests," she said a trifle impatiently. "It should be a most interesting afternoon."

I sat back while Madame Larre served my cereal. "You're making me curious," I said. "Who are these guests?"

"There are two ladies—Madame Grasse and her dear friend Miss Cavendish—and Dr. Schiller. They all live in Sussex Wold. It was Madame Grasse, by the way, who answered my questions about your welfare, although she has never been in Boston in her life. Neither has Miss Cavendish."

"Madame Grasse is a medium?"

She nodded. "In some small degree she has your mother's gift. But she does not have Bernadette's courage, or her power. But you will learn more about her at the séance this afternoon."

"Séance?" I looked doubtfully across the table at her. "I'm not sure . . ."

"Please—no doubts!" Lissi snapped. "The séance has been arranged especially for your benefit. You've no idea how much trouble it was to persuade Madame Grasse to come here today. Besides, there's your young man—Fulton. He, too, will be at the séance. I happened to mention it to him, and he professed an immediate interest. He said he had been involved in psychic research as an extracurricular activity at Harvard. So, naturally, I invited him to attend. He will be staying for dinner."

"Yes, that's all right," I said quickly. "But I still don't particularly like the idea."

"Wouldn't you like to communicate with your mother?" Her dark eyebrows had contracted into a small frown. "Or your father? You could, you know, through Madame Grasse."

"Look, it isn't that . . ."

"What is holding you back, Megan?" she demanded. "Did something happen last night to frighten you? If so, you must tell me about it at once. I need to know. It could mean the power is coming to you, as I am sure it must one day, because you are Bernadette's only child."

I was reluctant to tell her anything about what had happened last night. It would only make me more deeply involved.

Suspicion lingered in her dark eyes. She shook her head and returned to the subject of the séance. "Nothing will happen at this afternoon's séance that could disturb or frighten you," she said. "I'm sure of that."

We ate for a few minutes in silence; then Lissi looked up at me again and asked, "Why do you think this young man wishes to see you?"

"I guess it's something to do with my father's estate," I suggested warily.

"There was an estate?" She sounded genuinely surprised.

"Yes, of course. A few thousand, I guess," I said vaguely.

She nodded. "I'm pleased for your sake that he was able to leave you that, Megan," she said quietly, studying my face across the table. "But tomorrow we must talk about your future quite seriously. I want you to live here with me, and allow me to provide for you. I'm a wealthy woman, and you are my heir. We'll decide a suitable allowance for you, and a car of your own. You may want to return to college. I think you should. Anyway, that can be arranged. Perhaps in Quebec, where your mother and I studied. You and I must go to Montreal in a week or so, to select a wardrobe for you. I haven't been to Montreal in years. You've never been there—or to Quebec. I think you'll enjoy it."

She had changed the course of our conversation adroitly into safer channels, I realized. I was grateful for the respite, no matter how temporary, from more sinister considerations.

Chapter Six

Among the fresh red roses that had been placed in the library was a single yellow bloom which I knew had been selected for me. As I entered the room, Madame Larre was supervising Frances, who was placing the heavy library chairs around the table. I moved across to the small table beneath my mother's portrait, on which the flowers had been placed, and carefully extracted the single yellow rose.

"Do you have a vase in your room, mam'selle?" Madame Larre asked over her shoulder.

"I remember, I once had a vase that held a single rose. It was blue, I think. My aunt gave it to me."

"There's a vase like that in the reception room," Frances volunteered. "I could fetch it for you."

"No, no, it's quite all right," I assured her. "I'll find it." I turned back to the housekeeper.

"Why are the roses beneath my mother's portrait, and not on the table?" I asked. "They would look much more effective on the table."

"The big table must be kept clear," she replied. "Besides, the roses have a definite place beneath your mother's portrait. Particularly today."

"Why today?"

"Today is the anniversary of your mother's death," she said. "Red roses were always her flowers. That is one reason why the roses have importance today, mam'selle. The other is that you are here. If it is possible for Madame Grasse to contact your mother, today offers more likelihood of success because of you."

"If it is possible?" I returned. "Do you believe Madame Grasse can do the things they say?"

The housekeeper glanced at me sidelong with dark, expressionless eyes. "I believe so. I saw her do it once, about two years ago. I do not believe in such things as a rule, you understand. I have seen Madame Grasse attempt to communicate with the dead at other times. Strange things happen, things your aunt accepted, but I could not. But two years ago in this room Madame Grasse spoke to us with your mother's voice, and looked at us with your mother's eyes. She told us things about you in Boston that we did not know."

I stared at her. My flesh was beginning to tingle again. "What did she say . . . about me?"

"That your father would die this summer. She knew that would happen. She said that you were so alike that when you looked in the mirror it was she who looked back at you. And she said that Mam'selle Lissi must bring you back to the house this summer, because this is where you belong. You were her second self, she said."

She had said these things so simply and sincerely that I gaped at her in astonishment. "You're joking," I whispered.

"No, mam'selle, it is the truth. It was your mother speaking through Madame Grasse. I swear it. I was not the only one who saw and heard these things. It was as though your mother possessed her for those few moments. Then Madame Grasse began to struggle against what was happening to her. She desperately fought it. It was a terrifying thing to watch, and very strange, because sometimes we would hear a man's voice, very loud and obscene. Then Madame Grasse screamed and fell from the chair as though she were dead. Dr. Schiller revived her, but what happened that day has left her as you will see her this afternoon. She does not walk well anymore."

"Incredible!" I heard myself exclaiming.

"Mam'selle." Denise's voice came from just behind me. I turned.

"Yes, Denise?"

"There's a M'sieur Fulton to see you. He's in the reception room with Mam'selle Lissi."

I followed her to the reception room.

The newcomer was talking to my aunt near the windows at the far side of the room. He was tall and blond, and extremely good-looking. I had never seen him before. As I entered the room, he was saying in a deep voice, "Of course, you and I both know that it's also possible to produce stigmata, or marks that resemble the nail marks of the crucifixion, by means that have no connection whatsoever with extrasensory perception or clairvoyance." It was an interesting voice. His French was flawless. "I remember a case I read about in Boston where . . ." He saw me and broke off.

"Ah, Megan," my aunt said, gliding across the floor toward me. "This is M'sieur Fulton."

I smiled at him as he took my outstretched hand and bowed slightly from the waist. As he straightened, he grinned warmly.

"We haven't met before," he said, releasing my hand, "but my uncle has talked quite often about you."

"Your uncle?"

"Yes. John Carson. He's my uncle."

"Oh, I didn't know that."

"There was no reason for you to know that," he said.

"Perhaps you and Mr. Fulton would prefer to retire to the study to conduct your business," Lissi suggested. "It will be more private for you."

"It won't take long," Denis Fulton told me. "I have an important document for you to read and sign."

Lissi nodded. "My guests will start arriving at any moment," she said. "We will wait for you to return before starting the séance."

The study was next to the library. I had not been in there before. It was smaller than the other rooms. There was a typewriter on the desk, and modern steel filing cabinets along one wall. I suggested to my companion that he take the swivel chair behind the desk, while I drew up another for myself.

"I didn't realize there would be more documents to sign, Mr. Fulton. I thought I had signed them all before leaving Boston."

"You did," he said. "Practically all of them. This one, from the bank, I brought with me. It does need your signature, but to be quite truthful, it could just as easily have been mailed to you."

"I don't understand, Mr. Fulton?"

"My uncle is worried about you," he said.

"Why should he be worried about me?" I asked.

He smiled at me. He had an attractively boyish smile. "First things first. Read this and sign. Then we can talk. Okay?"

It was just a simple bank transfer to an account where better interest would be earned for some of the money my father had left me. I signed it and watched him replace it carefully in the envelope from which he had produced it.

"Well?"

"My uncle has been thinking of opening an office in Halifax for some time, Megan," he explained. "More and more New Englanders are coming to Nova Scotia every year on vacation, and many of them are buying property in the area. It has all the requirements. Good fishing—salmon, trout. The whole region is a sportsman's paradise. Did you know that, Megan?"

"No, I didn't." I returned his smile. "But you were telling me—or about to—why your uncle is worried about me."

"He just wanted you to know that in the event of your needing a friend, or help of any sort, that I'm not far away. No farther away than the nearest telephone, in fact."

"But why should I need help?" I asked.

He shrugged. "You never know," he said

enigmatically. "I don't know what could happen, but . . . well, it's nice to know, isn't it, that there's someone around you can turn to when the need arises." He sat forward and rested his forearms on the desk. His gray eyes searched mine. He frowned and looked away from whatever he thought he saw there. "Are you sure you're happy here, Megan?"

"Why shouldn't I be happy here?" I countered indignantly. "This is my home, after all. I mean, this is where I was born."

"But do you *like* it here?" he persisted.

"In many ways, yes."

"But not in all?"

I shrugged. "Nothing's ever perfect, is it?"

"So things are not going as smoothly as you would have me think?"

"Who said that?"

"It's this ESP stuff, isn't it? Your mother was a medium. Your father told my uncle she was. My uncle knew the contents of the envelope he had delivered to you at the airport. He told me what was in it." He studied my expression. "Has anything happened to you in this house for which there doesn't seem to be a normal explanation?"

"Why do you say 'in this house'?"

"Because in psychic research, the inexplicable, when we find an instance of it, is nearly always repeated in the same locality, in the same house, and to someone close to the person who had the first experience. If something even remotely like the experiences your mother had has happened to you, you must tell me about it. For your own safety and well-being, you must confide in me. That is why I'm here. To help you as a friend—if you will let me. Will you let me help you, Megan?"

I hesitated, debating with myself as to whether I should tell him or not; then, abruptly, I made up my mind. I decided to tell him what had happened to me the night before. And that was exactly what I did. Somehow, sitting here in Lissi's study, with the sun shining brightly through the windows, the story sounded quite ludicrous in my own ears.

However, Denis listened intently, without interruption, until I had finished. Then he shook his head and asked thoughtfully, "Couldn't the drawer have been stuck?"

"No."

"And there was no mouse?"

"No, I'm certain of it."

"So the sound you heard—the scratching sound—must have come from the planchette."

"How can you be so sure?" I asked.

"Well, what other explanation could there be? What other explanation is there for the warning to you in your mother's handwriting?"

"How can anyone explain a thing like that, Denis? Can you?"

"I'd like to see the message."

"I'll get it before you leave." There was a soft knocking at the door. "Yes?"

Denise's voice answered. "Mam'selle Ferrari has asked me to inform you that the guests have now arrived, and that coffee is being served in the reception room."

"We'll be out in a few moments," Denis Fulton told her.

"I'll tell her, m'sieur."

He looked at me. "Do you know anything about poltergeists, Megan? Or psychokinesis?"

My smile was weak and apologetic. "Not much, I'm afraid. Hardly anything, in fact."

"A poltergeist, the believers tell us, is a noisy spirit which throws things about, thumps, scratches, bangs on walls, and occasionally carries objects from one place to another. It can *bring* things to people."

"Like last night?" I thought of something else. "Denise did tell me that someone kept bringing the Ouija board back into my bedroom every time she put it where it belonged."

"Which was where?"

"My mother's room."

He nodded. "Psychokinesis, on the other hand, means the movement of physical objects without the use of physical means. By the mind. Notice the similarity in effect? Telekinesis is another word coined in psychic research to explain the ability of some spiritualistic mediums to do these things deliberately by force of mind."

I shook my head, only partially understanding his words. "And?"

He sighed. "It seems possible that your mother was that kind of medium," he said. "Are you afraid to attend the séance this afternoon? If you are, I'll find some excuse to keep you away."

"What about you?"

"Normally I wouldn't miss it," he said. "But, in the circumstances, whatever you decide . . ."

I thought about it for a long moment, then said, "It doesn't matter. I must say I feel a little better about it now that you're here." I smiled again. "I don't mind going." I stood up. "Now, shall we go?"

"Wait." He glanced quickly at the door. "There is something I have to ask you. Did you know your father came here frequently?"

"You're wrong." I shook my head. "He's never been back here since my mother died. That was thirteen years ago."

"So you didn't know he came here every second week?"

"I know he didn't!" I said with certainty. "He couldn't have."

"Okay," he said. "Different approach. Do you know where your father went every second Saturday? Religiously, every second Saturday, leaving home at six-thirty A.M. and returning in time for dinner?"

"He played golf," I told him. "He played golf every Saturday. It was his only relaxation."

He was frowning at me. "You're sure of that?"

"Yes, of course I am."

"I'm only asking this, Megan," he said reasonably, "because my uncle wants to know. Apparently it's important for him to know. Now, I'll just have to tell him what you told me. He has never been here since your mother died. Right?"

"Oh, I'm sure of that," I said. "Dad was a good golfer. He had a handicap of seven. I saw him once or twice on television playing in some of the open events. He was very good."

As we walked into the reception room, Denise was serving coffee. Lissi introduced us to the assembled guests.

Dr. Schiller was a big man with a strong face and sharp brown eyes that probed disconcertingly into mine. His brown hair looked too young for his age, and I suspected it was dyed. His long muttonchop sideburns were as gray as a badger's.

"I knew your mother, Megan," he said as he

took my hand. "She was a remarkable woman. Her death was a personal loss to all of us."

"The resemblance is extraordinary." Miss Cavendish was a thin woman in her fifties. Her hair was the same shade of brown as Dr. Schiller's, and therefore, to my mind also suspect. "Quite remarkable."

Madame Grasse wasn't at all what I had expected. She was a plump, pink-and-white woman about the same age as Miss Cavendish. Her hair was natural blond streaked heavily with gray. Her smile was pleasant, her eyes a bright and friendly blue. She sat in a wheelchair, her legs covered with a rug. I offered her my hand, but she caught it, and dragging me down to her, kissed me firmly on the cheek.

"If ever there was a Ferrari, this is one, Lissi," she cried. "Thank God! Bernadette would be so proud of her."

Lissi introduced her to Denis Fulton. "Not *another* young man from Boston!" Madame Grasse exclaimed. "How could the wheel turn full cycle so soon?"

Lissi frowned down at her. "He is an attorney," she said coldly. "He brought some documents for Megan to sign. He is also interested in spiritualism, which was why I invited him to stay and take part in the séance. Madame Larre is joining us, so Mr. Fulton will make the seventh."

"Yes, I see." Madame Grasse was smiling up at me. "This should be an interesting experience, Lissi," she said. "I am beginning not to regret that I allowed you to persuade me to come."

"Without you, Antoinette, there could be no séance in this house," my aunt told her. "Until now, you are our only link with Bernadette." I didn't like the way she said that, or the way she glanced at me.

We sat down. Denis sat next to me. "Is there some significance in the number seven relating to séances, Miss Ferrari?" he asked Lissi in his calm, deep voice. "I hadn't heard that before."

"It is just an idiosyncrasy of Antoinette's," my aunt said, with an indulgent glance at Madame Grasse. "It has no significance other than that she feels she has been most successful when seven believers have taken part."

"Are you a religious group?" Denis asked.

Dr. Schiller gave a booming laugh and answered for them. "If you mean are we religious in the sense that we believe in God and a hereafter—we certainly are. We've had proof of the existence of that other world many times. We've been granted glimpses of the people we loved and who have died before us. Our group has been granted examples of precognition. Can the gift of seeing, hearing, and in some small way understanding these other worldly things come from anywhere else but God, Mr. Fulton?"

Denis nodded. "So that means you are Spiritualists."

Schiller smiled. "We are seekers after truth, Mr. Fulton," he said. "As *you* have been, if your interest is in psychic research. In a way, so is ours. However, I think we might have gone farther than you. Much farther. Yes, I am sure you will soon come to understand what I mean."

Denis nodded. "And, of course, at the other end of the scale is the possibility of demoniac possession. Doesn't that worry you?"

"If we are firm and confident—if we *believe*—we have nothing to fear, m'sieur," my aunt interposed quickly. "*None* of us!" She glanced quickly at Madame Grasse.

Denis said, "The premise being that if we're not firm and confident and believe, we *do* have something to fear. Is that right, Mam'selle Ferrari?"

"That sounds to me like a leading question," Schiller interposed with a laugh.

Denis smiled at him. "Seeking truth, Doctor," he said. "With your training, you know the importance of truth, without which no evidence, scientific or otherwise, can be valid."

"Oh, I do," Schiller said firmly. "Especially truth I myself have seen proven. I know that as well as you know that psychiatry doesn't yet accept extrasensory perception in any form."

"Or demoniac possession?"

Schiller chuckled. "Your point, I presume, being that we should not accept the biblical notion of demoniac possession?"

"Doesn't the church, or at least one important section of it, still have the ritual of exorcism on its books? Wouldn't you say the church therefore still believes demoniac possession possible?"

"Not being a churchman, I wouldn't know," Schiller said with a trace of resentment. "What is a demon, so-called, anyway? The ancient Greek word *daimonion* was used to describe a spirit who could be either good or evil. Like 'angel,' the word meant a spirit generally, whether good or evil. In the Middle Ages and later, demons were still believed to have the power of taking possession of the minds and actions of people. The mentally ill were thought to be demoniacally possessed from ancient times almost to the present day. But this possession wasn't always an evil thing. Socrates believed his life and actions were controlled by his *daimonion*, which, communicating with him as an inward voice, told him what *not* to do. Of course, today we know a great deal more about such things. Through psychiatry, our knowledge of the workings of the human mind has made immeasurable advances."

I noticed Lissi was frowning slightly at Denis Fulton. She stood up. "I think we should adjourn to the library," she said firmly.

As we all rose to our feet, my eyes unexpectedly met those of Madame Grasse. She seemed paler than before. There was a frightened look in her eyes. Denis moved across to her. "May I help you, Madame Grasse?" he asked cheerfully.

The frightened look faded from her friendly blue eyes as she nodded and thanked him. He turned her chair, and we followed the others to the library.

Chapter Seven

We sat around the library table. Madame Grasse was at the head of the table. The drapes were drawn across the window, darkening the room. The air-conditioning hummed softly through dispensing vents.

"It may take a little time," Madame Grasse was saying to Denis and me. "We will start by trying to contact Naidu, an Indian maharajah who lived and died near Bhopal during the nineteenth century. Naidu is quite a pleasant, friendly spirit." She looked at me. "There is no reason for anyone here to be afraid of him. There are good and evil spirits," she went on. "A cheerful spirit like Naidu finds fear amusing. The spirit of someone who loved you, as for instance Megan's mother, finds your fear a cause for sympathy and greater love. But with an evil spirit, this changes about. An evil spirit feeds on fear. Fear strengthens evil and multiplies it to horrifying proportions."

She was slowly looking around at us, her blue eyes dwelling on each face. Then, watching Denis, she nodded. "There is something I want to say before I begin. It is something I have meant to say ever since the last time I was here, three years ago."

"Antoinette, is this really necessary?" my aunt asked impatiently.

"It *is* necessary, Lissi, and it concerns all of you," Madame Grasse said sternly. Her eyes fixed on mine. "On that occasion, we made our first contact with your mother. In all the years we sought her before that, there was no sign that she heard. Nothing to even indicate that she had ever existed. But suddenly she was here, and I had the impression that she was trying to warn me . . . us, about something. I began to grow afraid. I sensed evil. It was an evil that seemed to me stronger than any power of your mother's, living or dead. I could *feel* it approaching me. I tried to escape from it by waking myself from my trance, but I couldn't. The more terrified I became, the greater became its threat to me. I felt it seize me. It began not only forcing itself into my mind, but into my body! Something huge and cold and utterly ruthless! I could *feel* it! . . ."

She broke off abruptly, and stared past me as though at something none of us could see. My flesh crawled as I watched her. I suppressed a desire to leap from my chair and run from the room. Then, as I still watched her, her face changed again. She shook her head, and I knew she could see me again.

She looked down at her legs. "I remember falling from my chair, and Dr. Schiller helping me. The next thing I knew, I was in a hospital."

"You had a cerebral hemorrhage, Antoinette," Dr. Schiller said quietly. "As I've told you before, it was a rupture of a sclerosed blood vessel in your brain. I had warned you often enough that hardened arteries and cholesterol buildup were complicating your high blood pressure. The rupture was the end result of something that had been in the process of happening for some time."

"I know," she said. "But why was it triggered just at that moment?"

"Nervous strain. You were tense. You were under extreme pressure. Excited. I'd never seen you like that before during a séance. When you became frightened, that also showed. All these things contributed to what happened."

She looked from Dr. Schiller to my aunt. "Suppose . . . it happens again? Suppose the . . . evil presence I felt drives the others away? Suppose I . . . become afraid again?"

"This time we'll understand what is happening," Lissi said confidently. "We'll know what to do, Antoinette. We'll bring you back at once. You know you can trust us."

Madame Grasse looked back at me. "We will start by putting our hands on the table," she said quietly. "Ready? Palms raised so that the weight is on the fingertips. After the first few minutes, you won't notice any strain in holding the position. Now, lock your little fingers, left over right."

Denis winked at me slyly as he hooked the little finger of his left hand over the little finger of my right hand. Lissi, who was seated on my left, linked her finger with mine.

Across from us, Dr. Schiller sat next to Madame Grasse, with Alice Cavendish on his left and Claudette Larre, the housekeeper, facing Denis.

"Is everyone linked?" Madame Grasse asked. I will use first names from now on. If you are linked and comfortable, answer as I ask you. Karl? Claudette? Alice?"

Beside me, Denis answered "Yes," too, when she spoke his name.

"Yes," I said in answer to Madame Grasse's question to me.

"Lissi?"

"Yes."

"For your information, Megan and Denis, the end of the table is left open for communication. We have now assumed the shape of a magnet through our bodies and linked hands. Now, as a magnet draws steel to itself, so will the linked power of our bodies and minds now draw to us the loved ones we seek. Are we ready?"

"We are ready."

"Then concentrate on the thought of Naidu, Maharajah of Bhopal."

We all concentrated. For myself, it didn't do me much good. There was no way I could summon up the image of the lost maharajah, as hard as I tried. He was just too elusive.

Then Madame Grasse called the maharajah in a voice that to me sounded theatrically hollow and quavering. "Naidu, Prince of India. Answer, Lord of Bhopal. Are you there, Naidu? Why do you not answer me, you who always come when I call? Are you afraid, Naidu? Is it because you sense danger here? Or because there are among us this evening strangers who do not know you as I do? Answer, Naidu. . . . Answer. . . . Answer. . . ."

Her voice faded into silence. My eyes were closed. After some moments, I felt my head nod. I straightened myself with an effort.

My mind began to clear again, and I opened my eyes. I started, and my heart began to pound furiously. My companions were gone, as were the familiar surroundings of the library.

The air had grown unbearably hot. I could feel tiny droplets of perspiration forming on my forehead. Above me a fan of plaited cane swung monotonously back and forth. Fearfully, I stared about me.

I was standing in a huge, high-ceilinged room. All around me were heavy silk drapes and the curved arches of Oriental architecture. Beyond the windows, which were left open to catch the slightest breath of moving air, I could see that it was night. Oil lamps burned in niches in the wall.

Nothing moved in the room except the slowly swinging fan. My eyes followed a rope of plaited fibers suspended from it and rested on an Indian boy who, even though he was dozing, was automatically working the fan.

I walked tentatively toward the boy. "Where am I?" I asked him in English.

He took no notice of me, nor did the rhythm of his movement falter. He was a plump, obviously well-fed boy of thirteen or fourteen.

"Answer me!" I cried, reaching out to grasp his shoulder. I drew back from him in horror as my hand reached through thin air. The boy had no substance whatsoever.

The boy turned to one of the windows. I looked in the same direction just in time to see a black-bearded man drawing himself up onto the sill, then, obviously exhausted, haul him-

98

self into the room to collapse onto the floor. A second face appeared at the window. The boy watched silently. The fan continued its regular rhythm. The first man pushed himself up from the floor, and together with the second man, who was clean-shaven, came toward us. They both looked fierce and tense. They looked apprehensively about the room. Neither man, I noticed, was armed.

I was sure the bearded man had seen me; he was looking straight at me. I backed away instinctively, but he gave no sign at all that he had seen me. He whispered something to the boy, and I realized I understood what he was saying.

"Where is he?" the bearded man was demanding.

The boy pointed to a closed doorway. "He sleeps."

"Alone?"

The boy shook his head. "No."

"The maharani is with him?"

"Yes." The boy glanced at the second closed door. "There are many guards."

The bearded man patted his shoulder. "We will be careful, little brother."

"You said you would give me gold."

The clean-shaven man smiled at the boy. It was a mocking smile. His black eyes were cruel.

"Not yet, little brother," he said pleasantly.

"Not until it is done. Be quiet now. It will not take long."

The two men moved quickly, stealthily toward the first of the two closed doors. I fought it, but I found myself following the two men as though impelled by an irresistible power. They were closing the door behind them, but that was no obstacle to my entering. The door had no substance. When I put out my hand to open it, the door just wasn't there.

A great bed stood in the center of a room that was as large as the outer room. In the bed, a man and a girl were sleeping beneath a single silken cover. The two intruders were creeping stealthily toward either side of the bed. I saw them extract what looked like scarves of dirty white silk from their shirts. I ran to the bed.

"No!" I cried. "No! Wake up! Wake ..." But neither my voice nor my hand, with which I was trying to rouse the sleeping man, had any effect. It was as though it was happening in a dimension in which I didn't exist.

The sleeping man lay on his back. The girl's head was resting on his arm. She looked young, no more than about fourteen. The covers had been thrown back to her waist, revealing breasts that were still not fully developed.

The bearded intruder was standing at the head of the bed, behind the sleeping man. He had twisted the piece of silk into a tight cord, the ends of which were wrapped around his hands. He was poised there, breathing hard, his black eyes glittering. On the other side of the bed, the other man, also holding a silken noose, was approaching the girl.

Again I screamed a warning, and again no sound came. The assassin on the girl's side of the bed struck almost too quickly for me to see. He looped the silken noose over the girl's shining black hair, then, jerking it down to her throat, pulled it tight. Her body arched. The covers were flung away from her. Her slim fingers tore vainly at the noose. Her eyes were wide in horror. No sound came from her open mouth. Her wild plunging wakened her husband. But he had barely raised his head from the pillow when the other assassin's noose snapped tight around his throat.

I stood there as though paralyzed, watching something I was unable to prevent. No sound came from the helpless victims save the faint thudding of their legs and bodies as they threshed and arched on the soft mattress. Without releasing the pressure of the noose around her throat, her assassin was dragging the girl backward off the bed. His teeth bared in an animal grin, he threw her down onto the patterned carpet and squatted astride her naked back. He tugged her head back with the noose.

The man still fought frantically. His eyes were bulging, his mouth gaping.

I closed my eyes, trying to shut out what I saw.

"No, Megan!" a woman's voice cried. "No! Not you! No!"

Then, suddenly, the scene of the murder was gone. Behind my closed eyes another face had formed. Matted black hair streaked with gray straggled untidily across a woman's face. It was as if my own face, but grown old in sickness and despair, was staring back at me. Red veins patterned the whites of her blue eyes. Her hands gripped two vertical bars between which she looked at me. Her face had a gray, sick pallor. The bright youth of the Boston painting was gone. It was my mother!

She could have been a woman of fifty. All her youth and beauty had gone.

"Megan! Megan! What's the matter? Are you all right, Megan?" Now a man's voice was calling me. It was anxious, and vaguely familiar.

A hand was shaking my shoulder. "Megan, wake up!"

Then, gradually, through the milky haze, a mass of red began to emerge and take shape. I could see red roses in a vase. Behind it, a portrait slowly appeared, then the shelves of leather-bound books. I became vaguely aware of the great red-cedar table at which I was sitting, my body felt as if it had frozen to the chair on which I was sitting bolt upright. I felt so cold. . . .

"Careful, young man," a deep voice said warningly. "Sometimes the shock of being forcibly brought back can be bad. It can cause clouding of consciousness, mental confusion."

"She's in some kind of coma. Can't you do anything?"

"It's a trance. It's like a state of deep hypnosis. No, don't touch her. Leave her to me."

"Her hands are like ice." A hand closed over mine. I could feel its protective warmth. The room was clearing. The pale faces across the table were taking vague shape.

"In some spiritual mediums the trancelike state, when achieved, is just as deep. There is limited sensory and motor contact with ordinary surroundings. Her mother was like this. I think she's coming out of it now. Yes, she is. Most of them have subsequent amnesia of whatever occurred during the trance, no matter how terrifying it was. We can expect the fear we see now to disappear with her memory of whatever happened."

The speaker's name occurred to me. It was Dr. Schiller. I remembered the room and the people around me, but it was as though I couldn't take my eyes from the roses in the vase. Red roses were for my mother, the young woman in the portrait. I myself liked yellow roses.

Then, abruptly, the red roses were gone. There was a loud shattering sound.

Denis Fulton's voice exclaimed, "My God, what happened?"

"The vase fell off the table!"

"She was staring at the vase!"

"It didn't fall! I saw it! It was as though something picked it up and hurled it against the wall."

"Psychokinesis," Denis said beside me.

"Or a poltergeist at work. It *is* a spirit! I can feel its presence." I felt my head turn slowly to Madame Grasse at the head of the table. "Megan, your mother is in this room, isn't she? Is that what you're trying to tell us?"

It was an effort to speak, but I heard myself say haltingly, "I ... dreamed ... I fell asleep sitting here ... and had ... a nightmare. I'm sorry."

"Megan, are you all right now?" Denis Fulton's voice was genuinely concerned.

"I feel cold," I murmured weakly. "My arms are too stiff to move." But even as I said it, I found I could move them. The rigidity was gone, and the numbing cold was disappearing. "What happened? I mean ... what did I do?"

"Some hint of power came to you, Megan,"

104

my aunt's cool voice said. "You cried out. You went into a trance, and we believe a vision came to you. You call it a nightmare, but you were not dreaming. What you had was a vision, perhaps of the forgotten past, perhaps of the future. This happened to your mother when the power came to her. If we had asked you while you were in the trance, you would have told us what you saw. But now that is lost. You took us by surprise, Megan. We were concentrating on Antoinette and Naidu, but it was to you the vision came, not Antoinette. We should have realized it would be that way, because you are Bernadette's daughter. Bernadette appeared to you; I'm sure of that, even though the memory of it is lost. It *was* your mother."

"She's right, Megan," Madame Grasse said. "It *was* your mother. We made her angry, so she broke the vase. I can feel the vibrations of her anger."

"Do we go on?" Madame Larre, the housekeeper, asked from the other side of the table.

"I think Megan has had enough for one day," Denis said quickly, looking up at Schiller, who was standing beside me, his fingers on the pulse of my left wrist. "Doctor, you must agree with that."

Schiller frowned. He released my wrist before replying. "Megan doesn't appear to have suffered any ill effects from whatever happened. But Denis is right. We should stop at this point. We could possibly continue after dinner, if Megan feels confident enough. . . ."

"I don't think Megan should continue at all." Denis looked across at Madame Grasse. "What do you think, Madame Grasse?"

She glanced around uneasily. "I say wait. The room is full of anger, fear, and hate. I feel it distinctly. Bernadette is here, and another presence—one that seems to me alien and evil. I am beginning to see it now. It has cruel eyes, and . . ."

She had been staring at the portrait of my mother. On the table beneath the portrait I saw a single yellow rose lying in a pool of water. The red roses were scattered across the carpet near the shattered crystal vase. Suddenly Madame Grasse cried out in fear.

She had her hands resting on the wheels of her chair, as though poised for flight. The spell that had held her rigid and transfixed to my mother's portrait had broken. Now she was looking down at the wheels of her chair. It seemed she was struggling with them. As I watched disbelievingly, the wheels began to turn despite her obvious efforts to hold them back.

"Help me!" Madame Grasse screamed. "Help me! He . . ."

The wheels seemed to tear themselves from her hands, and she screamed again in terror as the chair spun like a top before it steadied, then, with gathering speed, rushed toward the opposite wall. Both woman and chair struck the bookshelves with terrifying force. One of the shelves collapsed beneath the impact, cascading books down on the woman, who, with the overturned chair lying across her paralyzed legs, was sprawled on the carpet.

She lay there motionless. Dr. Schiller was moving quickly around the table to her. Alice Cavendish, white-faced, was rising to her feet. Madame Larre was pushing back her chair. Denis was already by Madame Grasse's side, moving the chair away from her legs.

"Don't move her, Denis," Schiller ordered, dropping to his knees beside her. "She could be badly hurt."

Denis moved away to make more room for the doctor.

It was quiet in the room. Alice Cavendish and Madame Larre were talking in hushed, awed whispers. My aunt hadn't moved from her chair. She watched Dr. Schiller, her lips compressed in a thin and worried line. I wanted to do something to help, but knew I would only be in the way.

As I sat there, I thought of what Dr. Schiller had said. People who had visions such as I had

had while in a trancelike state had no memory of it afterward. That was just it—I remembered mine so vividly, every detail. . . .

"You have the power, Megan. You have it."

I gasped and started. I looked around for the speaker.

"The power has come to you, Megan, as it did to your mother."

It was Lissi. My boundless relief that it was her must have shown.

"What's the matter, Megan? Did you think it was someone else? Bernadette, perhaps?"

"I had a very bad dream," I murmured.

She smiled indulgently. "Don't deny the gift that has come to you, Megan. Grasp it, as I would. As your mother did. It does not matter that you lost the vision you had today. It was our fault that you remember nothing of it now. But there will be other visions, and we will be there to help you interpret them."

"But I was dreaming. I don't want the power!" I cried.

Alice Cavendish gave me a startled look. Lissi smiled at me. "You may refuse it if you wish. It makes no difference. With Antoinette Grasse's help, your mother will come back to you again and again. She will live again for us. You must realize how important that is to us."

"Not with Madame Grasse." I don't know

why I said it. It was as if someone had prompted me.

She looked surprised. "Why not, Megan? Do you feel you are capable of doing it without Antoinette? Well, why not? Your trance, the flowers—it was your doing. Is that it? Megan, answer me." She was staring at me intently. Her face grew paler as I returned her stare. In that moment I hated her. Perhaps she saw that in my eyes. She added wonderingly, "You were looking at Antoinette, as you were looking at the flowers."

I looked past her to Madame Grasse and the two men. Schiller was rising to his feet. I no longer felt the need to explain what I had said. It was as though the need were gone.

"This is terrible," Schiller said in a shocked voice. "She is dead. Antoinette is dead. Megan's trance, the vase of flowers, whatever Antoinette saw in here that she thought evil and cruel—these things proved too much for her state of health. I can't be sure until the autopsy, but it seems to me she has had a second cerebral hemorrhage. One that proved fatal."

"It can't be!" my aunt cried. "She can't be dead!" She turned her head to stare at me. "You *knew*. That was what you meant just now, wasn't it, Megan? It was *precognition*!"

"No!" I cried. "No!"

I started to my feet. The chair fell to the

floor. I was at the door. Behind me I heard Denis Fulton call sharply, "Megan! Megan, wait!"

I began to run up the stairs. Below me, I heard Denis call my name again, but I ignored him.

Chapter Eight

The sun was shining outside my windows when I wakened. Someone was tapping lightly on my door.

"Coming!" I called, slowly easing myself from the bed, still shaky after the happenings of last night. I hadn't been able to sleep, and had lain awake for what seemed hours, shivering and apprehensive of what would happen, of what I would see, when sleep finally came. In the end, I had heard the swelling early-morning tide begin to roar below my window and stream over the rocks toward the Minas Channel.

Denis Fulton was at the door, carrying a tray. The smell of coffee was welcome. He looked tired. "Maid's day off," he greeted me cheerfully. "If you don't mind, I've brought my own coffee along as well."

I was a little confused. "I thought you left last night," I said.

"Not without seeing you. No. After I gave a few broad hints, your aunt finally invited me to stay overnight. Possibly against her better judgment." His gray eyes studied me quizzically. "Well? Won't you invite me in?"

"Oh . . . yes, of course." I stood aside. "Come in."

"Thanks." Moving across the room, he placed the tray down on the table by the window. "Did you sleep all right?" he asked, straightening and turning to face me.

I gave him a wan smile. "Eventually. The tide didn't help matters any."

He grinned. "I guess not. I was in the room opposite yours. Even putting a pillow over my head made no difference." He was looking at me closely, with an expression of tenderness in his eyes. "Anyway, you look much better than you did last night. You look fresh, and quite lovely, if I may say so."

Aware of the flush that rose to my cheeks, I excused myself and went into the bathroom, where I splashed cold water onto my face to clear my head of the still-lingering fuzziness. "What happened after I came upstairs?" I called through the partly open door.

"Oh, the ambulance took her to the hospital in Sussex Wold."

"And the police?"

"No. Schiller's diagnosis was right. It was a

cerebral hemorrhage. He telephoned your aunt this morning from the hospital."

"So there won't be an inquiry?"

"No."

"We both saw the way the ... chair ran into the wall. Couldn't the ... accident have caused her death?"

"Not if two doctors, one of whom has been treating her for the complaint, say that she died of a cerebral hemorrhage. It's the second severe one she's had. And don't try to make too much of what you saw, or thought you saw, just before she collapsed, Megan. Did you know that at the outset of terminal attacks in cerebral accidents or disease, the patient usually becomes confused, the intellect is clouded, and there are convulsive movements, often quite violent, of the hands and body?"

"So?" I was hurriedly brushing my hair into some semblance of tidiness. "No, I didn't know that. But it's not quite the same, is it? I mean, we all saw what happened."

"When she cried out, that *could* have been pain or fear. There *is* pain, you know. And fear. Just as her convulsive movements as she grasped the wheels *could* have driven the chair across the room and headlong into the shelves."

As I returned to the main room, I could see

he was frowning thoughtfully. "Do you believe that?" I asked.

He shook his head. "Frankly, no. But what I think I saw isn't the kind of argument I would use to convince a coroner or a jury that Madame Grasse did not die from natural causes. The law deals only with tangibles. That is its only concern."

"I suppose we hypnotized ourselves," I remarked caustically. But I wondered if Madame Grasse had been murdered.

"Almost," he said earnestly. "Look, we had deliberately set up conditions that were ideal for mass hysteria, or mass self-induced hypnotism, which we helped along all the way with suggestion. Quite frankly, I suspect Madame Grasse was a fake. Mediums like her invariably introduce a spirit guide from the last century who lived in India or China and who was in a position of some authority or lived in its shadow. Madame Grasse didn't even show much ingenuity. Oh, yes, I agree we *did* see something unusual—something quite inexplicable." He shrugged. "But how could we hope to convince anyone else of that?"

"And the vase," I murmured. "How could that be explained? I mean, if, as you say, Madame Grasse is . . . was a fake."

He laughed. "It's been done before. The medium has an accomplice outside. A nylon thread, invisible in the darkened room. All it needs is one sharp tug." His smile faded. "No, I don't believe this was what happened yesterday. I believe *you* broke the vase."

"Me?" I was startled.

"Yes," he said soberly. "Psychic research is beginning to admit the possibility that there are people with unusually high powers of concentration. They can move objects with the sheer force of this concentration. Psychokinesis, in other words. You had just come out of your trance, or whatever happened to you, and you were staring fixedly at the roses. I was watching you."

"I remember that," I murmured thoughtfully. "You were saying something about psychokinesis when the vase went."

"Do you remember what you were thinking at the time?"

"The first thing I saw was a red mass, which gradually became a vase of red roses. I remember thinking that red roses were my mother's favorite flowers. I have never liked them. They're not mine. I prefer yellow roses."

"You see?" he said. "If such a thing as psychokinesis *is* possible, that was a classic example. The vase was struck from the table. It shattered, and red roses were spilled right across the carpet. Only one rose was left on the table. A yellow rose. I don't know where it came from. I was sure there were none in the vase."

"There *was* one. The gardener had it sent in to me. I was to take it up to my room. Madame Larre must have put it in with the others, despite the fact that Lissi insisted that the roses be red, as they had been especially chosen for my mother."

He sipped his coffee. "The whole emphasis of the séance was on your mother," he muttered, lowering his cup back onto the saucer. "As it was when Madame Grasse had her first stroke. I guess it was because of that that she could have imagined she saw your mother on this last occasion, when her fear prompted another—this time fatal—stroke."

"But it wasn't only that," I recalled. "She said: 'Bernadette is here. The room is full of anger, fear, and hate.' But I don't think she was referring to my mother. She said something about another presence, alien and evil. She could see it."

"That's right. She said it had cruel eyes. Immediately afterward the chair began to go haywire. She cried out to us to help her."

"She said, 'Help me! Help me. He . . .' She said *he*, I'm sure of that."

"It could have been her imaginary spirit guide."

116

"Naidu?" I shuddered involuntarily as I recalled my vision.

Denis was thoughtfully studying my expression. "Megan, telepathy, like psychokinesis, is another facet of ESP that is being examined very closely. When you came out of your trance, were you frightened?"

"Yes. I was terrified."

"You could have communicated your fear to her. It's possible. She could have had the impression that your mother was nearby, she being a 'believer.' Her sense of evil, of some cruel demon close to her, could have stemmed from your fear. It's a pity you weren't able to tell us what you saw. But, as all the authorities on the subject agree, there is no memory in the mind of the medium of what she has seen or described to others."

"But I'm *not* a medium," I said with feeling. "I dozed, and I had a nightmare. That's all."

He shook his head. "You weren't asleep, Megan. Schiller examined you. He examined your eyes, your hands and arms. You were absolutely rigid, and your eyes stared straight ahead when he raised the eyelids. Yet your breathing and circulation were normal. He told me before he left last night that your state resembled a cataleptic trance, except that you felt abnormally cold. He said he'd never seen

117

anything quite like it in spiritual mediums. Not of the same intensity."

"I remember exactly what I dreamed," I told him.

He stared at me in surprise. "You mean ... you remember what you saw?"

"Because it was only a dream, and I'm *not* a medium. Yes, I do!" I said defiantly. "It seemed very real."

"What did you dream, Megan?" he urged. "Tell me."

"We were concentrating on Naidu," I said. "I remember I began to feel sleepy. Nothing was happening. There didn't seem to be any sign of Naidu."

He smiled. "Come to think of it, he never *did* show up, did he?"

"Anyway," I continued, "it seemed I was somewhere else. I dreamed I was in a palace in India, and he was there. In my dream, I saw him killed!"

"Killed?" He was staring at me curiously. "How? What happened?"

"He was assassinated. In his bed. His wife with him. They were both strangled."

"I see." He nodded slowly, then, lowering his voice, said, "You can't stay in this house, Megan. The atmosphere is ... wrong for you. It's this house. John Carson thinks your mother

118

knew this. That's why she wrote that warning to you and your father."

I shook my head. "I must stay a few days at least, Denis. I owe Lissi that much at least."

"And I can't go back until I've finished the investigation into your family's affairs. So we'll keep in touch. I'll be nearby. Personally," he ventured, "I like the idea of that very much indeed."

"I thought you were in Halifax to open an office."

"That, too. But protecting you from happenings like yesterday is more important now. It's become my first priority. Do you mind?"

"I don't want to lose touch with you either," I said with feeling. "I need a friend in this place."

"I'll work something out," he said. "Maybe I can find a place to stay within a few miles of here. I have a car. And your aunt mentioned last night that there is a car you can use. In the meantime, I'll shop around for an accommodation and call you back. Okay?"

"Perhaps you could stay here," I suggested hopefully.

"I'll be spending some time in Sussex Wold." He smiled and shook his head. "No, really. I don't think it would be advisable. I'll be around, though. I won't be far away. I have a job to do that can be important to your future."

"What do you mean? What sort of a job?"

"It's safer if you don't know, Megan." His expression was solemn. "I can't tell you at this stage. You have to trust me."

"Why? I wouldn't repeat anything you told me."

He shook his head. "I have to think of your safety. I don't want you involved in what I'm doing, because of these crazy people and their psychic delusions. It's better you know nothing. It really is." He glanced at his wristwatch. "I'll have to go now, Megan. I have an appointment in Halifax this morning."

I stood up as well. "Shall I see you at breakfast?"

He smiled wryly, and took my hand for a moment. "No, I'm afraid not. There's so much to do, you see." He stopped at the door and smiled back at me. "Please be careful, Megan," he said in a low voice.

"Yes," I breathed. "Yes . . . I will."

"It's very important to me . . . that you be careful."

I don't quite know how it happened, but the next thing I knew was that we were kissing. I was in his arms, and he was kissing me. We were holding each other in a long, fond embrace.

Then, too soon, the moment had passed, and Denis had opened the door and was striding down the passage. I wanted to rush after him, but knew at the same time that that would be unwise. I let him go.

A few moments later I heard a car's engine start to life below my windows. I pulled aside the drapes and looked down just in time to see a red sports car slowing down at the gates. The top was down, and the wind was whipping Denis's thick blond hair. He swung the car out onto the road, and was gone.

Madame Larre was waiting patiently in the dining room when I came down. "Good morning, Miss Marshall," she greeted me. "You may start when you wish. Mam'selle Lissi isn't having breakfast this morning."

"How is my aunt?" I inquired. "I hope she's not too upset."

"She is not a woman who becomes distressed easily," she said carefully. "She is taking your cousins to the airport."

I stared at her in surprise. "The girls? I didn't even meet them."

"They are flying from Halifax to Boston this morning, I understand. From Boston they will fly direct to Europe. I don't think they ever really liked it here. Mam'selle Ferrari was quite determined that they should leave early this morning. She made all the necessary arrangements last night."

"But why?" I was still staring at her. "I don't understand."

She shrugged. "She had no further use for them. I don't know any more than that. They were a disappointment to her. As Madame Grasse was—except for the two occasions when your mother appeared to her."

"You mean, the girls have gone because they didn't fulfill my aunt's expectations? That they hadn't inherited my mother's powers? Is that it?"

"Let's just say that she feels all her problems are solved."

"I'm not sure that I understand your meaning."

Her expression was unreadable. Her thin lips twitched briefly. "It's obvious. She had what she has wanted ever since your mother died. She has the power your mother had within her grasp. She has you."

I sat back on my chair and sipped the chilled tomato juice Madame Larre had placed before me. "Do you think Madame Grasse could really conjure up spirits? I mean . . . like Naidu?"

She shook her head. "The séances are an obsession with your aunt. She has always been like that. Perhaps it is because she herself cannot communicate. Antoinette tricked her in the first place—for money. Your aunt can be generous where her weakness is concerned. I remember when Antoinette first came here. She had been holding séances in Halifax, and there had been many gullible people who had taken those séances seriously.

"But your mother was not satisfied that her spirit guide, a Chinese mandarin, was genuine. From necessity, you understand, Antoinette discovered Naidu. I noticed her reading a book in the library one day. It was a volume of Indian history. At her next séance, the Maharajah Naidu appeared. I was curious enough to check this person. I found your aunt doing the same thing, so we looked together, and there he was—an obscure prince your aunt couldn't expect Antoinette to know existed. I said nothing about having seen Antoinette in the library earlier. There wasn't much about him, just his name, dates of birth and death, his titles, and the principality he ruled—just enough to give Antoinette a spirit guide who had existed, in case anyone *did* check."

"And Lissi accepted that?"

"Yes. Yet she did find out a little more about him than Antoinette. She found another reference to him in a volume on the Indian mutiny, in which he played an important part."

"I would like to see that book," I said.

"You could find it through the library index.

123

There can't be many books dealing with that period."

In the library, all the traces of the drama of the day before had gone. The broken shelf had been fixed and all the books replaced. The table smelled faintly of polish, and the carpet had been cleaned. At the end of the room my mother's face was smiling faintly at me above a blue bowl of yellow roses.

The index was in a steel filing cabinet against the wall. I tried the *M*'s first and found what I wanted quite easily when I reached "Mutiny." The card read, "Mutiny, Indian. The Protagonists, 1857–1858."

I found the book without any difficulty. It was a very old book, over one hundred years old. I took it out into the reception room.

With the bright morning sunlight streaming in through the large windows, I settled into a comfortable chair and opened the volume. Eventually I found a subheading with the name Bhopal and took it from there. There was almost a whole chapter on Chandra Naidu, Maharajah of Bhopal. He appeared as a politician and a soldier choosing British protection to maintain his rule.

Then came the Sepoy mutiny.

Naidu believed the British must crush the revolt, and that in the process the British Crown would take control of India away from the East India Company, and either banish or execute the Great Mogul, titular emperor of the subcontinent. He assumed that when this took place the British government would give the power of the moguls to those princes who had helped put down the Sepoy mutiny.

Naidu was right, but he was not to live long enough to have his belief vindicated. His policies had made him too many enemies among the conflicting factions of his own race.

Following the desperate fighting during his ruthless suppression of the Sepoy rebels at the Chambal River, Naidu led his men back to his capital for rest and reinforcement. While there, to strengthen what he expected to be his bargaining power with the British, Naidu took as child bride Anice, daughter of the Nizam of the neighboring territory of Uttar.

On the night of November 15, 1857, two members of the Cult of Assassins, worshipers of the goddess Kali, whose practices Naidu had banned on punishment of death, avoided the guards and crept into the palace. In an antechamber they silently crept upon and strangled a palace servant before forcing their way into the maharajah's bedroom, where he slept with his bride. Using the silken scarves that were ceremonial weapons of execution of the cult, the assassins ruthlessly strangled both the Maharajah Naidu and his child bride, Anice.

Seen and captured by guards as they tried to escape, the murderers were slaughtered by the maharajah's infuriated soldiers as soon as the murders were discovered.

I put the book down and walked slowly out into the sunshine.

Chapter Nine

Over the telephone, Denis' voice sounded deeper than I expected. "Are you alone?" he asked.

"Yes. Lissi has gone to Sussex Wold to see Alice Cavendish. I guess they're finalizing details for the funeral tomorrow."

"Your aunt called me this morning at the hotel. There's to be another séance after the funeral."

"Are you going?" There was a sinking sensation inside me as I thought of it.

"Well ... that's something I have to talk to you about when I see you today. Has anything unusual happened since I saw you last?"

"No."

"Are you sure? No mysterious knocking, planchette writing?"

"The poltergeist is on vacation!"

He chuckled. "I'm glad."

"However, I *did* find a chapter on the life of

127

Chandra Naidu, Maharajah of Bhopal, in the library."

He sounded surprised. "You mean he was for real?"

"Yes. He was murdered in exactly the way I saw it happen. Or dreamed I saw it happen."

"It could be coincidence," I heard him mutter. And then something I couldn't hear.

"What was that?"

"Do you know why your aunt sent your twin cousins back to Europe?"

"How did you know that?" Now it was my turn to be surprised.

"I don't know it all yet," he said soberly, "but I mean to. And I believe I will very soon now. Trust me until then, will you?"

"Do I have a choice?"

"Frankly, no!" he said. "But *do* you know why she sent them off like that?"

"Madame Larre said it was because they had disappointed her. She said Aunt Lissi had no further use for them, now that she had me—"

"She said that?" he interrupted harshly.

"She more than hinted it."

"Not now that she has you!" he muttered thoughtfully. "Megan, just hold the line for a moment, will you?" After some moments, he picked up the receiver again and said, "Megan, are you still there?"

"Yes."

"Look, I'm sorry, but there has been a change of plans. Something's come up. I can't see you before tomorrow. Until after the séance. I'm sorry. I'll explain then."

"I won't be going," I stated flatly.

"It's to be held at Dr. Schiller's hospital."

"I still won't be going."

"Megan, be serious," he said soberly. "You must come with me tomorrow to Dr. Schiller's hospital. We must go through with it together. It's very important. Please."

"No!" I cried.

"Well, come to the funeral and let me talk to you there. I promise you, everything will be explained to you."

"No, I can't let it happen to me again—don't you see? I've stopped kidding myself that the last time was ... a dream. I saw my dead mother. I went back a hundred years through time to watch a man and his wife being murdered. I looked at a vase of roses, and the vase shattered. I looked at a woman, and she died."

"Megan, you mustn't talk like that," he said urgently. "You mustn't think that. It can't be the way you think. How can I convince you? Listen ... No, hold the line. I have someone here who can talk to you. Don't hang up. Please."

"Megan?" Now a deeper voice was speaking to me. "Megan, are you there?"

"Yes," I said hesitantly.

"This is John Carson. Now, listen to me. I arrived this morning from Boston. There are a number of things we have to discuss."

I shook my head. "I don't understand!"

"We've been going into the legal affairs of your mother's family, on your behalf. It seemed strange to me that you were not provided for when your mother died, so I decided to investigate the question of a possible legacy. Denis has been working on it, and among other things, he has discovered your mother's will. I can't go into details until the thing is proven, but there's a possibility of a conspiracy to keep from you a very substantial legacy. Now, we can recover this for you, but we need certain proof, information that Denis believes can be found only in Dr. Schiller's hospital."

"I don't care about money, Mr. Carson," I protested. "I'll get by with what my father left me. That's all I want. I still won't go there tomorrow."

"Are you frightened, Megan? Are you frightened of your mother's power?"

"I'm afraid I *have* my mother's power—don't you see?"

"You had a dream," John Carson said quietly, reasonably. "A bad dream."

"Other things happened," I said sullenly,

thinking of the knocking, the planchette, the vase. "Inexplicable things."

"Megan," he said, "I want to prove to you that you do not have any supernatural power, that you are a perfectly normal and very lovely girl. You would like that, wouldn't you?"

"Yes." All the same, my fear was beginning to return.

"Megan, I want you to go tomorrow. I want you to trust Denis. I believe that if you do, you will never need to fear anything like that again. I'm asking you to do this as a favor to me, and because I know I can trust to your common sense that whatever happens will not seriously affect you. You may feel nervous, but I know you have courage. Will you do it for me, Megan?"

"Will . . . you be there?" I had hesitated, and I already knew I was lost.

"If I were, it could spoil all Denis' work. They would suspect at once that he had another interest apart from psychic research or being with you. The things we expect to happen, and which we intend to use on your behalf, would never eventuate. On the other hand, Denis has your aunt's confidence and that of the group. He has already attended one séance, and has been invited by your aunt to attend this one. He is accepted. I'm not, and never could be, as your father's close friend. Well, Megan?"

"I'll go," I murmured weakly, with a sinking feeling inside me.

"You've made a decision you won't regret," he said with the cheerfulness of someone not directly involved.

Outside, the sun was shining with the brightness that follows the clearing away of early-morning fog. It drew me out of the gloomy house I was beginning to hate so much. Outside, I felt much better. Maxwell's father and another man were loosening the crust of soil around the rose beds.

"It's a fine day, Miss Marshall," Maxwell, Sr., said in English. "The beds are at their best now in early summer. There's a rare bed of tulips down at the edge of the trees. Perhaps you would like to see them. The woods are full of late-flowering daffodils this year."

I thanked him and walked on across the lawns. The tulips were a most impressive, colorful sight. The glimpse of the daffodils sprouting everywhere lured me beneath the trees. It was cooler in the shade. I walked aimlessly, absorbed with my problems.

I stopped abruptly. I had turned a bend in the path. Ahead of me, fringed with trees, was the tiny cemetery the chauffeur had talked about on the first day as he was driving me to the mansion. A newly painted picket fence surrounded the score or so of crosses and headstones. In front of me was a partly open gate. My first impulse was to turn away. Then I remembered that my mother was buried here, and thought that her closeness might trigger psychic reactions in me that I couldn't control. I forced this thought away from me, and walked on.

My grandparents' graves were situated side by side. I stopped at the grave beyond, and stared at the brief inscription on the headstone: "Bernadette Ferrari Marshall. Born 1935. Departed the World of the Living 1959."

I walked back slowly to the house. Lissi was there. At lunch, she mentioned "A little gathering with Dr. Schiller and the others to say good-bye to dear Antoinette in our own way."

"I asked Denis Fulton, Megan," she went on. "He said he would come. You seemed to gain strength from having him near you the other day, which is good. If your father had been as considerate and shared your mother's ventures into the unknown, their life together would have been happier and longer, I'm sure. But your father refused to believe. Do you like the young man, Megan?"

Her dark eyes probed my face anxiously.

"He's rather nice," I said evasively. "Quite considerate."

Lissi nodded; it seemed, with satisfaction. "After tomorrow," she said, "you and I are going to Quebec to forget what happened here."

"I told you yesterday that I must go back to Boston in a few days."

"To what?" she said emphatically. "There's nothing there for you. Nothing at all." She shook her head. "No, I have plans for you. It would be much better all around, for everyone, if you stayed here. . . ."

I listened as she overrode my arguments. That night I asked Madame Larre for sleeping tablets. I didn't hear the tide.

I woke late, and the morning dragged until lunch. With lunch the sea fog came in again, blanketing the sun. I wore a raincoat to Madame Grasse's funeral.

The Daimler groped through the opaque gray fog all the way to Sussex Wold, which I saw only as the vague shapes of buildings with a scattering of brightly lit shop windows and the lights of passing cars. Madame Larre sat erect and silent in the front seat. The fog had made us too late for the chapel service. The small cortege was already leaving as we arrived, so we followed it. It was raining before we reached the cemetery. Denis was waiting as Maxwell opened the door for us.

"We were starting to worry about you," he said as he helped Lissi out onto the gravel path.

"The fog delayed us."

Dr. Schiller and Alice Cavendish were standing behind Denis. The other mourners were climbing out of the parked vehicles. Schiller moved forward to shelter Lissi with his umbrella.

With Denis beside me, holding his umbrella over us, we followed the others to the graveside.

On either side, crosses and arched headstones appeared and disappeared in the writhing mist.

The service was brief, and, frankly, as far as I was concerned, couldn't be over soon enough. As the last clods of earth fell hollowly on Madame Grasse's coffin, I turned away. Alice Cavendish was the only one I could see who was weeping. Denis walked me back to the cars. I expected him to ask me to ride with him, but he didn't. He was hurrying me toward Lissi's car.

"Megan, you're not to be surprised by what happens," he said softly as we reached the car. "You must trust me. Please trust me, Megan." He turned away as I stepped into the Daimler.

We followed Dr. Schiller and Alice Cavendish. At the gates, as we turned back toward Sussex Wold, I could see no sign of Denis. At the hospital, iron gates were open. A gatekeeper in a blue uniform touched his cap as we drove through them. It was the afternoon visiting hour, with cars parked in lines outside the entrance to the large main building. Lights were on in the building and in the enclosed balconies.

Following Dr. Schiller's bright red taillights, we were moving around to one side of the main building. "Where are we going?"

"Dr. Schiller's residence," Lissi told me.

The residence was of stone, with a massive door. A covered walk led from the house to the side door of the hospital. I still saw no sign of Denis or his car.

Maxwell sheltered us with his umbrella to the brightly lit porch, where Dr. Schiller waited with Alice Cavendish. He ushered us solicitously inside.

We were drinking coffee, which had been served with hot biscuits and blueberry jam, when the doctor's housekeeper ushered Denis into the room.

He smiled apologetically as he sat down next to me. "It's getting thicker every minute outside," he said. "I missed the gates and drove halfway to the Ferrari house. I'm sorry if I worried anyone."

"It's all right, Denis." I was so pleased to see him.

"Are *you* all right?" he said quietly so that the others wouldn't hear.

"Now you're here, yes. I thought they'd start without you."

"Not a chance," he said. "I had that covered. I ..." He broke off. The housekeeper had returned. She walked to Schiller and spoke to him.

He said curiously, "What name?"

"Carson," she said. "John Carson."

"I can't recall anyone of that name." Schiller frowned.

"I think you should see him," Denis said suddenly. "But perhaps if you read this, you will understand why." Standing, he took an envelope from his pocket. He moved across the room to where the doctor was sitting.

Schiller said uneasily, "Do you know this man?"

"I should. He's my uncle, and I work for him. But this will explain the situation."

Schiller took the envelope and turned it over uncertainly in his hands. He glanced at my aunt. "What is it?"

"The paper I have just given you is a court order." Denis was no longer smiling. "It orders you to give us immediate access to Anne Saxon, a patient in your maximum-security ward for women. You have her in room seven, I believe."

I watched the color drain from Schiller's face. He glanced again at my aunt; then, extracting the document from the envelope, he unfolded it. "Anne Saxon? Suppose I can't do this? For reasons concerning the patient's condition? She has completely withdrawn. Anne Saxon is a schizophrenic. Her condition is chronic."

"In that case, a writ of habeas corpus will be served upon you." Denis was staring at him hard. "By the way, did you say Anne Saxon *is* or *was* a chronic schizophrenic?"

Schiller looked up at the housekeeper. "Show him in."

She nodded and hurried away. Lissi said angrily, "How does this inquiry of yours, if it is that, concern us?"

"I want you to see Dr. Schiller's patient. There is a matter of identification."

"No!"

"I think you should see her," he said seriously. "I think we all should." He glanced at the door. "Don't you agree?"

John Carson entered the room. "Why, yes, I do," he said. "Will you take us to see Miss Saxon, Doctor? Of course, I would advise you to do so—I'm sure none of us would welcome the entry of the police into the matter at this stage."

"I've no objection to allowing you to see the patient," Schiller muttered. "But you must understand that she is withdrawn, and that her condition is chronic. This is not my opinion alone. If you take her from here, it can only be to another institution."

"At the moment, Doctor," John Carson said coldly, "we are concerned with the patient's identity, not with your diagnosis or treatment of her condition."

He shrugged. "All right, I'll take you."

He took us. We left Schiller's house and moved into the covered walk. We stopped at a door, where a burly orderly in a white coat got up from his chair to let us in. He stared at us curiously, but said nothing.

We stepped into a long, narrow ward with locked doors on either side, each of them with a square opening blocked off by two bars. A nurse in a white uniform rose from a chair in the center of the ward as we came in.

Schiller said, "Anne Saxon in seven—is she awake?"

"Yes, Doctor. She was on the floor, but we got her up."

Schiller looked at John Carson, who nodded. "I'd like to look at her first, if you don't mind.

Then I'll call each of you in turn, and you will tell me if you recognize the woman."

I looked apprehensively around the brightly lit area. Near me a woman's face stared from the shadows at the back of her room. Someone snored steadily. The bars reminded me . . .

"Madame Larre." John Carson was standing outside one of the cells at the other end of the ward.

She walked reluctantly toward him. When she reached him, he asked, "Do you know this woman? Have you ever seen her before?"

"No, m'sieur."

Madame Larre came back to us. She had paled, I noticed, and her lips had tightened to a thin line.

Next was Alice Cavendish's turn. She gasped and shook her head. She said in what sounded like a slightly hysterical voice, "No! I never saw her before!"

"Mademoiselle Ferrari."

Lissi glanced at me, then walked across to the cell. I watched her peer in, then start back as a hand, hooked into a claw, reached out at her through the bars.

John Carson said, "Well, Mademoiselle Ferrari? Do you recognize this woman?"

"She resembles someone I once knew!" my aunt murmured uncomfortably. "No, I don't know her."

I had started to move forward, but Denis'

hand on my arm stopped me. "No, Megan. We don't need your identification."

"But . . ."

John Carson walked back with Lissi. "I have something to say to you, Madame Larre," he said sternly as they reached us. "And this applies to all three of you. All three of you lied. You know the woman as I do. Madame Larre, you recognized the woman. You know her name is not Anne Saxon, you know who she really is. And you, Miss Cavendish. You also, Mademoiselle Ferrari. You have more reason to remember her than anyone else."

I was seeing the bars. The bars in the doors. Suddenly I tore myself away from Denis' restraining grasp and was running toward the cell. Schiller stared at me foolishly as I ran toward him. He moved belatedly to stop me, but I avoided him. I looked in through the bars of the cell.

I screamed!

From the square opening in the door of room seven my mother's face looked out at me, as I had seen it in my nightmare. Her hands were gripping the bars. Her blue eyes were bloodshot in the light. Her untidy black hair was streaked heavily with gray. Her eyes looked through and past me without recognition. I heard Denis' voice calling me back, but, with perspiration beading my forehead, I was falling into oblivion. . . .

I opened my eyes in a white room. I was lying on a bed. I moved, and on the other side of the room Lissi's voice said sternly, "You must lie still, Megan."

"My mother!" I gasped. "I saw her again. It *was* her! You knew it was." I turned my head to look at Lissi; there was anger in her eyes.

"I knew she resembled Bernadette," she said. "But how could I recognize someone I saw buried? Or . . . thought I did. Years ago. . . ."

"Buried in a cell in an asylum!" I said bitterly. "Because you wanted her to become involved deeper and deeper in . . . supernatural things she didn't want, and couldn't control. You made her the way she is. As you would have me, if you could."

"No!" she whispered. "No."

Where was Denis?

"And who did you bury in my mother's place?" I cried. "I wish your 'power' would come to you, Lissi. I wish it would possess you. The way it did my mother."

Lissi came for me then, enraged and full of power. Her hands took hold of my throat, and she began to squeeze. . . . I couldn't even scream. . . .

Denis plunged into the room. With fury, he yanked Lissi from me, and ordered her out of the room.

She was gone. The door slammed behind her. "Take it easy, Megan," Denis said soothingly. "When you feel better, and John has the rest of it in hand, we're taking you back to Boston. But first there's something we feel you should know about your aunt. She really did think her sister was dead. So did your grandmother and grandfather. When we started checking, we found that quite a large inheritance had been left to you, but only on your father's death. They hated him, Megan. Lissi still does."

"I saw the grave today. It has her name on it." I was still dazed.

"Megan," he said quietly, "your father wanted to take your mother and you away from the Ferrari house. But your mother was already mentally ill. He put her in Schiller's hospital. He arranged for Schiller to write the death certificate and give her the name Anne Saxon, hoping, as Schiller had told him, that she could be cured. And to spare you the knowledge of her insanity."

"Why?" I breathed, still not quite understanding.

"Megan, a lot of money was involved, as you will find in due course. It costs money to keep a patient in such a place. Your father loved your mother and wanted to see her. He saw her every two weeks. He needed the money for this and for you as well. But it didn't work out. Your mother had willed her interest in the family estate to you and your father, but your grandparents were still alive when your mother officially died. So they changed their will. They provided for Lissi and you in equal parts, but your inheritance was to come to you only in the event of your father's death. He couldn't get a cent of it. Your mother's illness kept him a poor man for all those years, and he died poor."

"But the grave?" I could see it again. I could see the words that had been inscribed on the headstone.

"John will get an exhumation order tomorrow, but we don't expect to find anything. Schiller says there is no body. The coffin was empty."

"My mother was just as I saw her."

"Telepathy, perhaps. Who knows," he said. Suddenly, his arms were around me, and I clung to him. "Megan, darling, you must forget such things. You're leaving this place."

"And leave my mother?"

"We'll take her to Boston," he said. "Lissi won't try anything more. We'll try other therapy on your mother, different opinions. You can afford the best, Megan."

"We can."

There was comfort in the way he held me. In the way his head bent and his lips found mine.

The Secret of the Chateau

CHAPTER ONE

HAD KICKED off my shoes to wiggle my toes better, and sat curled up in a deep chair beside the window of my hotel room while I recovered slowly from a feast of Paris shopping. So much had happened to me so fast that now in my last few hours in Paris all I wanted was to relax, take a deep breath, and recover from the shock before I encountered new, and as yet unknown, problems.

I lay back in the chair and stared down at the passing scene. My bags were already packed, and the parcels of my day's shopping were still tantalizingly unopened; they would be even more exciting to unwrap when I reached Auvergne in another day or so.

By night the scene below my window was something to remember. The nobly proportioned Champs-Elysées swept to the Arc de Triomphe that crowned the Etoile. Streamers of light bathed the façades of buildings on either side of the great boulevard. The trees swayed and dipped in a playful breeze and four lines of parked cars glinted in the light.

Twelve fine avenues radiated from the Etoile like the spokes of a wheel, but I liked the Champs-Elysées best.

It seemed incredible that only ten days before I had been living quietly in New Orleans on the other side of the wide Atlantic, not quite sure whether I could live on the few thousand dollars my grandfather had left me on his death, or whether I must go to work and earn my own living. I even considered selling or renting the house in which I'd been born and lived for the first twenty-one years of my life.

Ten days ago a visit to Paris had been an elusive dream that every American girl secretly desires, but seldom realizes. But that had been before I received Uncle Maurice's letter.

I closed my eyes briefly and could see it quite clearly again, written in round, childish letters:

My Dear Denise,
    I have no doubt this letter will surprise you, but I

5

hope that you will not reject what it asks, for it is the plea of a man who has grown old and lonely for the companionship for a few brief months of his only living relative—yourself. In the years since the war I have written to New Orleans seldom. It is no longer easy for me to write. Yet I received many letters from your grandfather, and in all of them he spoke so highly of you that it is my dearest wish to meet you. Denise, I want you to come to Auvergne and stay with me for a little while. To one so young as you a few months is unimportant. To me each moment is as precious as life itself.

If we find when we meet that the affection of kinship binds us, then I will return with you to New Orleans to be near you. I am a wealthy man, and I promise that you will not lose by the association. I remind you again that you are now my only living relative. May your choice be the wise and generous one that I believe, from what your grandfather has said of you, it will be. I am enclosing a letter of credit through the National Bank of New Orleans for an amount that I hope you will find adequate for your fare to Paris, plus a week's vacation there before you come to Auvergne. However, that decision is yours alone, dear Denise. If you have some new tie in America, perhaps a romantic one, and decide against it, then please accept the money as a present for your twenty-first birthday which my calendar tells me is due next week, and forgive the presumption of an old man whose loneliness prompts him to appeal to you.

Maurice Gérard

The bank draft was for five thousand American dollars. Only one letter came. I wired my acceptance, and someone replied for Uncle Maurice; his secretary, I supposed. A reservation had been made for me at this great hotel on the Champs-Elysées, and after a week there a car would be sent for me. The week was up today.

It remained only for the car to come and whisk me away to Uncle Maurice. To the Château-les-Vautours—the Chateau of the Vultures. I was not sure just where the chateau with the rather sinister name came into the family of Gérard. Maurice had said that he was wealthy, and he had sent me a large sum of money, but I could not quite believe my uncle had the kind of money to own a chateau. My grandfather had always spoken of the family as farmers.

even in their grandest days, when one of them was a favorite
of Napoleon, there had been no chateau in the family.
Merely farmhouses and an elegant town house in Paris that
had long since been lost.

Perhaps my uncle was steward of some great family's
estate? I sighed and sat up.

It did not matter about the chateau. Though that had
been an attractive thought. To be heiress to a French
chateau—that really was something! Still, I *was* in France.
In the France whose essence I had breathed through my
grandfather's word pictures since childhood.

My grandfather had a saying: "Everyone has two countries, his own and France."

He used it often, but I don't believe it ever applied
to him, for he had only one—France. When he decided
to leave his home in Auvergne after World War I, he
brought my grandmother to New Orleans to bear their only
child, my father. New Orleans was as close to France as
he could get on foreign soil.

I remember him as a very craggy old gentleman, dark-
skinned and fierce, with unruly white hair and eyebrows
that met across his brow, writhing into knots when he was
annoyed, which was most of the time. Except when he
looked at me; then his face would change, warming and
becoming gentle. He thought me a scatterbrain, and perhaps
he was right.

I loved my grandfather. My father was killed at the
Normandy beachhead, and my American mother died soon
after my birth, so in the French manner my grandfather
became my only family, and I his. We closed out my mother's
relatives, for the French love to be enclosed in the small,
safe confines of the family. In France it is only the family
that counts. Always the family.

The Gérards came from Auvergne, in the south of France.
They had been sturdy, independent farming folk for genera-
tions. Love of the land and horses was bred into them.
They were neither of the aristocracy nor of the tenant
farmers, neither wealthy nor poor, but pure bourgeoisie.
One of them chose to follow the rising star of Napoleon
Bonaparte, and became one of his distinguished cavalry
leaders.

The family fortune, such as it was, was built upon that
Gérard's devotion to Bonaparte. At the time when my grandfather left for New Orleans, the family had been reduced
to three male Gérards, my grandfather Henri, his elder
brother Jean-Paul, and Jean-Paul's son, Uncle Maurice. At
the family conference the family assets were divided equally

7

between the two brothers, Jean-Paul taking the farms, Hen the liquid assets. And now with my grandfather's death t male line was reduced to one, Uncle Maurice.

I had never met him, nor even seen a photo of hir He had neither married nor allowed his photo to be take because he had been crippled and disfigured fighting as partisan against the Boches and troops of the Vichy Gover ment of Pétain and Laval. German soldiers had caught hi and his band in one of the occupied tow in the north, and had burned them out with flame-throwe when they refused to surrender.

The way Grandpa told it, Uncle Maurice had killed for of them, and had spat in the faces of his captors as the dragged his burning body clear of the flames, and had sur the *Marseillaise* all the way to Gestapo headquarters. B then, Grandpa was always inclined to exaggeration whe his loves or hates were concerned.

Yet Uncle Maurice must have been a high officer in t Maquis, for the Germans kept him alive and patched his burned body for questioning at that infamous hous 84 Avenue Foch, Paris. How severely he was tortured durin the questioning, or whether he had given them the inform tion they sought, we did not know. Uncle Maurice neglect to inform us in those rare letters he had learned to wri with his left hand.

Grandpa, of course, drew his own heroic conclusions. B in any case the Gestapo officers at their headquarters the Avenue Foch must have had other things to wor about besides my Uncle Maurice. For the Allies were drivi toward Paris.

Uncle Maurice was taken away hastily, together with oth Maquis, to imprisonment somewhere near Berlin. He seeme marked for speedy execution, for already the Germans we systematically killing off all prisoners who had been tortur by the Gestapo, lest later they give information again their torturers.

My grandfather thought he was dead.

He was astonished when the first brief letter came an almost illegible scrawl sometime in 1946. There we just the two of us by then in New Orleans, and I w a baby, and a girl, so I guess he was pleased that anoth male Gérard still survived in France. When I was old he never tired of telling me about the first letter fro Uncle Maurice.

But I liked my Uncle Maurice the better for his lett to me, for in it he did not sound at all like the embitter man I had imagined. He sounded kind and generous, a

8

very, very lonely. He sounded in fact about the way any girl might wish a wealthy uncle to be. I liked the reminder that I was his only living relative.

I began to think quite seriously of the Chateau of the Vultures. What a name! But names can be changed. How would it feel to be the mistress of a chateau in Auvergne? It seemed a remote possibility that he actually owned it, but . . .

I liked the thought.

Je suis comme ça! I am like that. It is because I am my grandfather's granddaughter. He taught me the value of a franc, among other things. In France, he had told me often enough, every man has a right to be himself. It is good. It can make France Cocaigne, that fabulous if imaginary country where everyone does as he pleases. A land of individuals. And half my blood is French. . . .

I jumped as the telephone on the small table buzzed. I uncurled myself lazily from the chair and sat on the arm while I picked up the phone.

"Oui?"

"This is Achard, Mam'selle Gérard. There is a man downstairs who says he is a Monsieur Gérard's chauffeur. You know this man? I mean, it is always wise to check if . . ."

"It's okay, Monsieur Achard. I am expecting the chauffeur. He is to take me to my uncle's chateau in Auvergne."

"Ah! Would Mam'selle wish me to send the man upstairs?"

"If you would, M'sieur. And someone to help him please. I have been shopping all day and have many parcels."

"At once, Mademoiselle!"

I put the phone down and checked my make-up hastily. My face looked back at me anxiously from the mirror, an oval face neither beautiful nor plain in repose, but somewhere in between. My hair is sleek, black, and has a bluish sheen. And I know I have a good body, high-breasted and narrow of waist, with the kind of shoulders that show to advantage in a low-cut gown. My legs are long. My eyes are the kind of brown that you'd expect of my French ancestry and dark hair, and they are large and clear. They slant slightly at the corners, above high cheekbones. Not beautiful, I know, but not bad at all, really.

Je suis comme ça!

I let the doorbell ring twice before I answered. The man out there filled the doorway and it took me a moment to recover when I looked up into his eyes. They were amber, cold eyes, like the eyes of a dead puma I had seen killed in

9

the swamps of New Orleans. Devoid of expression, they studied me only briefly before they slid away, cruel eyes set in a brutal face that had at some time suffered a badly broken nose. But the nose went with the thick, blubbery lips that were an unexpected, almost womanly red, and bunched, twisted ears like a wrestler's.

"You are Uncle Maurice's chauffeur?" I asked nervously.

He nodded heavily. "Monsieur Gérard bids me welcome you home to France, Mademoiselle. He sends you his good wishes. I am to bring you home to Châtaigneraie and the chateau as quickly as I can with regard to your safety, for he grows impatient to see you."

His voice was nasal and very light. It did not go with his face or the great breadth of his shoulders, or with the huge hands that held his chauffeur's cap as though it were something he wasn't used to holding. His upper body was built like a wedge beneath those wide shoulders. He had the build of an athlete and was obviously very strong.

I muttered something about my uncle being very kind, aware of the bellhop's curious eyes as he stared from one to the other of us.

"Your uncle is one of the heroes of the Resistance, Mademoiselle," he said, as though the war that had ended when I was born was not yet over. "A great man M'sieur Gérard. Great. It is a pleasure to serve him, Mam'selle. He has instructed me to guard you well on the way to the chateau. I am Albert Bernard, and your servant."

I nodded. "Thank you, Albert. These are my things."

He growled something at the bellhop, put on his peaked cap, and picked up my four heavy suitcases, two in each hand. He stood waiting respectfully as though the cases were featherweight.

The bellhop gathered my parcels, and I took a last look around the suite that had been my home for a whole exciting week in Paris. Compared with the chateau, I decided, this place must seem insignificant. Bound for a real French chateau, I could leave it without regret; it would still be here on our way back. I retrieved a pack of American cigarettes that I had forgotten, and preceded my colossus and his assistant out into the passage.

It was quite a formal leave-taking. Monsieur Achard saw me out, with the doorman and the bellhop fussing as though I were a countess. It occurred to me disconcertingly in the foyer that all this would be a bit of an anticlimax if Uncle Maurice's car proved to be an ancient heap, or one of those tiny European beetles that parked in droves along the avenues of the Etoile.

10

I stared down anxiously from the entrance. Albert was putting my bags into the luggage compartment of a sleek and gleaming limousine that would not have shamed De Gaulle. A black Mercedes-Benz, it would have cost poor grandfather almost the whole of his life's savings. Grandfather, I decided, had made a bad deal when he allowed Jean-Paul to have the farmlands.

Albert held the back door open for me. I sank luxuriously into the deep cushions. The doorman was bowing, Monsieur Achard was bowing, and the bellhop was bowing with them both. I waved at all three.

"There is a pillow, and rugs," Albert said in his nasal whine. "Later, if Mademoiselle tires, she can sleep quite comfortably. It is a long drive, but I will endeavor to make it a smooth one."

"I'm sure you will, Albert," I said. "Thank you."

I glanced around the interior as the motor purred into smooth and powerful life. The Mercedes could have been custom-built for De Gaulle, in fact.

"There is a radio, if Mademoiselle likes music," Albert informed me, his peculiar eyes watching me obliquely through the rear-vision mirror. "If pressed, the green button opens a small compartment, its door becoming a table. In the rack inside you will find wine from the estate, and vintage brandy. The thermos contains hot coffee, and the plastic compartment holds food that Monsieur Gérard chose for Mademoiselle."

"My uncle is spoiling me," I murmured.

"It gave him pleasure, Mademoiselle. As it does me in the telling. Mademoiselle must excuse me now. I must give my attention to the traffic."

Nostalgically, I watched the newly familiar boulevards sweep past. Occasionally heads turned to stare at us; people kept trying to see what kind of person rode in the back seat. Paris became a skyline of flashing neons, then a glare in the northern sky as we moved into the southern suburbs.

"We are on the highway now, Mademoiselle. It takes us through Etampes and the fringe of the forest of Fontainebleau. It is a great pity that it is not daylight, for just ahead lies L'Hay-les-Roses. The finest rose garden in the world, they say. And this is May, the time of roses."

"Perhaps I will see them when I come back," I said, staring into the darkness beyond the street lights.

"Perhaps," he said. He made a sound like laughter. "But roses do not last forever, Mam'selle."

I rolled down the window and could smell the perfume on the night air as we passed. He was right. The blooms

11

looked perfect, in the first flush of their beauty, under brilliant floodlights. It was the same in the great park of Sceaux, and in the gardens of houses on the outskirts of Etampes as we drove through.

Darkness drew about us again beyond Etampes. We entered the forest of Fontainebleau. A sign beside the highway read: "Stag and boar crossing," but we did not see any.

The sound of the motor became a deep and powerful drone. The air rushed past my windows. I leaned back again as Etampes dropped far behind. I began to translate the distance between Paris and the chateau from kilos to miles. Three hundred and fifty miles!

"Albert, can we really reach the chateau tonight?"

"But of course, Mam'selle. In time for breakfast. Eight hours from Paris. We left at nine, we should be at the chateau by five in the morning. We must be there, for Gabrielle will have prepared breakfast for us. She will have a tantrum if we allow it to spoil."

He said it with such solemnity that I laughed involuntarily. "Who is Gabrielle?"

"Madame Bremen, Mam'selle. The master's housekeeper, of course. You do not know of her?"

"I know very little about my uncle's household, Albert. His letters always said very little." And that was overstatement! "Tell me about the chateau and its people, Albert."

"It is not for me to tell," he growled. "It is better that you sleep, if you can. There is nothing to see here."

"No towns?"

"Orléans. It is not very much. Between lies the forest of Orléans. We cross the valley of the Loire at the city. After that there is nothing for you to see until we reach the Massif, and it will still be too dark then to see anything at all. It is much better that you sleep."

I said: "Ah yes, the Massif. I've heard that the mountain scenery is magnificent."

"Who told you that?"

"My grandfather. Monsieur Gérard's uncle."

"What people think of the Massif is a matter of opinion. You will see enough of the Massif Central from the chateau, no doubt. But the chateau lies south of Aurillac."

"Châtaigneraie? Is it as desolate as they say?"

"That again is a matter of opinion. The Châtaigneraie was once so fertile that it became overpopulated. The fools wore the earth out, stole its fertility, wasted its generosity. Now they are gone. There are only firs, pines, beeches, and beneath, the furze and the ferns. Yes, the Châtaigneraie could be described as desolate. Except on the Gérard estate. There are few people and no villages elsewhere for many kilos. It is a country of limestone caves that go deep into the earth. It is damp. It is impoverished. The people have not changed much in two hundred years, Mam'selle. That is the Châtaigneraie. Sleep now. It is what your uncle would wish."

I asked another question, but he pretended not to hear. The car rushed on smoothly through the darkness. Ahead the beams of the headlight stretched out, showing us the highway and dense forest on either side.

My watch said that it was eleven o'clock. The lights ahead that I could see distantly must be Orléans. They did not look impressive. I yawned, and found the pillow and the rugs, kicked off my shoes and curled up my legs. It was comfortable on the seat, and I began to realize that my day's shopping had tired me. The deep drone of the engine was soothing, so was the rush of passing air. Before me Albert Bernard's broad shoulders moved slightly as he drove. He drove very fast, but I had lost my fear of him and I like speed. He was certainly a good driver, and he seemed devoted to my uncle. Presently my eyes closed. . . .

The sound of metal against metal woke me with a start. The engine was silent, the car stopped. I sat up in sudden unexplained panic to stare about me. We had stopped at a gas station and a man with disheveled hair was struggling sleepily with the pump. I could not see Albert, but as I looked about I saw him coming from a small café attached to the gas station in which a single light burned.

He opened the car door with one hand, balancing a tray expertly on the other great palm.

"Mademoiselle is awake?"

I yawned and adjusted the rug to cover legs that seemed to interest him. "I woke just now. Where are we, Albert?"

"Outside Limoges, Mam'selle. I have brought you coffee. It is fresh, better than the coffee in the thermos. If Mademoiselle will allow me?"

He pressed the button and the compartment opened, the door becoming my table. He put down the coffee. It smelled delicious.

"A little brandy, Mademoiselle? It is very good brandy."

"Just a little, thank you."

He opened the plastic container, revealing a cold chicken, crisp leaves of lettuce, a red tomato.

"It will please Gabrielle if Mam'selle eats a little of the chicken—though they make splendid omelettes in the café here, and the woman will prepare one quickly if that is more to Mam'selle's taste?"

"I'll stay with Gabrielle's chicken, thank you, Albert."

"Good," he said. His thick lips parted in what I supposed was a smile. Through the open door keen air touched my face.

"Are we in the mountains here?"

"A thousand feet up, no more. But you will see the Massif soon. The river beside us is the Charente. The building ahead is the prison. Many Maquis were imprisoned here during the war, and taken to Paris for torture by the Gestapo often enough. Fine porcelain is made here. There is a rare deposit of fine clay at Limoges—kaolin. Its like is not found anywhere else in the Western world, only in China."

I nodded, and glanced at my watch. "Then we have made good time to Limoges?"

"We will reach the chateau at five, as I promised Monsieur Gérard. There is a rest room at the café if Mam'selle wishes to stretch her legs?"

I nodded and stepped out into night air that had a distinct bite. The prison was a dark bulk against the sky ahead, a single light showing above arched iron grille gates set in a massive stone wall. I shivered. Albert had probably been one of the Maquis, Grandpa's heroes of the Resistance. I wondered if it was here that beatings had made his face the way it was.

When I came back Albert was waiting beside the door and the attendant had gone back to bed.

"Will you help me with the chicken, Albert?"

His lips writhed into the grimace of a smile again. "I have eaten, Mam'selle. While the woman prepared your coffee. An omelette. The moon is full and rising, and half an hour beyond Limoges you will see the Massif as we turn toward Puy-de-Dôme and Mont Dore. At Tulle we turn south to Aurillac and the Châtaigneraie. From here on the road will be clear, and we can drive fast."

I nodded. "Then I'll eat as you drive."

He drove carefully through the city of Limoges, so that I did not have to worry about my coffee spilling. The coffee was good, and so was the chicken. I persuaded him to finish the chicken. He ate wolfishly, driving with one hand and tossing the bones carelessly out the window. I lit a cigarette and leaned back, gathering the rugs about me again.

A full moon was rising behind a peak to the southeast and I could see the saucer-like depression of an extinct volcano clearly in silhouette. Limoges fell behind rapidly, and now Albert hunched over the wheel silently, intent upon the road ahead.

I smiled, remembering Grandfather's glowing descriptions

14

of Auvergne scenery. The Massif was volcanic, and there were many such peaks as the one the moon revealed to me. He had spoken often of the limestone country of Châtaigneraie, but had never thought it desolate. Just beautiful. Staring ahead I wondered if Grandfather and Great-Uncle Jean-Paul had been among the improvident farmers who had despoiled it, the way Albert said.

The car dipped and rose. It soared smoothly now with only the rush of passing air indicating our speed. But we were going fast. The tires whined as we swooped around a curve, and I sat up higher to see the speedometer. Momentarily I blinked and gripped my seat. The crescent of yellow touched the figure 120. Then I remembered that the speedo showed kilos, not miles. Still, seventy-five was fast; Albert was holding the car on that speed, rock-steady.

He said abruptly, as though he sensed my interest, "A few kilos ahead we turn east toward the town of Brive. We drive through Tulle to reach Aurillac."

"You drive well, Albert."

The strangled sound of laughter came back to me. "I should! In the old days I often must drive much faster than this. And the cars we had—you would not ride in them today. Yet it was better to die in a road accident than at the hands of the Gestapo."

"You drove my Uncle Maurice?"

"No. I knew of him, of course. Who did not? But when we met for the first time it was at Gestapo headquarters in Berlin. They put him in my cell, marked for execution. He was so ill, so close to death it did not matter to him. But they delayed too long. I will never understand why, for others were shot. Many others. But the sands ran out. The Russians came. Hitler died in his bunker. We were still alive when the Gestapo leaders went underground and the Russians released us. I stayed with him to nurse him. So I came to the Châtaigneraie with him. There was nothing left anywhere else for me, nothing. I had a young wife once, and a child. But my wife was arrested when I was caught. They sent her to be a field whore for their troops. They shot her when she tried to escape. That happened often with the young women sent to the camps."

I shuddered. "It's so hard to imagine. And the child?"

"She was two years old. By mistake, she was sent to Dachau as a Jewish child. She was killed there."

The memory silenced him. And me.

I watched the moon rise higher. The mountains were beautiful by moonlight, full of soft purple and violet shadow in the valleys. The Mercedes started climbing, swooping

15

around curves, soaring over ridges to rush down the other side, seldom reducing speed. But suddenly the mountain slopes seemed ominous, the valleys gloomy chasms where fear lurked. Twenty years and more, the war was not forgotten here. And it was a vastly different war from the heroic pictures that my grandfather had painted from his imagination. Despondently watching the mountains pass, I began to wonder how the war had affected Uncle Maurice.

We rushed through sleeping Tulle and turned south. Aurillac lay ahead, a town of twenty thousand people. We passed through and gathered speed again.

"The Châtaigneraie," Albert muttered, still beset by memories.

A damp darkness seemed to hem us in on either side. The highway was secondary now but still quite good. We climbed, then descended. A stag, startled by the lights, leaped from beside the road and fled blindly, crashing through undergrowth.

My ears buzzed from a long descent before we rose again. I lost the sense of distance and time. Albert seemed indefatigable and huge over the wheel. I became aware of a lightness of false dawn in the east.

"We are now on the estate," Albert's voice said abruptly. "A few more kilos, Mam'selle, and you will see the lights of the Château-les-Vautours. . . ."

Suddenly there were buildings ahead. Dark, for there seemed no street lights. I glimpsed thatched houses, fields, and rows of grapevines. . . .

"The Château-les-Vautours," Albert grunted.

"Where?"

"Look left, Mam'selle, on the slope. The road curves beyond the village. The village is called Tocsin, the alarm-bell, as it was once when the chateau was Maqui-held. Its people are your uncle's tenants. Few strangers come to Tocsin these days, except by chance."

But I lost interest in the village as such. I stared at the light showing on the slope above the village. The Mercedes slowed then, bumping over what felt like cobbles. I glimpsed faded signs above small shops on either side. A bakery, an inn, a butcher's shop, clothing displayed primitively in a dirty window. A dog ran out barking defiantly, but retreated hurriedly as the Mercedes rushed down upon it.

The macadam road became gravel, rutted and narrow. I watched high stone walls and open iron gates materialize in the headlamp beams. The Mercedes stopped and Albert slid out to close the gates behind us. I stared back at him, frowning. He was closing a great padlock on a chain

16

hat might have once held a drawbridge, locking the great gates behind us. Ahead the chateau light still seemed far away, but as I glanced at it the single lighted window became two, then three as other lights came on.

Albert slid back into the driver's seat.

"Why lock the gates, Albert? Weren't they open when we came in?"

"They were left open for us to enter, Mam'selle. By the gatekeeper whose cottage you see on the right. It is safe to leave them open by night, for nobody from the village walks by night here. The villagers are superstitious."

"Safe?" I frowned. "Why is it necessary to lock them at all?"

His broad shoulders shrugged as he meshed the gears again. "Monsieur Gérard gives the orders, Mam'selle. Not I. He likes these gates locked. He does not like people to come to the chateau. He does not like people near him, especially strangers. It is permitted for the villagers to come to the chateau by day when they have business here, or when they work in the fields. The gates are opened then. But not by night."

"You make my uncle sound like a recluse, Albert."

Again the shrug. "Perhaps he is, Mam'selle. Yes. Whether he wills it or not, recluse is what the war has made of him. . . ."

Vineyards on either side became an orchard, then gardens with roses in full bud, for here it was cooler than on the lowlands. The lawns between looked smooth and well kept. The Mercedes' lights shone on many windows, then abruptly before it turned, upon the fallen stone of a disused wing of the chateau. We turned onto smooth gravel, and stopped. In a doorway above curved stone steps a woman's figure stood awaiting us. I stared at her, groping for my shoes. She looked huge, more like a man than a woman. Her bulk filled the doorway as she peered down at us. Albert slid out of his seat to open the door for me.

Above me the chateau loomed high, reminding me of the prison at Limoges.

The woman dwarfed me as I climbed the steps. I said: "You must be Gabrielle?"

She nodded curtly. "The master bids me welcome you to the Château-les-Vautours, Mademoiselle. A room is prepared for you. Breakfast in fifteen minutes, for that great oaf Bernard is fifteen minutes early. But first the master will greet you. He is waiting in the library."

I smiled at her, trying to see in the dim light what kind of face went with that deep, almost masculine voice.

I saw it suddenly as she turned, dark-skinned, the lips thin the eyes narrow, the white line of an old scar crossing th left cheek from near where black hairs sprouted on he upper lip.

I said: "I think I'd like to freshen up before I see m uncle. My suit is wrinkled, my make-up must be all ove the place. . . ." I said it as one woman might to anothe though to me her femininity seemed a doubtful quality

She replied without looking at me. "He said at once Mademoiselle. He means at once. If you do not look lik a Parisienne, that is not important. In his day he has know enough of such. This way please."

"But . . ." She walked on as though she had not heard

Somewhere I could hear the sound of diesel motors. decided they must be the source of power for the lightin It did not seem very bright, though in the great passag down which I followed her there were a lot of electri light globes in a cluster set in a chandelier of shining crysta Perhaps it was the height of the passage, I thought, th made the light dim. But when she stopped outside a grea oak door on my left, she turned her head before she knocke and looked at me deliberately.

"The master likes the dark, for reasons you will understan in time, no doubt. It is best that you do not show surpris when you see him, for he is sensitive about such thing even after all these years. He was once a very handsom man. Now . . ." She broke off.

"I know that he was scarred in the war, Madame," said calmly.

"Do not speak of it," she said roughly. She knocke "I warn you, not a word to him!"

"Come in," a deep voice called. "Is she here, then? Gabrielle opened the door. "She is here, M'sieur."

"Leave us," the deep voice ordered. It changed subtl "Come in, Denise. Welcome to the Château-les-Vautours.

I entered, nervous. The light from the passage showe me the interior of a room lined with shelves of book A shadowy figure sat behind a great table, but the roo was otherwise in complete darkness.

"Uncle Maurice?" I ventured, approaching warily.

"So you are Henri Gérard's granddaughter, Denise." Th words had an elusive accent. "Welcome, my dear. In th dark everyone is equal. Is it not so? But perhaps und the circumstances we should have light, eh? So let the be light."

A reading lamp on the table blossomed abruptly. It di closed the room, and the shape of a small, but sturd

an, square-shouldered, his left hand resting carelessly on
the table as he stared at me. He could see me very well,
had no doubt. But I could not see his face at all, for
the lamp was shaded to keep the light from him while it
shone directly at me.

"Grandfather always showed me your letters. You were
a hero to him, Uncle Maurice," I said. "I feel that I know
you, and have known you all my life." I came round the
table impulsively, and bending, kissed him quickly on the
cheek.

I recoiled instinctively in a horror that I could not quite
conceal, for to my lips his cheek felt like the fur of an
animal. And he too had recoiled from my kiss as though
it affected him in the same way. He sat very still, staring
at me.

He said slowly then: "You must pardon me, Denise, if
I seem unresponsive. It is a long time since any woman
kissed me. Particularly a young woman such as you. Walk
back to the door. There is a light switch there. Use it,
and you will see that there is no reason to fear me as
you do at this moment. I am neither an animal nor the
devil. I am just a man, and your uncle."

It took effort to stop at the door and not run through
and back to the Mercedes. But I did stop. I switched on
the light and turned slowly to look at him.

He sat very still, very straight, watching me. A squat
man with a military bearing. His hair was thick and snow-
white. The rest of his face I could not see at all, for a
mask of black velvet covered it. Through it I could see
the shape of a face, but that was all. The nose was there,
a straight ridge down the center of the mask. The velvet
was slit above the nostrils so that it pressed in a narrow
band across his upper lip, allowing him to breathe freely.
It parted again at the mouth, which I decided now was
laughing at me, though no sound of laughter reached me.
But the velvet mask disclosed white, even teeth before it
draped over the chin and disappeared inside an open white
shirt.

"I don't understand," I muttered. But I did, the picture
was clearing for me. Of course, the scars of burns! My
lips had touched velvet instead of skin. . . .

He shrugged. "It is simple, my dear. I was scarred during
the war. I do not speak of it, I try not to think about
it. Sometimes I think it was a mistake to grasp at life. . . ."

I came back to him involuntarily, touched by compassion.
"But Uncle Maurice, with plastic surgery. . ."

"It is beyond that," he said curtly.

19

"But you are healthy and strong. In America there are surgeons, reconstructive surgeons who could . . . who do perform, well, almost miracles with scars and burns."

"In America, yes! Though I doubt they can help me," he said. "But perhaps if . . . we decide that I go to America I will allow you to persuade me to see one of your surgeons."

"You must!" I exclaimed.

His teeth showed again briefly in that faceless smile.

"Perhaps," he said. "We will see. You have the confidence of youth, Denise. And you are a very lovely young woman. It encourages me. You are good for me already, I think. I hope you will stay here for a while. Then, we will see. There are problems to overcome. It is not easy for me to leave France. But perhaps with your help, I may. In the meantime, Gabrielle has food and hot coffee for us. Come."

He stood up and bowed, put my hand upon his arm and patted it affectionately. I allowed him to lead me from the book-lined room. Walking beside him I tried not to think of what lay behind the smooth black mask. Or of the fact that the arm my hand rested on ended in a claw of stainless steel. . . .

CHAPTER TWO

"ARE YOU AWAKE yet, Mam'selle?"

The hoarse whisper woke me in fear, with my heart pounding. I cried out something, I did not know what, and heard quick movement close to the great bed in which I slept. A whisper of hoarse laughter sounded in the darkness.

"Who is it?" I gasped. I sat up quickly.

"It is I, Gabrielle Bremen." I heard her moving toward the window. "You have slept beyond lunch. It is midday. I will draw the curtains for you."

The heavy drapes that had made my room like night were drawn back revealing Gabrielle grinning at me. In the midday light she looked even less attractive than she had in the morning. As her thin lips parted in that mirthless smile, I noticed her teeth for the first time, yellowish and darkened by the stains of tobacco.

Her eyes gleamed, slitted as they slid over me, so that

I drew up the covers hastily. I wished that I had worn a thicker nightgown than this Paris creation.

I muttered something about being sorry that I had slept so late, but she shook her head.

"It is of no importance. Except that the master thought the shooting might frighten you. So I brought you something light to eat, and coffee. There is red wine if you prefer it."

"Thank you." I glanced at the tray on the table near my bed. "You are kind, Gabrielle."

"I?" she said. "Kind?" She laughed again, coming back from the window to stand at the foot of my bed. Her eyes, I noticed, had not left me, or lost that curious, speculative gleam.

"Yes," I said. "If you had called me, I would have come down."

She shrugged and turned back to the window. Beyond her I could see mighty mountain peaks, a line of them vanishing into hazy distance against a pale blue sky.

For a woman of her bulk she moved with a catlike silence that surprised me, for the floor was of oak, polished by time and usage, with only scatter rugs, and she wore heavy shoes under her old-fashioned black dress. I took the opportunity of her distraction to slide silently from the bed myself, and seize my robe. I pulled it on hurriedly and was closing it when she sensed the movement and turned her head quickly to stare at me.

I pulled the robe tight, feeling warmth in my cheeks that I knew was mostly anger.

I forced myself to say calmly: "You said something about shooting just now?"

She went on staring at me. "You are beautiful, Mam'selle. But I suppose men have told you that often. Would you believe that once men thought the same of me? I was very tall and slender then. I—" She broke off abruptly, and laughed. "Now I have offended you, I suppose. It is because it is a long time since I have . . . attended anyone like you, Mademoiselle. I am sorry." Her tone changed quickly while I felt anger darken my face and sought the right words. She added hastily: "But, ah yes, the shooting! Come see for yourself. There is a good view from your window and it is worth seeing. After lunch each day the master shoots. He is a very fine marksman. And it is about to begin. Bernard has thrown the grain, and already the vultures are hovering."

I allowed my anger to subside before I moved to the

21

window. Above the garden, high up, floated a score of black birds, circling slowly.

"I did not know there were vultures in Europe," I muttered. "Does my uncle shoot them?"

"Not the vultures! Certainly *not* the vultures. They are black vultures, rare now in Europe. They nest in the forest above the chateau. Each day the master feeds them. They give this place its name, Mam'selle, so it would be a pity to destroy them, would it not?"

"Then what . . .?"

"Look on the lawns below you, and watch closely."

I saw the grain suddenly, wheat scattered across the lawn in a wide swath. A dozen or more plump pigeons were strutting about, pecking at the grain among the mown grass of the lawn. And as I watched another group flew in, alighting eagerly with spread wings to join the parade.

"There are many flocks of pigeons living wild in the forest," Gabrielle's voice explained pleasantly. "Soft little creatures, and very stupid. For they never learn. We also breed them for the rare occasions when through fear or by the thinning of their numbers they stay away for a while."

But I was staring at the pigeons intently. There was something wrong. A few seemed unsteady on their feet. As I watched, one tried to fly, but fell and flopped feebly about on the grass.

"Mostly," Gabrielle explained, staring down beside me now, "they are too fast for the vultures. Only the hawks and falcons in the forest can take them on the wing. But here it is different. We help the vultures a little. Albert soaks the wheat the night before in a liquid the master has taught us to prepare, and that way it is easier."

"You mean—the wheat is *drugged?*" I asked, horrified.

The flat, heavy sound of the first shot cut across my indignation. A pigeon disintegrated abruptly into torn flesh and spurting gray feathers.

The pigeons I had watched alight took wing frantically. But those nearest to their slaughtered companion merely moved away slightly from the flying debris of flesh and feathers. They went right on pecking as though nothing had happened. A second shot slapped, and a third, and I saw the blue smoke then, rising above a window at the other end of the chateau.

I watched fascinated, revolted, but unable to look away. Feathers littered the lawn. The last group of pigeons had flown at the first shot, but the earlier and greedier birds

22

seemed unable to escape, despite the frantic flapping of one or two frightened ones.

"He never misses," Gabrielle gloated exultantly. "Never! It is worth seeing, is it not, Mam'selle?"

Her fingers gripped my arm with the strength of a man, hurting me. I pulled my arm away. I turned, the spell of fascination that had held me at the window broken now.

"I think it's horrible!" I gasped.

"Horrible? But why, Mademoiselle? He uses a rifle. And the birds down there are wild birds. Is that not better than slaughtering tame pigeons with shotguns, the way Englishmen and Americans do? With him it is an art. The birds he has shot feel nothing. The rifle is of heavy caliber. And is it so different to feed the drugged live pigeons that remain when he has tired of shooting to the vultures, than it is to release falcons upon them to tear them to pieces in the air. Oh, look now! The vultures are coming! Their leader is coming in. Always the same bird. He likes his meat alive, though the others are content with the fragments. . . ."

The shooting stopped as the vultures settled. She stared down absorbed. A big black bird with a bald head had alighted near one of the fluttering, helpless pigeons. I watched him seize it by one leg. As I stared down he gripped it with one claw and tore at its flesh. Bloody feathers clung to the hooked beak.

I turned away quickly, sickened. "You are a sadist, Gabrielle," I whispered. "And so is my uncle."

"A sadist? I?" She looked at me. Her eyes, were almost black. It was hard to discover the small pupils. But as I gave her back look for look, they filmed suddenly, disguising their intent from me. Her eyelids lowered, and she looked away. "Oh no, Mademoiselle," she said in a changed, almost servile voice. "You are wrong. Truly, you are. I am always sorry for the pigeons. They are so plump and pretty—yet so silly. Like children, the way they strut and pose down there, and coo. Why, I often feed them in the early morning, saving the crusts of bread and crumbs for them. They almost eat from my fingers."

"For what purpose?" I asked furiously. "To make them the tamer for *that*?"

"No!" She shook her head. "No! I am sorry that they must die. But if they did not die the vultures would starve, and I would be even more sorry for the vultures. For starvation is the worst death of all. It is a matter of necessity. And death is not so horrible. Death can be—beautiful. . . ."

She bit the words off short and turned away from me.

23

"If I have offended Mademoiselle, I am sorry. It was not intentional. Your coffee has cooled, I will bring a fresh pot at once."

"Don't bother," I said. "I've lost my appetite."

"A glass of wine will revive it while I am away. They are but birds, after all." She shrugged. "What we have watched is of no importance. One should not look at what one finds disagreeable. It is best forgotten."

She picked up the coffee jug and went out, closing the heavy door silently behind her.

She is insane, I thought, staring at the closed door. No woman in her right mind would think as she does! The woman could be dangerous. My uncle should be warned.

I hurried to the door to lock it against her return. I stopped, appalled. My bedroom door had no lock!

I came back slowly to sit on the edge of the bed and stare at the door. I would protest to my uncle about that, and about his cruelty to the pigeons. I would . . .

The train of frightened thought broke. This was my uncle's chateau. Here he was master. Gabrielle was only an employee. So was Albert.

My uncle had shown Albert how to mix whatever drug soaked the wheat for those poor birds. The twisted mind of Gabrielle might find enjoyment in the killing of the pigeons; but it was *my uncle*, not Gabrielle, who must enjoy killing them.

Had my uncle's suffering so long ago, his self-imposed isolation ever since, destroyed his sympathy for the suffering of other creatures? If it had, I thought, I could understand it. The Gérards were sensitive, so was it not possible that Uncle Maurice's seeming coldness and indifference now was a defensive veneer that he had built to keep out further hurt? I began to find excuses for Uncle Maurice, sitting on the edge of my bed watching the door. Yet even as I reasoned, I felt unclean for what I had just witnessed. I wanted a shower. No, a bath. But that would have to wait until Gabrielle had surely gone. Gabrielle in my *bathroom* would be too much. I turned to stare at the bathroom door. Like the bedroom door, it had no lock.

As I stared at it, frowning, I heard my bedroom door open, and turned my head quickly. She had made no sound coming along the passage, but Gabrielle was coming in now carrying a jug trailing fragrant steam.

She smiled at me with what she probably thought a conciliatory smile.

"Mademoiselle will feel better for this. Louise made it.

Louise is a girl from the village who works here. She makes good coffee."

I nodded curt thanks. I allowed myself to unbend slightly. "There are servants here, then?"

She nodded. "The servants come from the village. Maids, a woman who prepares the meals I order. Another woman does the laundry. Pierre Labrousse acts as gatekeeper, and his wife Marie is the cook. They have a daughter, but she will not work here. She has a lover they say, in the village. She is attractive to men, in a silly way. At nineteen, girls are like that. Our maids come and go all the time. Only the older women stay. It is difficult for older women to find other work in the Châtaigneraie."

"You have quite a household," I muttered, wishing only that she'd go. "I must not keep you here, then."

"At times the whole village works on the estate. It is seasonal work in the fields or vineyards, of course. If you require a bath, Mademoiselle, press the bell beside the door and I will come up and prepare it for you while you undress."

I forced myself to smile. "Thank you, Gabrielle, but I am quite capable of preparing my own bath."

Her eyes slid down. "As Mademoiselle wishes."

"I will come down presently, and bring the tray. Where will I find my uncle?"

"In his room."

"Does he go out much at all?"

"Yes, often." Her eyes met mine suspiciously. "Why do you ask?"

I shrugged. "It is not good for anyone to spend his life indoors."

"He goes for long walks in the forest often enough. Hunting. Or fishing in the streams in the valleys up there. There are deer and wild pigs in the forest, trout in the streams. They help our table."

"And the pigeons, of course," I could not resist saying.

"Yes, the pigeons. And pheasant, and often quail and wild fowl."

"Perhaps he will take me hunting one day," I said tentatively.

"You?" Her eyes slid over me, acquiring a malicious-seeming look. "Yes, perhaps he will. I would like to be there when he does!" She moistened her thin lips with the tip of her tongue. Her tone gave it a meaning I didn't like. She added: "Yet a shot pigeon turns your stomach?"

"That was not hunting. . . . I have no lock on this door. I must speak to my uncle about that."

"Why? Are you afraid?"

My temper flashed. "No, I am not afraid!" I said indignantly. "Why should I be afraid here? I am quite capable of looking after myself. But a lock on a girl's door is a common courtesy where I come from. No girl likes to be disturbed dressing, or in her bath."

"I see. In America, of course, things are different from here." She made a sound like a hoarse giggle. "Well, perhaps he will have Albert put a bolt on specially for you—though I doubt it. The only doors with locks in the chateau are the doors of the rooms the master uses most. The library and his bedroom. And of course the outer doors, which are locked fast each night by the master and Albert, like the lower shutters." She giggled again. "Mam'selle, once the lights go out and the chateau is locked, nobody can get in, or out. You are safe here. Unless, of course you are afraid of your uncle, or Albert, or me—for we three alone sleep within these walls."

"You must be busy, Gabrielle. I won't keep you longer," I said. "Or the coffee will grow cold again."

"So. Very well, Mademoiselle. I will send one of the maids up later to make your bed. With orders to knock before she enters, so that she does not disturb you—dressing or in your bath."

"Thank you, Gabrielle," I said coldly.

I sipped a little of the coffee, and ate some of the food, while hot water ran into the old-fashioned bath. The sound of a cheerful whistle drew me back cautiously to the window. A thin man in blue levis and a red shirt was raking the lawn beneath my window with a bamboo lawn-rake. He had gray hair and wore a black beret rakishly. I supposed he must be the gatekeeper, Pierre Labrousse.

He was raking the gray feathers into a heap. There were no longer any vultures hovering in the sky above the chateau, but presently I discovered one sitting hunched on the branch of an oak tree beyond the garden. Replete. . . .

As though he sensed someone watching him, the thin man looked up at my window and saw me.

"Good morning, Mademoiselle," he called up gaily. He had a barrow down there, and he had picked up a handful of the feathers. He flung them into the barrow and swept off his beret courteously. Blood and a few feathers clung to his fingers, but he did not seem to notice.

I nodded to him, and withdrew. I hurried into the bathroom. I was not satisfied until I had eased myself into the steaming water and lay submerged to my chin. And

26

only after I had scrubbed myself until my skin tingled did I feel clean and relaxed again.

I dressed carefully with a chair propped against my door. As I passed the stairs I could hear Gabrielle Bremen's deep voice talking to someone in the kitchen, but the rest of the great house was as silent as the grave in the warm afternoon sunshine. Uncle Maurice, I decided, would be in the library.

I knocked timidly.

"Who is there?" his deep voice asked harshly.

"Denise, Uncle Maurice. Am I disturbing you?"

I listened to a brief silence before his voice said curtly: "One moment, Denise."

I waited, overlong, it seemed, before I heard his step. Curtain rings rattled, and then the lock clicked as he opened the door.

"Come in, my dear." He was smiling at me, the black velvet mask precisely in place, though I suspected that he had needed the time just now to put it on. His eyes smiled at me benevolently above it. They were brown, I saw now, studying them briefly for the first time in daylight. But they were not the dark, soft brown of my grandfather's. They were much lighter, with reddish-brown specks.

Yet as our eyes met, I could believe what Gabrielle had said about him being handsome once. His brows were dark and well shaped, his forehead broad and intelligent. The bone structure beneath the mask seemed symmetrical. . . .

I looked away. "I was not sure whether you might be working. If you are busy, don't hesitate to send me away."

He laughed. "After taking so long to bring you here to me, Denise, how could I do that? My work, as you call it, is of no importance compared to that. I hope you rested well?"

"Oh, yes."

"Good. Come in, child. Wine? Yes, I insist. We drink our own wine from the estate usually, except at dinner. We have a taste for it, though this is not an area of good wines. The vineyards are too high, the sun too weak here. For myself, I like a good Pouilly-sur-Loire."

I laughed as he drew out a chair for me. "Really, Uncle Maurice! An Alsatian—almost a *German* wine?"

He looked at me for a moment before he laughed, an odd expression in those brown eyes. "The Rhine grew fine grapes long before there were Nazis in Germany, Denise," he said quietly.

I breached an awkward pause by smiling at him. I watched him relax again before I said: "Grandpa taught

27

me what little I know about wines. He did detest anything German. To his mind there was only one wine—Bordeaux."

"Of which our local red wine here is a frail offspring," he said. He chuckled suddenly. "And what wine do *you* prefer, young lady? Bordeaux?"

I laughed a little ruefully. "Burgundy," I admitted.

Behind the black velvet I sensed that he was smiling. "Well, well! Then you will find our own Château Vautours Bordeaux too sour for your taste. Not that I blame you. I prefer Burgundy to it myself." His eyes twinkled. "Full-bodied, earthy, lusty Burgundy is for sturdy natures like yours—and mine when I cannot get wines of Alsace."

I had not noticed him touch anything but my chair and his own, but someone tapped on the door and a rather nervous feminine voice called: "You rang, M'sieur?"

"Yes. Mademoiselle would like some Burgundy, Louise. One of the '45 bottles. Slightly chilled, please."

"Yes, M'sieur."

I raised my eyebrows at him. "Forty-five? Grandfather used to say that was the best year for Bordeaux. A vintage year. You must have a good cellar, Uncle Maurice."

"It is well stocked. You shall see it later when I show you the chateau."

"Thank you. Most of all though, I would like to see the farm at Vaison where grandfather was born. And Great-Uncle Jean-Paul and you, of course."

His brows drew together briefly. "Ah yes, of course, Vaison. It is twenty kilos from here, and there is not much to see any more. It was worked out, neglected, partly destroyed during the war, the buildings crumbled. When I bought this estate, the tenants came with me—some of them. Labrousse, a few others. I still hold title to the land at Vaison, and there is a caretaker there, but it is no longer in use. However, since it interests you, I will have Albert drive you over one day. You can report its condition to me. I have not seen it for many years."

Remembering Grandfather's glowing accounts of Vaison, I frowned. "It seems a pity . . ."

"Here is our Burgundy." I hadn't heard the girl coming, but there was a gentle knock at the closed door. "Come in, Louise. The door is not locked."

A girl in a black dress like Gabrielle's came in nervously, carrying a tray. She was young, no more than nineteen or twenty. A slim girl with a good figure, dark-haired, dark-eyed, but rather plain and without make-up of any kind on her broad peasant face.

"You may leave it, Louise. I will serve it."

"Yes, M'sieur," The gleaming crystal glasses rattled slightly as she put the tray down, and I saw that her hands were trembling, her dark eyes wide with nervousness.

He looked at her sourly. "Stop shaking, girl," he said testily. "I am not an ogre."

"Yes, M'sieur," she muttered. "No. . . M'sieur. Is there anything else, M'sieur?"

"Unless Mademoiselle would like a little cheese to bring out the flavor of the Burgundy?" He looked at me inquiringly.

I shook my head, and smiled at the girl reassuringly. "No thank you. I've just had lunch."

"Then that is all," he said. She turned away hastily, her eyes averted, and he said sharply: "Wait!" He looked at me. "You have not met Louise, Denise. She is the daughter of one of our tenants in the village. Jean Guiet. A good man. Louise, this is Mademoiselle Gérard, your new mistress."

"Mademoiselle." She bobbed her head in a slight bow, her eyes still wide and frightened.

I said: "How are you, Louise?"

She murmured something too low to be heard. My uncle frowned. "If Mademoiselle requires anything, you are to attend to her, Louise. Whenever she wishes. Do you understand?"

She glanced at me, her eyes more interested, and a little relieved, I thought.

"But of course, M'sieur, Mademoiselle."

"You may go, Louise."

"Thank you, M'sieur."

He watched her go out before he reached for the wine and sighed. "She fears me of course. Mostly it does not matter. They all do. It is this . . ."

He touched the mask, and the steel artificial hand reached carelessly for one of the crystal glasses. I watched fascinated, not sure what to say. It looked like one end of a handcuff. It closed on the stem of the glass with a slightly grating sound, but the glass lifted, was set down undamaged. I let my held breath sigh out carefully lest he hear.

"While we drink our wine," he said, so precisely that I knew he had noticed, "you must tell me about my uncle, your grandfather. And your home in America. Tell me everything you can remember. Your grandfather told me much in his letters, but letters are never enough. He said once that you have a taste for the good things of life, and that beauty must get them for you, since you were not at all cunning. You have intelligent eyes, Denise."

29

"I am not sure where to start, Uncle Maurice," I murmured, embarrassed.

"Then start with New Orleans. Is it like Paris, now that you have seen both? Is it really as French as they say?"

I laughed. "It is not like Paris at all, part of it is American. As for the French quarter, the Vieux Carré, it is more French than Paris because it is Old French, as Grandfather used to say. It is full of little crooked streets, sidewalk cafés, and restaurants. It has not changed in appearance in a hundred and fifty years. . . ."

He asked the questions for the most part. We sipped our wine. The sun steamed in through the large windows and beyond them I could see the neat rows of vines in the fields, then mountain slopes and forest.

I forgot the pigeons and Gabrielle's rudeness and the things I had meant to say to him. To me he was pleasant and courteous. If he had sharp questions to ask, it was interesting to answer them. He had a keen mind, that was obvious. And after a while I forgot the mask too, and the strange artificial hand that was like a claw of stainless steel. . . .

When he leaned back at last and smiled at me, I discovered that I was slightly hoarse, and that there was not much left to be said about my life with Grandfather in New Orleans. He laughed softly.

"You are a very sensitive and observant young woman, Denise," he said approvingly. "You have the gift of description, as well as an excellent memory. Already I feel that I could walk through your home in the Vieux Carré from attic to cellar, or rather basement as you Americans say. And I would recognize each thing that I passed, and feel at home. It is a pity that your grandfather is not still sitting in his rocking chair, dreaming his dreams of a France that I am afraid ceased to exist many years ago. A France that lost its spirit, its very soul, in the war. To become decadent, to become far more Americanized than your New Orleans."

"You must be wrong," I muttered, appalled.

He shook his head. "No, Denise. That is the truth. That is the way France has become. Greatness has gone from France. Now she walks a line between democracy and communism, swaying first one way and then the other. Not even sure of her own mind."

"But De Gaulle—" I protested.

"—is too austere," he interrupted, "too aloof from reality ever to have become the kind of leader France needs. De Gaulle is no great orator expounding a vision that Frenchmen could be prepared to follow really. He thinks like an aristocrat, and acts like one. He has lost touch with the little people. He cannot offer them a dream of greatness, because he is not of them. Yet that is what France needs today, obviously."

I stared at him, frowning. "A rabble-rouser?"

"France will never be great again until she finds herself a leader from the people. If West Germany falls to communism eventually, as she may, it will be too late. France and all Europe will be communist. France needs a new leader now. And even now it may be too late. Denise, I like the word pictures you paint for me of New Orleans. You have decided me. There! I will go to America with you and live in New Orleans. Yet this will take thought, and time, for there is this. . . ." He touched the mask with the tips of his fingers. "And there is also this. . . ."

He turned his left hand over slowly, extending it to me palm upward so that I saw the undersurface of the hand clearly for the first time. I stared at it shocked. The palm of the hand, the balls of the four fingers and the thumb were deeply scarred, with red ridges of scar tissue showing.

"Your hand was burned, when . . .?" I glanced at the black velvet mask, horrified.

His eyes smiled at me. "A little later, Denise," he said in a quiet voice. "In Paris at Gestapo headquarters. They pointed out the advantages of still having one hand that I could use freely, even though I had lost the other. Then to persuade me to tell them the things they wanted to know, among other things they held my hand upon a hot stove, palm down. That is not important now. But to the authorities who issue passports it is a problem. And to the American authorities also, no doubt. For neither my face nor my fingerprints are of use for identification any more. So you see, it is difficult. I had the same difficulty when I returned to Vaison after the war. Then, I had to learn to write with my left hand. That meant that money, assets I had, were difficult to obtain or convert into cash, for my signature had changed. Yet with the help of friends who had not forgotten me these things were overcome. Just as we will overcome the problem of reaching America. For I still have my friends, some now in high places. And I have you, my niece, American-born, to vouch for me with the American authorities. You will do that for me, Denise, eh?"

"Of course, Uncle Maurice."

He stood up. "I will show you the chateau and the vineyards now. The Château-les-Vautours is at its best at this time of day." His eyes smiled at me.

The glance of those friendly eyes, the touch of his scarred

fingertips as he moved back my chair with old-world courtesy, disarmed me.

I followed him silently out into the corridor.

CHAPTER THREE

SITTING OPPOSITE UNCLE Maurice at breakfast, I remembered how well I had slept on my first night at the Château-les-Vautours. I had opened my eyes only once to peer at the chair propped against my bedroom door. Nibbling crisp, newly baked bread and creamery butter, with the fragrance of Gabrielle's coffee in the air, I felt full of an almost animal vigor that I supposed sprang from my night's rest and the mountain air. On that one occasion last night when I had wakened, the scene outside my window had seemed so serene, so peaceful, that it had quickly lulled me back into the arms of sleep.

The moonlight outside my window through the parted drapes had disclosed the mountain slope and the edge of the forest beyond the fields in clear, luminous detail. I had stared out at it for long moments, savoring its beauty before I closed my eyes and sighed contentedly and went to sleep again.

Uncle Maurice's Château-les-Vautours must be far more beautiful, I decided, than the farm at Vaison that Grandfather had painted in such glowing pictures. It was on a far grander scale, a relic of a past magnificence. Only the older portion, that which had crumbled into fallen stone and powdered mortar had been built for strength in medieval times. The chateau as Uncle Maurice lived in it now had been built as two additional wings in the elegant pre-Revolutionary days of the late eighteenth century. The towers were there, but they had not been built for defense, but for ornament.

The chateau had been looted and partially burned during the Revolution, Uncle Maurice had told me yesterday afternoon. There had been heavy fighting here between Royalist and Revolutionary troops, fighting that had ended in an orgy of rape and murder when the badly disciplined Revolutionary troops finally overcame the defenders.

Uncle Maurice's expressionless voice had painted word pictures that were not easy to forget and that left nothing to my imagination. In fact they had the ring of truth that made me suspect that during his days with the Maquis Uncle Maurice had seen more than his share of similar violence.

It was then apparently, after the withdrawal of the exultant Revolutionaries laden with the loot of the chateau, that the vultures had first appeared in numbers to feed upon the unburied dead. The years of the Revolution and of the Napoleonic Wars must have been verdant years for vultures, for they had stayed on at the chateau, no doubt finding the two great wars of the present century equally fruitful.

The pigeons had been bad enough, but I found the vultures even more revolting now that I had their complete history from Uncle Maurice.

But this morning there were no vultures in sight, and a truck was unloading villagers in one of the fields to begin a day's work among vines already carrying the tiny grapes of the summer harvest.

We idled over our coffee, watching the villagers begin their work. Both Albert Bernard and the man I had seen raking the lawns were up there on the slopes with them apparently directing the work of about a score of people, women as well as men.

Uncle Maurice began talking about the possibility of becoming an American citizen. He knew a great deal more about that than I did, I discovered quickly.

"I think perhaps my best chance would be to apply for a visa as a non-quota immigrant, Denise," he confided thoughtfully. "I understand your consular officials have authority to grant visas to prospective immigrants. It is there that you can help me, if you will. For an American citizen has the right to petition for the admission of certain relatives. It is true that this does not apply to an uncle, but there are, it seems, no hard and fast rules for the affidavit of support by the citizen for the foreign relative, so no doubt your support will help me."

"Then I will certainly make one," I said, smiling at him.

"Good girl." His left hand reached out to pat mine affectionately and I felt the ridges of his scars against my hand. "You know, I suppose, that there are certain conditions of entry that make such things selective?"

"I know there are certain clauses in the Immigration Act against the entry of people who may not become good citizens. For instance, although there is no rule as to the amount of money a sponsor should have, yet a potential non-quota immigrant must satisfy the consular officials that he is not about to become a charge upon the state."

He laughed. "I think that is hardly likely, my dear Denise.

Even without the sale of this place and Vaison, I am a wealthy man, as I have already told you. I can prove that easily enough to your consular officials. I have credits in South America and in Switzerland that must ensure that neither you nor I will ever become a charge on your American state."

I said: "You must have done very well from Vaison before you moved here, Uncle Maurice. Grandfather always spoke of Vaison highly, but not as a source of great wealth."

He laughed softly. "There are other ways of making money than grubbing in the soil of France to grow grapes and potatoes, Denise." He touched the mask with the tips of his fingers, his inscrutable eyes studying me calmly. "Such disfigurement can make a man aggressive as well as solitary. And solitary men have time to think and plan. Wealth is power, Denise. I decided that wealth might be some compensation for what was done to me. Starting with a modest capital, I built it rapidly in the years of reconstruction after the war." He glanced around. "This place was a ruin. I bought it cheaply and restored it. I sold everything that could be sold, and invested. I suppose you would say that I invested heavily. And there were certainly good friends of mine who thought at the time that I invested foolishly in that period of reconstruction. Yet I did nothing without careful thought. I never invested a franc where I could not see a certain profit some time in the future. My friends laughed, thinking I was over-optimistic, that I chased rainbows where they saw only cloudy sky. But the rainbows formed, and my friends began jealously to call my foolishness by other names. Friends are like that."

"There is little chance of *you* ever becoming a charge on the state!"

"No chance at all," he smiled. "For I have learned a great deal about investment. And your rules for non-quota immigrants also include a clause which says that where a potential immigrant whose services are determined to be beneficial economically to the United States is concerned, certain preferences are available to him. Have no doubt that we will take full advantage of that clause, Denise!"

I nodded. But his face darkened suddenly and he added: "But there is still the matter of the photos. Three of them, I understand. Giving a full front view of the features without a hat or anything else that might disguise details . . . of this."

I said impulsively: "Anyone who sees your scars and knows about what you suffered must understand and feel sympathy, Uncle Maurice."

"Perhaps. Yes, perhaps so. Well, we will know soon enough,

no doubt. For very soon I must ask you to go to Paris for me, and speak to your consular officials and try to find out these things in detail." For the first time since I had met him, he showed hesitation. He grew silent, watching me intently for what seemed a long while before he leaned forward and said in a low voice, "In the meantime, can I trust to your discretion, Denise?"

I said sympathetically: "You know you can, Uncle Maurice. At all times."

"Then you must say nothing of this to the others, Denise. Not a word. Do you understand?"

I stared at him blankly. "To . . . the others?"

"To Albert Bernard. To Gabrielle." He frowned, studying my surprise.

I said: "But they are just your servants, Uncle Maurice."

"Nevertheless, they have shown me great loyalty. And I cannot take them with me when I leave. It is not possible. Foreknowledge would disappoint them. It would breed bitterness. It would be the same if you mentioned it to the Labrousses, or in the village. It would create discontent. In reality they will be all right. . . . And I need to go to America now. It is something I have felt ever since I met and spoke to you. Perhaps there I can find a surgeon who can give me . . . hope?"

"I am sure you can, Uncle Maurice."

He nodded. "I am beginning to think so. And we will use that also to get to the United States. It gives me more reason for wanting to live there. A valid reason. I am becoming selfish enough to want to look like a human being again. Do I have your promise, Denise?"

I said slowly: "You have it, Uncle Maurice. I'll not say a word, except at the consulate in Paris."

His eyes smiled at me again, and he nodded. "The word of a Gérard, eh, Denise? Good girl. But now, there is perfectly good sunlight going to waste outside. And my selfishness keeping you indoors! I am sorry. What would you like to do today, eh? A drive into the surrounding countryside perhaps? You drive, of course? I have heard that all American women drive cars."

"Oh yes. But if you'd like to come with me?"

"I?" He shook his head silently.

"Then I'll drive myself. I'd like to see the village. And the farm perhaps. Vaison? May I?"

He frowned, considering. "Vaison? I planned for Albert to take you . . ."

"Please?" I appealed.

He gestured abruptly. "What have you done to me in

35

such a short time, Denise? It seems that it has become difficult for me to refuse you anything. Very well. Take the Mercedes. There is a road from the village to Vaison. You will see the turnoff, but it is not a good road. I advise you to drive back to the Aurillac highway and turn south, a road to Vaison is clearly marked five kilos south of where you enter the highway. To the Mercedes a few kilos are nothing, and that road is greatly superior to the other."

"Thank you, Uncle," I said, delighted. "How do I find the farm at Vaison?"

He chuckled. "Like this place, it overlooks the village—or what used to be the village—of Vaison. But surely your grandfather told you that?"

"Yes, of course." I flushed. I was not sure what had prompted me to ask that question, but he did not appear to have noticed that I had put it almost suspiciously.

"You will find Vaison a lot different from the way he described it to you—yet no doubt it will be unmistakable."

"You're sure you do not wish to come with me?"

"No," he smiled. "One does not throw off the habits of a recluse easily, my Denise. Or lose one's embarrassment at the way people stare at an . . . an oddity. But I will make use of your visit to Vaison, since it is your wish to go there. Ask that lazy rascal Jacques Marceau for a report on the condition of the place, and the number of stock, sheep and goats, as well as cattle, that he has out to pasture on the slopes. And use your eyes to inform me how much wine he has in the cellars and what fields if any are cultivated and bearing grapes."

"Certainly."

"Gabrielle will give you the keys to the garage and the car. And no doubt Jacques' wife Marie will prepare lunch for you at Vaison. Do you need money? Is there something you might care to buy in the village?"

I shook my head, and laughed. "No thank you, Uncle Maurice. I have money left over from Paris; you were more than generous. My grandfather taught me to be thrifty. He said thrift was a characteristic of the French provinces."

"That is true. But if you need money during your stay at the chateau—you have only to ask. And one day, when you and I reach America, the thrift my uncle taught you is one lesson you may perhaps enjoy forgetting."

In my room I paused only long enough to find a notebook and pen. If I was to bring Uncle Maurice a report on the farm at Vaison, I might need them.

Uncle Maurice had shown me through the great kitchen and the cellars below yesterday. As I came in, one of Gabrielle's helpers was serving Gabrielle where she sat at the table against the window. She was eating a huge breakfast of bacon and fried eggs, an empty bowl that had contained porridge beside her, the cream with which she had garnished it in a huge crockery bowl on the table. And Gabrielle I noticed with distaste was no fastidious eater, for fragments of egg clung to the piglike bristles of her moustache, and stained the front of her black dress.

She looked up at me, frowning.

"What do you want down here? Not work for those idle hands, I don't suppose?"

"If you need help, say so, Gabrielle," I retorted angrily.

"That's easy enough to say, knowing *he* would not allow it." She seemed in a vile mood this morning, for the pleasant-faced woman who had been serving her was trying to give me a warning with worried dark eyes, her back to Gabrielle as she stood near the great wood-burning stove.

"If you needed help, I'd give it," I snapped. "And nobody would stop me from giving it. Neither my uncle nor anyone else. I did not come here to make too much work for anyone."

Her eyes slid away again from mine abruptly; she noticed the egg on her dress and started to remove it with the first thing that came to her hand, which happened to be the corner of the already soiled tablecloth.

But she said without looking up: "We've wondered about that, Albert and I. Oh yes, we've wondered why you did come to the Château-les-Vautours, Mademoiselle."

"I came because my uncle invited me. He mentioned that it was lonely here, and he felt the need for someone of his own family near him." In my anger I had almost said more than that, but I remembered my promise, and left it there.

"And that was the only reason, eh? Your uncle's loneliness? The loneliness of a man you'd never seen?"

I stared at her with growing anger. Her voice had been sharp with suspicion.

I said coldly: "I don't suppose you could be expected to understand it—but I have sympathy for another's loneliness, having been lonely myself."

She sniggered nastily. "I see. Well, you and your uncle have one thing in common—you both have sharp tongues. And no doubt in time one of you will comfort the other." One of those abrupt, almost psychotic changes of mood that I had noticed before touched her. "But then, I who am only a servant here have no right to say such things. I am sorry. I have had a bad morning. First that fool Bernard, who must have his breakfast early before Marie

Labrousse gets here, and then a stove that refused to warm. It would not, of course, occur to the great fool to warn me last night that he would be working people in the fields! And then I must burn my arm, and Marie Labrousse even more stupid than usual this morning." Ruefully, she showed me the red mark of the stove on her brawny arm. "Small wonder that I am not charitable this morning. Would you not agree, Mademoiselle?" Her voice had become almost whining as it supplicated my understanding.

I nodded curtly. "We all have our bad moments, Gabrielle. But I meant what I said."

She studied me briefly, before looking away again. "Mademoiselle is generous. I but jested, and have no need of your help. If I need help there are women in the village glad to assist me for a few francs."

It had not sounded at all like jesting to me, but I changed the subject. "My uncle sent me for the keys of the Mercedes. Otherwise I would not have troubled you so early in the morning when you are busy. I think he mentioned the garage key also."

She stared at me quickly, her lips tightening. "You are going out in the Mercedes with him?"

"No. Alone."

She stared at me incredulously for a long moment. "Alone?"

"What's wrong with that?" I demanded with a rush of returning anger. "I have been driving cars for years. There is less traffic here than in America, Gabrielle."

"So," she said with a peculiar bitterness: "Already he allows you to drive where you will in the Mercedes, unaccompanied! Have you turned his brain? It is a mistake. It is a great foolishness, as he will find out. He will see!"

But my patience had run out. "Are you going to give me the keys, Gabrielle?" I demanded. "Or must I go back to your master and tell him that you refuse, that you do not trust me to go to Vaison alone."

She got out of her chair so quickly, and with such a look of cold malevolence in her eyes, that I took a step backward involuntarily. But the look vanished almost at once. She merely nodded.

"Oh, I will give you the keys, Mademoiselle, never fear, since that is what you say my master orders. Go where you will. Take what risks you will in such a lonely place as Vaison. Only, if something happens to you, don't come running to Gabrielle for sympathy."

I stared at her. "Risks? In Vaison? What are you talking about?"

But she strode to the door as though she hadn't heard me and walked toward her own room.

I looked at Marie Labrousse and forced a smile. "Gabrielle is not in a very good mood this morning."

"No, Mademoiselle." She studied me from where she worked. A pleasant, plump woman, with a broad, rather stupid-looking face, thin hair straggling from beneath an old-fashioned white maid's cap. "All the same, there is truth in what she said. I would not go alone to Vaison for all the treasures of the Louvre."

I stared at her. "But why, Madame Labrousse?" Uncle Maurice had not seemed to think there was any danger in the trip.

She hunched her shoulders and shuddered. "Because of the girls who disappeared, Mademoiselle. Girls from the village. Young girls like you, and pretty. Two of them in a year. Pouf! Gone! Like that—and never seen again. One as she walked back to the village from the farmhouse. The other in the very village itself on the way home from visiting a neighbor. It is little wonder that nobody lives in the village any more. And of course the other one. The strange woman no one had ever seen before."

"She . . . disappeared also?"

"No, Mademoiselle. She was found in the old mill. All this was long ago, you understand. Before we came here. Not long after the master returned from Germany."

"You talk in riddles, Marie," I muttered impatiently. "You say this one was found, that unlike the others, who no doubt tired of Vaison and left for brighter places, she did not disappear into thin air?"

She shrugged and bent her head over her work again. Out in the passage I could hear Gabrielle coming back, jangling keys angrily.

"That one appeared from nowhere, Mademoiselle," Marie Labrousse muttered without looking up. "Some children playing found her lying in the old ruined mill near the farm. Nobody at Vaison knew her, or had ever seen her before. Nobody knew how she came to the village or the mill. But she was there, Mademoiselle, lying naked and dead on the floor. Unmentionable things had been done to her, and she had her face twisted in a mask of indescribable horror and agony as she died. There was an uproar, naturally, the gendarmes came and the reporters. But they never discovered who she was or where she came from. They never even found her clothing."

"But that is . . . horrible!"

"Yes, Mademoiselle. It was horrible. Of course there were

39

many displaced persons in France at the time. So assuredly she was one of them, and that made her identification difficult. Families had been broken up and dispersed or killed, you understand. So although they published her description, nobody came forward to say they knew her." She glanced uneasily toward the door. "These things are best not spoken of, Mademoiselle. That was sixteen years ago, five years after the war ended. A long time ago to one as young as you are. I was a girl then and unmarried myself. I was glad to come here. I would not go back there to live again. Or ever venture there alone. . . ."

Her voiced trailed off as Gabrielle came in. Gabrielle scowled at me and thrust out the keys. "Here! Now you cannot say I refused you, Mademoiselle. Nor, if harm comes to you, can you say I did not try to prevent your going."

"Thank you," I said. "For the keys. I am quite capable of looking after myself."

She said nothing with her lips, but her scowl spoke for her. She followed me at a few paces to the back door and stood there as I walked toward the garage. When I glanced back as I unlocked a padlock that might have held the *Queen Elizabeth,* she was standing with her hands on the doorposts, watching me; a grim female colossus in her black dress, her hair drawn back tightly. I shivered suddenly and was glad to walk inside where I couldn't see her, and she could no longer see me. I had an uneasy suspicion that Gabrielle was picturing *me* lying on the floor of the old mill as Marie Labrousse had mentioned.

The Mercedes purred pleasantly at the first light touch, and the sunshine outside was warm and pleasant. I glimpsed Uncle Maurice at the window of the study staring out at me over his black velvet mask. I decided that I was becoming accustomed to that, and to Uncle Maurice.

I blew him a kiss, and he waved to me and turned back, to his books, no doubt. I did not look at Gabrielle again. I had had enough of her for one morning.

In the fields the workers looked up, leaning on their hoes to stare at the Mercedes. Albert reared up his bulk from behind the truck, shading his eyes as he tried to discover who was driving the car. I could tell he recognized me, and it seemed to surprise him. I think he called out something, though as I picked up speed, I could not hear the words. He took a couple of great strides after me, then stopped abruptly and turned toward the chateau, hurrying between the rows of staked vines green in the morning light.

Right then I could not have cared less about Albert, or any of the other members of my Uncle Maurice's strange household. I was free as a bird, and driving a wonderful car, and the day ahead was all my own. Then I remembered the hapless pigeons on the lawn below my window. It jolted me slightly out of a complacent enjoyment of my freedom.

Perhaps that is why, although I slowed at the village, studying the old-fashioned houses and shops curiously, I decided impulsively to drive right on through. Everyone at the Château-les-Vautours seemed intent on keeping me from the ancestral farm at Vaison, except Uncle Maurice. Gabrielle with her dire warning of danger at Vaison, Marie Labrousse with her tale of atrocity, murder, and kidnapped girls, Albert staring at me beneath his hand and heading for the chateau in such a hurry that he forgot it would be quicker to take the truck. Perhaps between them they might even persuade Uncle Maurice that it was better to stop me going to Vaison alone. Albert might even come after me in the truck, since they expected me to stop at the village. I decided to drive on to Vaison and stop at the village only on the way back.

The houses were medieval, lining the single street of the village. Fowls scattered as the Mercedes appeared. A sow followed by her litter of piglets disappeared hastily through the open front door of a house. Outside the baker's shop a burly man with flour on his arms, in white apron and cap, stood talking to a butcher in an apron and with a scabbard full of knives on his belt. They both looked up at me, startled, and the baker swept off his cap and waved. There was a small bistro, I noticed, and in the shops a few women were about their morning shopping.

I would have said from sixty to eighty people lived in the village of Tocsin, though *how* they lived might take quite some research. Where the street widened into a square, several ancient cars stood parked beneath huge peppercorn trees out of the warm sun. A white goat with a stained beard was surveying one of the cars curiously, as though deciding where to commence eating the upholstery. He turned amber eyes on me as I passed, curious but unafraid.

There was a side road that led toward the high mountains from the village. The left road leading from where it intersected the main street had a crude finger-post with the single word "Vaison" upon it, but across the road was a more specific sign pointing the way to several mountain villages and health resorts.

This road, I decided, must be the reason for the village of Tocsin's existence, since the field work at the chateau surely could not wholly support the population of the village. I remembered Grandfather's stories of people who came

41

to Auvergne; sufferers from gout, liver troubles, catarrh, arthritis, and rheumatism, who came to these remote mountains and valleys to take the "cures." In every valley, if I could believe Grandfather, there were hot and cold mineral springs with magical healing properties still surviving from the once active volcanic disturbances of the old Massif. Some of these people must pass through Tocsin village on their way to the springs. Others, no doubt, came to hike through the mountains, absorbing their beauty in the spring and summer, or seeking winter sport on the snow-covered slopes.

Yet the cross-road seemed little used, and that section leading toward Vaison seemed to agree with my uncle's warning against it, for as I passed I noticed that it was narrow and deeply rutted.

The village dropped behind me. I drove steadily, admiring the scenery as one new vista of mountains after another opened before me. At times the Mercedes skirted breathtaking drops of many hundreds of feet, at others it climbed steeply, or swooped down toward green valleys. I saw no houses after leaving Tocsin, but ten kilos from the village I met two hikers trudging toward me, brown-skinned young men in shorts, shirts, and berets, heavy boots on their feet and rucksacks on their backs.

Usually, I am wary of hitchhikers, but perhaps because of the sunshine and my mood of cheerful self-confidence, I stopped when they signaled me, to see what they wanted. They looked good types of young men, suntanned, polite, both in their mid-twenties.

One swept off his beret, showing white teeth in a brown face as he smiled at me.

"Good day, Mademoiselle. Pardon—but we came down to this road through the mountains a couple of kilos back there. I am afraid we are not quite sure where we are. We entered the mountains near Saint-Nectaire not far from Mont Dore. If Mademoiselle would be so kind as to inform us where this road leads, we would be grateful." He spoke with an accent that I could not define. Germanic, I thought.

"It is a side road between the highway south of Aurillac and the village of Tocsin, Messieurs. Tocsin is ten kilos east, Aurillac much further to the west. I could give you a lift as far as the highway."

He glanced at his companion and then smiled at me. "You are very kind, Mademoiselle. But we will not trouble you. We prefer to walk. With us walking is pleasure. The world these days moves on wheels too fast to see itself, or be seen. The tourist in a car sees only the outline of distant

42

mountains. The hiker sees the insect on the blade of grass. Tocsin, you said?"

I nodded. "It is only a small village, and the road ends there, except for a side road from Vaison that crosses this and goes into the mountains. There is a bistro, and some shops. If you go the other way there must be villages along the highway before Aurillac." I changed gear, ready to move off.

"Thank you, Mademoiselle. But one more moment, please?"

"Yes, M'sieur?"

"This village you speak of, this Tocsin, it is an old place, yes?"

"The houses appear to be very old. Medieval in fact."

He nodded. "Good! And a side road runs through to Vaison, you said?"

"Yes, but there is nothing at Vaison any more, I have been told. There was a village once, but it is deserted now."

"Not quite deserted, Mademoiselle. A family remains there in the village, another at an adjacent farm. We were at Vaison recently." He glanced at his companion again. He said in a lower voice: "So there *is* a road through to Vaison?"

"Not a good road," I said. "I was warned not to use it, because it is in poor repair."

"Mademoiselle is not from Tocsin, then?"

"No. I am an American."

"An American? Yet speak French like a native?" His smile broadened, and his friend smiled with him. "Mademoiselle is a tourist, then?"

"No, I am staying with a relative at Tocsin."

He nodded. "We, Jules and I, are interested in architecture and old buildings. At Vaison we heard that there was an interesting chateau twenty kilos north of Vaison, though at the time we did not have the opportunity to visit it. Could it be, of your knowledge, in the vicinity of Tocsin?"

"There is a chateau, but it is privately owned, not open for inspection," I said quickly.

The young man shook his head. "A great pity, Mademoiselle. The chateaux should all be the property of the state. And open for study. But perhaps the proprietor might allow us to study it and make some sketches, or perhaps take photographs?"

"I doubt it. The owner is a recluse."

"Well, at least we must see it, since it is not far away. I presume that the chateau can be seen from the village, can it not?"

"Oh yes. The village is on the estate."

"It is obviously the chateau we heard about in Vaison," his friend said, speaking for the first time. "What was its name, Jossi?"

The other man's dark brows drew together in thought. "An unpleasant name, I think, but it eludes me. Perhaps Mademoiselle . . . ?"

"The Château-les-Vautours?" I suggested.

"That is the place indeed. Did not the owner come from Vaison, bringing his people with him?" His dark eyes quizzed me pleasantly.

"Yes," I said. "The farmlands at Vaison were worked out. Or so I have heard."

"A man with foresight then, the seigneur," the man called Jossi murmured. "He must be very wealthy to have acquired a chateau. Is he an artist perhaps?"

"Are artists wealthy in France?" I asked.

"Oh no. On the contrary, Mademoiselle. Mostly they are very poor. So are many farmers in this area. The Châtaigneraie is a backward place indeed. So perhaps he is an-dustrialist? A man made wealthy by his investments and profits of his factories? There was such a man, a friend of my father. . . ." His dark eyes studied me and his hand moved toward his breast pocket, but fell away. "No. That would be too strange a coincidence."

His friend laughed abruptly. "Jossi, you have shown the photo to so many people since we started our hike, what does one more matter. And Mademoiselle is amiable. . . . Go on, man. Show it to her. Perhaps she has seen him. Perhaps this Château-les-Vautours is the place where your father's friend has hidden himself all these years. Did not the young lady say the master of the chateau was a recluse? Go on. Show it to her."

"Well, if Mademoiselle does not mind?" He had drawn a wallet from his pocket and was taking out a photograph. "If Mademoiselle has seen this man at Tocsin I would be overjoyed. He was once my father's friend, my father has grown old and there is a debt between them."

I took the proffered photograph curiously, frowning. It looked like one of these black-and-white photos that official-dom, whether Immigration or Police, use. A photo that showed no more than the face.

I studied it, frowning. It appeared to be the face of a strikingly handsome man of about thirty years of age, a darkly serious face, thoughtful, aloof, brooding. I stared at it, finding the hint of something familiar that eluded me. . . .

"Unfortunately, Mademoiselle," the young man was saying, "the photograph was taken years ago. During the war in act. Yet men do not change so much when they have features such as his, such good bone structure. He may have grown old gracefully. That photograph was taken around 1944, over twenty years ago. My father's friend was then near thirty. He would look, I imagine, a little more like this. This is a sketch I have made from my imagination, with regard to the photograph. His hair must have become gray no doubt, and perhaps thinned a little. He must have acquired lines at the corners of his eyes and mouth, and become more austere, more embittered by the years."

The sketch was of the same size as the photograph. I stared at it, surprised. Age as the artist had added it had made that handsome face look even more distinguished. It ore a remarkable resemblance to the photo, but that elusive something that momentarily had seemed familiar was gone.

"As you see in the sketch, his eyes are brown," he said slowly, watching me intently.

I nodded. "I see that. It is a good sketch. Very good, M'sieur."

"But you have not seen him? Can you recognize in the sketch or the photo nobody now at Tocsin, or at the Château-es-Vautours?"

I laughed. "M'sieur, your father's friend has a striking face. If I had seen a man like that I would certainly remember him. You will find nobody remotely like that at either Tocsin or the chateau. You must excuse me now. I have a long way to go."

"You are sure of that, Mademoiselle? There is no one who resembles this photograph at the Château-les-Vautours, or in the village?"

"Not that I have seen."

I watched a shadow of disappointment fall across the man ossi's stern face. "Thank you, Mam'selle. A thousand pardons or delaying you. May the rest of your journey be smooth."

"It was no trouble, Messieurs. If you are still in Tocsin his afternoon, we may meet again."

I meshed the gears as the other man said something to im in a language that I did not understand. But as the Mercedes moved off, I heard the reply distinctly, expressing ossi's disappointment.

"No, Jules. She told the truth. He is not there. . . ."

The dust swirled, hiding them. I frowned as I drove, mulling over our conversation. I reached the highway and drove south. I turned into the road to Vaison still trying o track down that resemblance that had eluded me.

The two young men with their stern brown faces puzzled me. Glimpsed in the rear-vision mirror of the Mercedes as I

45

drove off, as they strode in step toward Tocsin they had looked more like soldiers than student of architecture. There had been an alertness, a wariness about them that alarmed me now when I thought about them. Despite their politeness those had been tough young men, trained to perfection. They must have been, now that I thought about it, to have walked over the Massif from Mont Dore.

They had been, in fact, not at all the kind of young men a girl should stop to chat with along as lonely a road as that linking the highway to Tocsin.

Driving now past ruined farmhouses and derelict barns where the undergrowth had crept in from the forest to overrun deserted farmlands, I decided that I would not make the mistake of stopping along any lonely French road again to speak to strange young men.

CHAPTER FOUR

SO THIS IS what Vaison is really like, I thought. Poor Grandpa. If he could see it now.

The ruins of the houses on either side of me, unlike the stone buildings of the village of Tocsin, had been originally constructed of roughhewn timber erected on foundations of stone in a few instances, but mainly over earth floors. The thatched roofs of straw were long since gone, leaving only the rafters rotting in the damp to mark where the eaves had been. The chimneys of a few houses still thrust up, chimneys of red, handmade bricks.

The gardens had rioted into vines that climbed sagging walls, or ornamental shrubs and trees that had grown so tall that now they almost hid the low walls of the houses. Yet it was early summer, and roses and other flowers bloomed, stunted by lack of attention, but nevertheless giving a hint of past beauty.

I shook my head, staring about from where I stood beside the Mercedes. That fallen building was the inn, I decided. This the house of Berthe Cloete, the flighty widow whom all the respectable wives of Vaison had feared might run off with someone's husband. Over there must be the baker, and next to it the home of the miller, for I could see the overgrown road turning in beside it that led down to the river and the

46

mill that Grandfather had described to me so often, its great paddle wheels turned by the rushing water, and in their turn revolving the huge old-fashioned grinding stones.

Could it be here where I stood that once the villagers had paraded on feast days, dressed in their traditional costumes, the young women in black dresses with brocaded sleeves, their bright aprons lending color, with tall, double-winged headdresses? Could it be here that Grandfather had paraded with my grandmother on his arm, dressed in his own best black suit and brocaded vest, the distinctive black hat of the region on his head?

I sighed, remembering how he had put it on to show me many times when I was a young girl, wearing it with such pride for my awed inspection. To me, Grandfather in his Sunday best had seemed a king.

Now Grandfather's generation had gone, and Grandfather with it. Now, people like Gabrielle Bremen and Marie Labrousse could speak of Vaison as a place to be feared, where murder had walked, and young girls disappeared never to be seen again.

No wonder Vaison was deserted. Yet not quite deserted, for hadn't the strange young men I had met on the Tocsin road said that someone still lived here in the village?

I stared about curiously, leaving the Mercedes where it stood, the ignition key held tightly in my hand. Yes, there was a house with a new roof down at the end of the village near a small bridge. And as I stared at it, I saw the thin blue smoke rising from its brick chimney, and then the freshly thatched roof of another house nearby.

Both roofs were of straw that had not yet changed color with age, so someone in Vaison still grew wheat in the fields, and no doubt used the old mill down by the river when the grain was harvested for grinding, the straw dried for thatching or to feed stock.

Uncle Maurice apparently still had tenants, and should be informed of it in case he did not know. I decided to make myself known to them at once. After that I would drive out to the farm to see Jacques Marceau and prepare my report for Uncle Maurice.

I walked that way briskly, my footsteps sounding surprisingly loud and hollow on the worn cobbles of the street between which grass and weeds sprouted. Other than the birds which chirped and flew among the ruins of the deserted houses I saw my first sign of life. A goat came out curiously from between the two houses to stare at me malevolently with clear, amber eyes, his straggling beard swinging rhythmically

47

as he chewed a mouthful of grass and weeds, some of which protruded from his lips.

I edged carefully around him, not sure whether he meant to attack me or not, or what I might do to defend myself if he did. But his glance became disdainful as I edged around him, and he bleated suddenly and trotted away as though as he had lost interest in me.

I walked on warily. The first house had no doors or window glass. The doorway gaped like an open mouth, the windows like sightless eyes reflecting the gloom within.

On a rough bench outside the door on my right shining buckets stood upside down; except for one that contained clear water, and had an enameled mug bound with wire to a wooden handle for a dipper.

Examining it, I decided that there was still no plumbing in Vaison. Even the drinking water must be drawn from wells, or carried from the river as it had been in Grandfather's day.

A peep in through the empty doorway disclosed a great table and heavy chairs. In a stove embers glowed fitfully in the draft from the chimney. A man's heavy woolen sweater with a high neck was thrown carelessly across the back of a chair. There was no electricity here so far from other habitation, for a kerosene lamp stood in the center of the table, and on a battered open cupboard containing plates and cooking utensils a candle was stuck to a saucer, fluted with wax droppings.

"Is anyone here?"

Nothing moved inside. I turned away, frowning. The goat had come into the passage between the two houses. He stood with lowered head, his feet spread truculently as he studied me. I made for the door of the house opposite, and hammered on it with my closed fist. The door hurt my hand and the sound of my knocking against the heavy, closed door seemed insignificant.

Nobody answered.

I withdrew and looked at the goat, and he shook his head, showing me his sharp-looking horns, and took a couple of steps toward me.

"Nobody's arguing with you," I told him nervously. "Play traffic cop if you want. I'll find another way around, thank you!"

I walked to the back of the houses and stared about. Grapevines were trained over ramshackle outhouses on wire-netting. Rows of vines in a small field had been pruned and tended and were covered with healthy green leaves, the tiny grapes hanging in bunches below them. Another field had been plowed recently and left to fallow. I looked for the horse that had done the plowing, but discovered instead a track marked with cart wheels parallel with the river, going toward the mill.

I studied the mill with nervous distaste. Its roof also had been thatched recently. It stone walls reared high beside the river that rushed in part beneath it. I could not see any movement there, or sign of life. But I could think of no other place where the tenants might be, unless they had gone to the farm. I think I would have welcomed an excuse to keep away from the moss-covered stone walls, but I could find none that seemed reasonable in bright sunlight. And in the end the goat decided me, coming from between the houses with his head down as though stalking me. I walked away, keeping an eye upon him, but when I walked toward the mill he merely shook his head disgustedly and went back between the houses.

"So you think you're smart," I muttered. "Waiting for me in the shade! But I have no intention of returning to the car *that* way. I'll take the other road beside the miller's house, and the next time we meet, my bearded friend, I'll be safe inside the Mercedes."

It was pleasant walking in the sunshine. Daffodils sprinkled the bank beside the river, and honeysuckle trailed bunches of yellow flowers from thick vines climbing a willow tree. Bees hummed all about me, and somewhere unseen a bird that I could not name was bursting its throat in song. I had been right about the mill, I saw as I approached. A bag of wheat was propped just inside the doorless entrance, the great wheel clanked unmusically as the water turned it—though above me as I stood in the entrance I could not hear the millstones grinding. I stepped inside, out of bright sunshine into deep shadow.

A ladder led up to a hole in the thick floor above, where I could see other bags of wheat stacked for grinding. The sun was shining in on them through an opening in the outer wall, where a pulley and a rope showed in dark silhouette against the sunlight, like a gibbet.

"Is anyone here?" I called.

There was no answer. Except for the sound of the mill-wheel it seemed to have grown very still. The birdsong had stopped, and I could no longer hear the bees, only the harsh grinding as the wheel turned, and the steady drip of water from the paddles.

I stared in sudden horror about me. Here on the stone floor children playing had discovered the body of a murdered woman. Momentarily my horrified imagination saw her lying there, and I started to back away slowly toward the door and the sunlight. Only as I turned then to run outside I sensed movement somewhere close, and a hand that smelled of tobacco clamped tightly over my mouth and nose, cutting off the terrified scream that rose in my throat. Dragged backward on my knees, I felt something sharp prick my ribs beneath my right breast. I was firmly held against some rough material, feeling the heavy beat of a heart behind my head. I struggled frantically.

"Be still!" a man's voice hissed. "Or I will have to kill you. Where is he? Where is he, damn you? Where is Gebauer?"

But the mill walls started to spin slowly about me, and I could not have answered. Sickened, fainting, I felt myself sagging in his grip. The knife at my ribs seemed to thrust deeper and there was nothing. . . .

"Mademoiselle! Mademoiselle, please!"

The voice penetrated my dazed mind only slowly. Two rough hands were rubbing my wrists and the sting of brandy in my throat made me cough.

"Mademoiselle, in the name of heaven, wake! Lord, was there ever anything so contrary as a fainting woman since the world began? Madeleine, bring more brandy quickly. Pierre, get out of here. If she sees *you* when she opens her eyes she'll be gone again. D' you hear? Out!"

"Of course, Etienne," another male voice muttered. "At once. I am sorry. But . . ."

"*Out!*"

The hands put my wrist down gently. The bottle came back, hurting my lips when I resisted it, dribbling the spirit against my teeth. Some went into my mouth, but more ran down inside my blouse between my breasts, stinging against my skin. I choked and tried to force the bottle away.

"She is coming back," the voice muttered. "Madeleine, help me with her."

"The poor girl," a woman's voice murmured sympathetically. "The poor defenseless lamb. Try some more brandy, Etienne."

But I was not *that* defenseless. I managed to thrust the bottle away, turning my head aside from it. I opened heavy eyes reluctantly and tried to sit up.

"No more . . ." I whispered. "Please . . ."

"You are safe," the male voice said reassuringly. "Nobody here intends your harm, Mademoiselle. You are among friends."

I looked around sickly, trying to focus the figures bending over me. One was a woman with thin gray hair and a face that suffering had lined deeply and indelibly. She limped as

50

she moved, but her eyes were kind and sympathetic, contradicting the thin lips that parted over discolored teeth.

"There, dear," she murmured. "Everything is going to be fine now. Nobody will hurt you."

"Madeleine is right. We mean only to help you."

The man was young, in his mid-twenties, looking as fit and tanned as my hikers of the Tocsin road, only far more handsome. His eyes were a steady gray, his features well-formed and pleasant, despite the anxiety that showed plainly enough in his expression as he studied me.

"I'm all right," I muttered, trying to sit up.

His arm helped me at once. "It is better if you rest for a little while. It is always better to lie still when one faints."

"No. I'm . . . fine."

Right then I wanted only to be in the Mercedes, driving away from there, for my memory was returning. I shuddered, remembering the prick of a knife, a hand clamped like a vise over my mouth and nose, the fierce muttering of a voice that held deadly hatred. . . .

"Mademoiselle has had a fright," the woman said gently. "But it is over now. All over. You were not harmed. You fainted, that is all."

"All?" I looked at her indignantly. "He tried to kill me!"

"My dear Mademoiselle Gérard, are you sure that you did not dream it? When I found you, you were alone. You had fainted. You were, as you Americans say—out cold. You were lying just inside the old water mill, looking, I must say, very helpless and pathetic, and beautiful, but quite unharmed. The old mill has a bad reputation with the people who used to live here and most of those people are now at Tocsin, or the Château-les-Vautours. They believe the mill haunted, as a matter of fact. And I have no doubt they have told you murder was done there. So are you sure that you did not imagine something, and in running from your . . . ghost, fall against the bag of wheat where I found you?"

I stared at him silently, somewhere between tears and cussing. Of all the supercilious self-opinionated young men I had ever met, this one deserved the blue ribbon! If he had designed the words to annoy me—he could not have done better.

When I had recovered sufficiently I said slowly and sarcastically: "I know exactly what happened to me, M'sieur. And I neither dreamed nor imagined it. I do not care greatly whether you believe me or not, for I am sure that the gendarmerie at Aurillac will. I am interested to learn, however, how you know my name."

He shrugged. "When I carried you here from the mill,

51

I felt it was necessary to know your identity. Your handbag was in the car. Naturally, I checked."

"You carried me here?" For the first time I took more careful note of my surroundings. I was lying on a very hard couch in the living room or what seemed to be a kitchen, for there was a stove against one wall, and I noticed for the first time an appetizing smell coming from a great iron saucepan.

"After I had examined you for a possible injury, of course," he nodded, repressing what I decided was a smile. "And I thought all American women dieted themselves foolishly slim. You proved to be the exception—I could barely stagger by the time I carried you here."

"You!" I ejaculated in English, "are the most . . . !" I bit that off and glared at him. "A man attacked me in the mill, M'sieur. He held his hand over my mouth and threatened to kill me. He had a knife. . . ." I put my hand up quickly to my ribs as I remembered, and winced instinctively. "I think he wounded me with it. Here."

He chuckled. "You may speak English, if you wish, Miss Gérard," he said in that language. "And complete what you started to say about me. I speak English. German also." He shook his head. "But you are certainly not wounded. I examined you very carefully before I moved you from the mill. There is a slight bruise, where you just showed me, but the skin is barely broken. However, when I brought you here I put a little antiseptic on the scratch, and it is no more than that, and I covered it with a little sticking plaster."

I stared at him. "You did? You certainly have a nerve!"

He shrugged his shoulders, smiling at me. "How was I to know that you were not a diabetic, and in shock? That you had fallen into a coma? Or that you had not really been injured? It was as necessary to examine you as it was to check your papers. Fortunately you were suffering from nothing worse than a faint. I am glad of that. I had no wish to find you injured."

"Thank you, M'sieur," I said sarcastically. I was starting to feel better. Through the thin material of my blouse, I could feel the small square of adhesive plaster. I moved aside the blanket that covered me and sat up groggily, easing my long legs carefully off the couch, and adjusting my skirt.

Watching admiringly, he said quietly: "You would be very foolish to go to the gendarmerie at Aurillac with such a story, Miss Gérard. You are safe, and unhurt, and they have more important work to do than drive out here for nothing."

"Having my life threatened by a maniac with a knife

may not seem important to you—but it is to me," I said acidly. "And I'm equally sure that it will be to the police at Aurillac, M'sieur. If it is not, however, I am sure that the American Consulate will obtain better results in Paris."

His fine, dark brows drew together in a frown. "You are a very determined young woman, aren't you?"

"When someone threatens me with a knife, and promises to kill me if I cry out—why, yes *I am.*"

"Very well," he apparently came to a decision. "Madeleine knows no English, so I will tell you something. The man you . . . ah, met in the mill is her brother. He is a little—" He frowned, for the first time groping for the English word. "The Moors would say that Allah has touched his mind. It was unfortunate that he saw the Mercedes drive up. These cars have a certain meaning to him and he forgets himself. He—"

I interrupted him. "But France is full of Mercedes. If he feels that way he should be put somewhere where he can't harm anyone. And don't try to tell me he didn't mean what he said. He wanted to kill someone—a man called Gebauer."

"A man named Gebauer," he said quietly. "Who invariably drove a Mercedes. Yes." He sighed. "S.S. *Haupsturmfuehrer* Franz Gebauer, an infamous, wanted war criminal whom you as an American citizen have probably never heard of. Well, there are many people who want to kill Gebauer. He made Madeleine's brother the way he is. He made Madeleine a cripple for life. He was responsible for the deaths of many thousands of innocent people in a Polish concentration camp. His specialty was strangling young women with his hands, though that was something he did for his own pleasure, since it was not an efficient medium of mass extermination. He had very strong hands, and . . . appetites. Yes, I have to admit that Pierre would kill Gebauer if he had the chance. And Gebauer always drove a Mercedes. It was that association of ideas that was responsible for the fright he gave you. I can't believe that Pierre would have harmed *you*. When you fainted, it brought him back to reason, and he ran to me for help."

"He . . . did?"

"Yes. He was terrified, he thought he'd killed you. He ran away, and would not come near you. He fears the dead, and no wonder, for he saw too many. That is why I had to carry you alone, Miss Gérard."

"He was no more terrified than I was," I muttered with feeling. But I shuddered. "What you have told me is horrible, M'sieur."

"Métier . . ." he said, smiling, as though I'd asked a question. "Etienne Métier, at your service, Miss Gérard."

I ignored that. I said, thinking about it: "But these things happened long ago. The Japanese also committed atrocities, but in America we have tried to forget. Surely this . . . Gebauer died long ago?" I remembered what Marie Labrousse had said in the morning: *It is better to speak no longer of these things.*

He gave me a curious, distasteful look. "Then you believe that Franz Gebauer should remain scot-free? For the extraordinary thing about Gebauer is that he has been able to elude—what do you say, the music?—until now."

I looked at him. "You mean he is still alive and free?"

"Yes. I mean just that, Miss Gérard. Do you believe that he should remain so?"

"No," I said. "No, a man like that might kill again."

He nodded slowly. "You are so right, Miss Gérard. For he not only *may* kill again—but we believe that he has. Many times. And therefore will again, and again, until he is caught, and tried."

I stared at him. "*We*, M'sieur?"

"We who seek him, Miss Gérard." He hesitated for a moment. "I am an agent of the French Government. Madeleine and her brother are two of the few people left alive who knew Franz Gebauer, and may be able to identify him. That is why you must not go to the police. I would have to contact Paris to prevent Pierre's arrest, which would mean taking the police into our confidence. And then," he shrugged, "news travels fast in small towns. And of course it would be most inconvenient for you, because I would have to see that your visa was canceled, and that you left France at once."

I stared at him, for once seeking words that would not come. He smiled. "In anger you are very beautiful, Miss Gérard."

"You," I managed, "are the most insufferable . . . !" I choked, studying his complacent smile. "You appear from nowhere! You are apparently trespassing on my uncle's land, in one of his houses—no, two of his houses! Your friend threatens my life! You produce a horror story intended to arouse my sympathy for the man who attacked me, so that I will not go to the police. You even threaten airily to deport me! You say you are an agent of the French Government? I doubt that. If you are an agent, you must be the worst in history. You've not only confessed to me, a perfect stranger, that you are an agent, but you have also told me about your mission." I drew a deep, indignant breath. "I don't believe one word of it!"

If anything, his smile broadened. "Oh, but we are not perfect strangers at all, Miss Gérard. I know a great deal about you. It is my business to find out about any strangers who come to the Châtaigneraie to stay. If I thought it necessary I could tell you a great deal about your life in New Orleans with your grandfather, Henri Gérard, a most estimable old gentleman incidentally. Or your examination results at Newcombe College in New Orleans, and your friends there. Your American Central Intelligence Agency is always most co-operative with my department in the matter of any search for war criminals."

He took a wallet from his pocket, opened it, and handed me a small folder.

His name, photo, and signature were there. Name: Etienne Métier. Rank: Captain. Department: Army, Military Intelligence. Status: Bachelor. Age: 28. Occupation: Special Operations Executive . . .

"Papers, of course," he said, holding that infuriating smile, but withdrawing the folder, "can be forged. Though it hardly seems likely, does it, that I would go to that trouble. However, if you contact your consulate in Paris I feel sure they will check on me at once and assure you that the details shown in this folder are quite genuine. I also feel sure, Miss Gérard, that your own people will then ask you to co-operate with me."

I shook my head uncertainly. "I . . . don't know what to say, M'sieur! I suppose I must believe you, but have no doubt that I *will* check. And since I intend to go to Paris again soon, that may be within a few days." I said it defiantly, watching him still with deep suspicion, but he merely nodded and smiled.

"Good. And I am not such a fool as you think, Miss Gérard. In my job I have to deal with many people. An agent has to be something of a psychologist, in that he must learn to assess people quickly, and separate those he should trust from those he should not. Mistakes, I assure you, can be fatal. I believe that I can trust you; I believe that if you give your word you will keep it. I also believe that you could not have much sympathy for a man like Franz Gebauer."

"No." I gave an instinctive shudder.

"That being so, I must ask you to promise that you will forget all this. You will not speak of it again until Gebauer has been found and arrested."

I frowned at him. "What makes you believe that this

man . . . Gebauer, is in the Châtaigneraie? After all these years."

He studied me, frowning, for a long moment, then shook his head. "I have not said that he is in the Châtaigneraie."

"But *you* are here, M'sieur. And your witnesses."

"Do I have your promise?"

I shrugged. "Do I have an alternative?"

"The visa. A form of polite deportation. Incommunicado, naturally. That is your choice."

His eyes had grown angry abruptly, and his smile was gone. I looked away uneasily. I said in French: "I have no wish to make things more difficult for you, or your friends; or to help . . . a war criminal. Does the promise include my uncle Maurice? Since you know so much about me, you must know that he was one of the leaders of the French Resistance and must therefore be the first to help you if he could."

"What I need from you is a promise, Mademoiselle," he replied in the same language. "There are to be no exceptions."

I sighed. "Very well, M'sieur Métier. You have my word. I will not mention it to anyone, including my uncle."

"Good girl," he said in a relieved tone. "But be careful, if you are questioned about today. The last thing I would wish to do is place you in any danger."

I frowned, remembering. "I was asked to report on conditions here to my uncle. How can that be done without mentioning that these houses are occupied? That someone is working the vineyards and the fields here? If I do not report it, you can be sure that sooner or later someone else will." I remembered the two hikers suddenly. "I heard there was a family living in the village before I came here. Two hikers I talked to on the Tocsin road mentioned it."

I expected him to be interested in the hikers, for I was becoming agent-minded, and had decided as I thought about them that they were probably also of the French Intelligence. But he merely shook his head disinterestedly.

"Pierre and Madeleine have been here for some months. Their name is Bourget, and they rent the house and the fields behind it from Monsieur Marceau at the farm. The Marceaus know me as their nephew. I am an artist, and I have rented the second house for greater privacy while I work. I also help Pierre in the fields when I can. It means a few more francs for your uncle, and we are improving the property for him, which should please him. That is all you need to know about us, and that is all that you would have learned if things had happened differently."

I slipped my feet into my shoes again and stood up.

"An artist is supposed to paint, M'sieur. I would have asked to see some of your paintings."

He grinned at me again. "And why not, since now we understand one another better. I was an art student before I became what I am. I hope to paint one day in earnest. At present it is a relaxation, and also with an easel out there a good way of seeing who passes, or moves about the countryside. I work in the other house. Come, take a look before you leave."

He seemed so eager suddenly that I could not resist.

Madeleine called to us, offering me coffee which I refused. She wiped her hands on her apron and smiled at me, and shook hands.

"I am sorry about Pierre, Man'selle. Except when he is angry, or remembers his wrongs, he would harm no one. And then, only those who harmed us long ago. I swear it . . . ."

"I know," I replied gently. "And thank you for helping me recover."

She muttered something, and looked away quickly, tears in her eyes. "Mademoiselle is kind as well as brave."

I wondered why she had said that as I followed Etienne Métier across the passage between the two houses. Anyone more scared than I'd been in the mill would have died of fright. The goat wasn't in sight. The sweater lay across the chair where I had seen it, but he led me through the great living room into one of the other two rooms that comprised the house. The light was good inside, the gaping windows empty of both curtains and glass.

An easel with a half-finished painting on it stood beside the window. A dozen small paintings, unframed and painted on wallboard, stood against the wall. I stared at them, surprised by the original use of color and form composition. Figures working in a field stood out in sharp relief. Bowed and weary figures in somber clothing against a background of richly colored yellow fields, of green forest and towering, snow-clad mountains blue with distance. I studied the signature: *Métier*.

"These are very good," I said involuntarily.

"You like them? I will do better one day, if life is kind, Denise."

I glanced at him, startled by the use of my first name. "Yes, I'm sure that you will," I muttered. "I must go now. I have much still to do."

"I would like to paint a portrait of you one day. Do you think that you could be so kind to someone you met under such unfavorable circumstances? I would be most grateful?"

57

I stared at him in an unusual confusion, my cheeks full of color. But if he noticed, he gave no sign. His gray eyes pleaded with me anxiously.

"It is a lot to ask, I know. The portrait would be yours, the pleasure of painting it mine. You have a good head; a face that mirrors every emotion. Please Denise?"

If it was mirroring my emotion now, I hoped he couldn't interpret it!"

"Perhaps," I muttered. "But we may never meet again, M'sieur."

"Promise to sit for me, and I'll see that we do," he said with confidence.

"My uncle is . . . something of a recluse," I stammered. "He does not encourage visitors to the chateau, M'sieur. You see . . . he was injured in the war. He was so badly scarred that . . ."

"Tortured is the word, Mam'selle," he said. "Not injured. I know the record of Maurice Gérard. I know it very well indeed. I would like to meet the man himself one day. I may if you'll consider sitting for me."

"I'll think about it . . . ."

He nodded. "I have embarrassed you, I think. But I will come to the chateau one day soon to discover what you have decided."

"No, you mustn't! My uncle would resent it," I cried in panic.

"To the village then?" His dark eyebrows rose appealingly.

"Very well, to the village. Have someone from the village who works at the chateau let me know that you are there."

"Thank you, Mademoiselle. You are very kind. I will walk to the car with you. I don't suppose that from your kindness you would permit me to call Pierre? He would like to say that he is sorry." He walked beside me quietly out into the passage between the two houses. Madeleine came to the door and waved to me, and I waved back. "If you speak to him with me, you will see how harmless he really is. A pathetic little man who has known great sorrow and suffering . . . ."

"Pathetic? Harmless? Why he almost . . . !"

"Pierre! Here. Mademoiselle is leaving now."

At the end of the passage between the two houses, where the goat had watched me so balefully, a shadow appeared abruptly, soundlessly, against the brighter light. I stopped, staring, my pounding heart preparing me for instant flight. But my fear passed as I studied him quickly. He *was* small; small and thin, almost frail. He wore trousers and a jacket of rough blue serge, and a beret of the same dark material.

Beneath it his face studied me with even more fear in it than I was sure showed in mine.

Etienne Métier's hand on my arm moved me slowly forward, with that small figure giving ground before us, until we all three stood in the bright sunlight.

"It is all right, Pierre," Etienne murmured soothingly. "See for yourself. She is quite well again. Nor will she harm you. She is a friend, Pierre. She thinks as we do. You must remember that she is our friend, and one of us. Do you understand?"

"Yes, M'sieur."

Even his voice seemed different, quavering, lighter, nervous where it had been deep and full of hatred. I stared at him, disbelievingly. His narrow face was deeply lined, his eyes very dark, and full of tears as he looked at me. His lips and his hands trembled. He was like a child waiting to be reprimanded, trembling on the verge of shame and contrition.

He was no taller than I, and very little heavier, for I could see the sharp edges of bone revealed by the open throat of his jacket, and his wrists and hands were as bony. He pulled off his beret as I approached and his untidy hair was snow-white. He looked in fact exactly as Etienne Métier had said. Pathetic, harmless . . . .

But those bony hands, I knew, could have easily choked the life from me, or driven home that knife to the hilt. They had held me easily despite my frantic struggles.

"Mademoiselle," he muttered. "You understand, do you not? It was the Mercedes . . . seeing it here, and nobody in it. And then when I searched—seeing someone moving in the shadows inside the mill . . ."

"I have explained all that, and she understands," Etienne said quietly. He glanced at me, his gray eyes suddenly appealing.

I forced myself to say: "Yes, of course. It's all right, Pierre. I am unharmed. Now that we understand one another, and we are friends, let us forget it, for it could not happen again."

"No, Mademoiselle," he said humbly. "As you say, it could not happen again. I am sorry. You are very kind, and I, Pierre Bourget, would give my life to keep you from the harm we have known. Thank you, Mademoiselle."

"Good-by, Pierre."

"Good-by, Mam'selle."

He bowed from the waist with a peculiar, furtive grace, and turned away to disappear between the two houses as silently as he had come.

59

"You see," Etienne said complacently. "He is not an ogre, Denise."

He seemed intent upon making the use of my first name a habit. "No," I said. "He is not an ogre. And he *is* pathetic, M'sieur. But *not harmless*. Never harmless. There is great strength in those bony hands and that thin body—believe me, I *know*."

Etienne chuckled. "All right, all right. He is a man."

CHAPTER FIVE

I LEFT THE FARM at Vaison with mixed feelings, for I had found the steward Marceau a surly fellow, the expression on his rather stupid face and in his mean black eyes suspicious, to say the least. Mixed with an almost whining obsequiousness when he addressed me as my uncle's niece, I quickly sickened of the company of both Marceau and his wife, who seemed to share his stupidity and meanness without any other distinction at all.

He showed me his cellars with their great barrels of wine, his stores of grain and other farm products, the bacon hanging to cure, the pickled pork. He produced his lists of stock, and his accounts, and I made a few notes from them.

I drank some of Madame Marceau's indifferent coffee from a cup that I would have liked to wash for myself first, for neither Madame nor her house looked very clean. I managed to avoid accepting their surly invitation to have lunch with them from the great iron pot bubbling on the back of the stove.

Compared to the farm, Madeleine Bourget's house had been spotless, and the smell from her great iron saucepan mouth-watering as I though about it nostalgically now. For this was the *pot-au-feu*, which you will find in no restaurant in France; it is the dish of the peasant farmer. Grandfather had told me about it often enough. In every farmhouse in the Châtaigneraie the great iron pot would be found on the back of the stove, simmering day and night uninterruptedly. And each day its contents became richer and more fragrant as fresh meat and vegetables were added. Its aroma filled not only the kitchen, but the whole house.

"A bit of cheese is good, or a slice of sausage," Grandfather used to boast to me with a faraway, hungry glitter in his dark eyes. "But give me a ladle of *pot-au-feu* with a loaf of bread and some Vaison wine and I'll ask no more."

We would, no doubt, have had our own *pot-au-feu* in New Orleans, and been the envy of all our French neighbors, except that in New Orleans our stoves ran on electricity instead of wood from the forest, and Grandfather always counted his cents twice before he paid the electricity bill. To burn electricity in the stove night and day, even beneath a *pot-au-feu*, would have been torture to his thrifty soul.

My nose had discovered the *pot-au-feu* in Madeleine Bourget's cottage, even in my sickness and fear. But I had no wish to sample that of the Marceaus at all.

Instead, I excused myself and went for a walk over the estate. Walking through the vineyards I had never felt Grandfather closer to me. For he had tended these very vines, and the others that had died long ago from neglect, or now ran stunted and fruitless over rank weeds and through undergrowth, or climbed trees that had thrust up in the years between. The red cattle and the long wooled sheep I could see on the mountain slopes were probably the progeny of those that he had taken up there to graze.

I found the deep pool where he had learned to swim with Great-Uncle Jean-Paul in the years before the First World War, and a cave in the mountain nearby where they had played at bandits. I found an oak that lightning had riven many years ago and on which he had carved his initials, though the encroaching bark had long since covered his feeble attempt at boyish publicity.

All this gave me a good deal to think about as I walked slowly back over the neglected farm to the Mercedes. So this was Vaison, a shadow of what it had once been. Yet I could see at the same time Uncle Maurice's reasons for the neglect. There were fields where nothing at all grew, where the last traces of topsoil had long since eroded away to the solid clay beneath, and the raised bones of limestone.

No doubt it would take a great deal of money to make Vaison fertile again. Even the vines that Jacques Marceau had fertilized and cultivated grew poor, sour grapes. The stock brought only the lowest market prices. Vaison, I decided, could never in one man's lifetime be made as fertile as the fields of the estate at the Château-les-Vautours.

I began to think with admiration of Uncle Maurice, who had not only been a hero of the Resistance, fighting all those horrible things Etienne Métier talked about, but had the common sense to refute the old ways, and even discard the ancestral farm of Vaison itself, while by shrewd investments he had done very well indeed.

I should forgive him his faults. I could almost, but not quite, forgive him the slaughter of helpless pigeons.

But I wished that he had a better housekeeper than Gabrielle. One who would set a great iron pot upon the back of the huge stove in the kitchen, fill it with rich meat and vegetables for a *pot-au-feu,* and allow it to mature without ever quite going off to boil.

With my appetite whetted by the long and trying morning, I decided that I would ask my uncle why we did not have a *pot-au-feu* at the Château-les-Vautours.

The Marceaus stood near the house, watching me silently as I drove off. At the village I looked for the Bourgets and Etienne, slowing the Mercedes to a crawl, and presently saw all three of them working among the vines; Etienne was shirtless, his athlete's chest, back, and arms tanned a healthy brown. I touched the horn ring, and they paused, straightened to stare across at me. Madeleine and Etienne waved, and poor Pierre took off his beret with a sweeping gesture.

I put my foot down then, satisfied, and sped back toward the highway. I stopped at a small bistro along the highway, in a village similar to Tocsin. Still prodded by my thoughts of the *pot-au-feu,* I asked if the dish was available. The pleasant-faced woman who came to serve me laughed.

"Who would want to buy *that,* Mademoiselle? It is merely the soup of the poor peasants hereabouts. We have fresh, hot loaves and farm butter. We have cheese and sausage, coffee. Wine. The proprietor's wife makes the best omelettes in these parts, if Mademoiselle would care for an omelette?"

I settled disappointedly for the omelette. I decided that Grandfather's teaching had made me a peasant at heart, and that the next time I drove to Vaison, if I did go there again, I would dine with Madeleine Bourget.

It was mid-afternoon when I reached Tocsin. The village drowsed in warm sunshine, and on the slopes the villagers still worked in the vineyards above the chateau.

I parked the Mercedes among the old cars beneath the peppercorns. Window shopping in the village did not take very long. I made a couple of small purchases in the dark interior of the yard goods store, and bought some cakes at the bakery. I remembered that in France in the provinces a lady does not enter the wineshop alone, but as I walked past the proprietor came out, smiling and curious, a plump man with the ruddy complexion of one partial to his own wares.

"Bonjour, Mademoiselle. Welcome to Tocsin. I am Henri Cloete. I hope Mr. Gérard your uncle is well?"

"My uncle is quite well, thank you, M'sieur."

"Would Mademoiselle care for a glass of wine? In the house, of course. My wife is inside."

I smiled and thanked him. I told him I had just had lunch.

He shook his head. "A great pity then. Violette and I saw you drive out this morning, Mademoiselle. I brought a bottle of our best Burgundy from the cellars in case you returned. But no matter. Perhaps some other time, eh? Not many strangers come to Tocsin these days. If one may call Mademoiselle a stranger."

"I thought you must have some passing trade, from people going to the spas, or into the mountains, M'sieur Cloete."

He laughed ruefully. "You saw the signs at the road, of course. But that road is seldom used, Mademoiselle. Mostly visitors go into the Massif spas by the direct road through Aurillac. If they come here, it is unfortunately by accident. We exist only because of the good will of your uncle, M'sieur Gérard. What work there is here comes from the estate. Like fleas upon a cat, we would starve without him our host. For we must live upon the estate or one another, and we are few."

I frowned. "But surely some tourists come here. Why, I passed two hikers on the road this morning. They asked the way to Tocsin."

He shook his head, smiling. "Tourists? It is not yet the time for tourists. When they come, it is in June during the summer weekends. And often enough they do not stop in the village at all, but drive on through. If the chateau were open to visitors it might be different."

"These were two young men, hiking, M'sieur."

"Then they tired of their walk, Mademoiselle. They did not come here."

"Are you sure?" I asked, surprised, for Jossi and Jules had seemed the kind of determined young men who would do just what they said.

He laughed. "I am quite sure. They did not come here. Were they friends of Mademoiselle?"

"No . . ."

"Perhaps they sought the other road. To the Massif, or perhaps to Vaison, and cut across the fields to reach it. When young people hike, they do not always follow the road, Mademoiselle."

I nodded. Not that it mattered, or had any importance to me. So I shrugged, and declined his offer of wine again. I went back to the car and drove out of the village and up the slope toward the stone wall that surrounded the grounds. The gates that had been open when I left were closed

now, but when I sounded the horn impatiently Pierre Labrousse came hurrying out to the cottage.

"Mademoiselle has enjoyed her drive on such a fine day,
eh?" he called cheerfully. "Albert Bernard said you drove to
Vaison. How is the old place? It is a long time since Marie
or I have seen the village. We lived in the house opposite
the bakery. A fine house it was too. Mademoiselle noticed it
perhaps?"

"The houses opposite the bakery have no roofs now, Pierre.
They are decaying away slowly," I told him. "Only two
houses in the village are occupied."

He shook his head sadly. "A great pity, Mademoiselle. But
we are better off here as the master says, no doubt. I was
born in that house in Vaison, and my father before me. And
now the only people who live in the village are strangers,
rootless people who care nothing for what our fathers built."

"They have improved the houses they live in, at least,"
I said defensively. "And they are working the fields. They
are good people, people who will not disgrace Vaison."

"And one of them is an artist, eh, and very handsome?"
His eyes became sly.

I glanced at him suspiciously. "I thought you hadn't been to
Vaison lately?"

"Marie heard it from Gabrielle, Mademoiselle. There is
not much that happens in the Châtaigneraie that Gabrielle
doesn't know about. Or Albert Bernard either, despite his
look of stupidity."

He said it with such a vindictive note that I looked at him
quickly. "You do not like Gabrielle or Albert, Pierre?"

He looked startled, and his eyes avoided mine. "I did not
say *that*, Mademoiselle. Why should I dislike them? The master is no longer the man he was when I knew him as a
young man before the war. His suffering changed him, and
since he is no longer as other people those two must be his
eyes and ears . . . . I will close the gate when you have
driven through, Mademoiselle . . . . Marie and I and Mathilde
live well here. We are content. I meant no disrespect to anyone, I assure you."

"I understand, Pierre," I said.

I drove through and kept going, and in the rear-vision
mirror I could see him closing the gates slowly; his head
turned as he glanced after me nervously. I was sorry suddenly
that I hadn't told him he was entitled to dislike whoever he
wished, since France was a free country. And that I didn't
blame anyone who disliked Gabrielle, though the slow-think-
ing Albert Bernard seemed harmless enough.

I saw Albert presently, still up there in the fields and look-

ng at the car as I stopped at the garage and got out to open
the doors. The villagers looked with him, until he gestured
savagely, and they returned reluctantly to their weeding.

Marie Labrousse came to the kitchen door to empty veg-
etable peelings into a bin as I came from the garage carrying
my parcels and the cardboard box of cakes from the bakery.

"Mademoiselle had a pleasant drive?" she smiled.

"Quite pleasant, Marie. I stopped at the village on the way
back. They had just finished baking and I bought some cakes.
I'd like some with coffee, when you can."

"But of course, Mademoiselle. In a few minutes. Shall I
bring them up to your room?"

I frowned. "Does my uncle like cakes?"

"That he does, Mademoiselle. He has a very sweet tooth."

"Then bring coffee for two, or send Louise to the library
with it, and a plate of cakes, please. My uncle is in the
library I suppose?"

"Yes, he is in the library, Mademoiselle. But Gabrielle is
with him. It might be better to wait." Her eyes became
uneasy suddenly.

I frowned. "I see no reason why Gabrielle's housekeeping
reports should keep my uncle from enjoying these with me.
But I will go up to my room first. I'd like the coffee in about
fifteen minutes, Marie."

She nodded and shrugged dismally. "Fifteen minutes, Mademoiselle," she agreed in a low voice.

It was time, I decided as I walked angrily upstairs to my
room, that someone taught Gabrielle her place at the Château-les-Vautours and the way I felt right then it might as
well be me.

My anger carried me up to my room, and I could barely
restrain myself from going down again at once. But I managed to control it until I had freshened up and put away the
things I had bought at the village.

I could hear Marie moving about in the kitchen as I came
downstairs, and the voice of the girl Louise. Cups and plates
clattered cheerfully. Marie, I decided, would make a far
better housekeeper than Gabrielle Bremen, who still seemed
more man than woman to me in any case.

What my uncle could see in that grim and autocratic
woman I couldn't understand. Yet Marie had spoken of any
intrusion on their privacy in the library almost as though they
were lovers. That was quite ridiculous. If my uncle fancied a
female friend, with his wealth, even with his disfigurement,
surely he would look for someone far more attractive than
Gabrielle. And in his way my uncle was something of a connoisseur of the pleasures of life. I was sure of that.

Voices murmured behind the closed door of the library, so Gabrielle was still in there. But the thought of Gabrielle in my uncle's arms was so incongruous that I had to smother a giggle as I thought about it now. And then, as I raised my hand to knock I heard Gabrielle's voice, raised in sudden anger.

"They know, I tell you! Albert is sure of it! He watched them camp under the crag near the waterfall. Why do you think he has suddenly become so anxious? You know what it means as well as I do. Or has that girl turned your brain?"

"So Albert looks at them and decides that they know," my uncle's voice said.

"He crept close enough to take a good look at them. He says they are trained men. And if he says so, that is what they are."

My uncle laughed. "It is nonsense. You are reading too much into something with a perfectly innocent explanation. Get out of here now. Denise is back. I heard the car. Out."

"Have you become a fool who does not listen?" Gabrielle's voice rose higher, strangely shrill and afraid. "Remember it is not only you, but *us!* Remember that!"

"Do you think I am likely to forget? You've reminded me often enough. I'll take a look at them tonight. There's a moon. Then we'll decide."

"Take us with you then, Albert and me. And if there is a decision to be made we can make it and carry it out as it should be done. Without delay."

He was silent for a long moment, and I found myself frowning while I waited for his reply. Trained men? Trained for the military? I tried to figure out why Gabrielle was so excited.

"If they are what you think—they may expect us to come to them. Have you thought of that?" my uncle said sarcastically.

"How could they? They do not know they were seen."

"Albert has grown older. We all have. We are not as good as we used to be, Gabrielle."

"Speak for yourself, not for Albert and me!" her voice declared angrily. "We are good as ever we were. Take us with you tonight and we'll prove it to you."

"Very well." His voice lowered and I lost the words. Then he said clearly: "Go now, Gabrielle, before she comes."

"And that is another thing. We don't like her being here. You'd better think about that. We've stuck together for a long time now. But remember, this could end."

"That is a thought that has also occurred to me," my uncle said coldly. "You've had your say, Gabrielle—now get out.

I'm taking you with me tonight. For one day that is enough. Don't anger me."

"You do not frighten us," she said defiantly. "You are no longer the man you were."

But she started toward the door quickly. I was not sure why, but I grew afraid. I realized I had been eavesdropping on something I had not been supposed to hear. And Gabrielle with her suspicious nature would be the first to think that I *had* heard if she found me here. I ran hastily to the stairs as quietly as I could, my heart starting to pound with some unnameable fear. By the time the door opened I had turned and was coming slowly down the last few steps, my feet soundless on the thick carpet.

She saw me at once and glared angrily as she strode toward me.

"So you're back," she snorted truculently. "Did that fool Marceau send us bacon and pork? And what has happened to his wine? He seems to think that we keep him for nothing over there!"

"He is coming in the truck tomorrow. He said he would bring it all then."

She relaxed a little. "Ah. He said so, did he! The worthless rogue should have been thrown out long since. Your uncle is too soft where people who knew him before the war are concerned. The Marceaus, these people at Tocsin all presume on his indulgence. It is a foolishness."

I said stiffly: "My uncle seems to know what he is about, Gabrielle."

Her eyes sharpened. "He does, does he? You should never have been allowed to drive to Vaison alone."

"Why not?" I demanded. She seemed to rub me the wrong way every time I spoke to her.

She studied me briefly. "Vaison is not a good place for young girls to enter alone, Mademoiselle. I told you that this morning. Well, you are back and unharmed, which no doubt will please your uncle. He is in the library if you want to see him."

She stalked away, a giant figure of a woman, full of her own secret gloom and anger. I stared after her. I was not quite sure what to think about her, for she *had* warned me as she had said. And although I had no intention of confessing it to her, I *had* walked into danger at Vaison. Great danger.

I tapped lightly on the library door and Uncle Maurice's voice said pleasantly enough: "Is that you, Denise? Come in, my dear."

He was standing at the window examining a rifle, a long, wicked-looking weapon with a telescope clipped above the

67

slender barrel. As I watched him, remembering the pigeons again suddenly, he glanced up and our eyes met. He laughed abruptly.

"Does the sight of weapons startle you, Denise?"

I forced myself to smile, supposing that he had seen the thought in my eyes as I remembered the pigeons.

"No, of course not, Uncle. That's a big game rifle, isn't it? An American one."

His eyes expressed his surprise. "So you know about weapons? Where did you learn that? Surely not from your grandfather?"

"Some friends of ours used to shoot in the Everglades. If you are fond of hunting, you'll find more sport in Florida than you will in Auvergne, Uncle Maurice."

His brown eyes studied me thoughtfully. "For a rifle such as this?"

I considered the question. "There are still a few puma in the Everglades. And bear, and of course alligators. There are plenty of varmints, small game that are not protected, like woodchucks and crows and foxes that you might use a rifle on. And, of course, plenty of wild fowl in season for a shotgun."

He looked at me incredulously. "And you have done all this?"

I laughed. "I'm afraid not, Uncle Maurice. Oh, I've shot at a puma, but someone else killed it. I was quite good at varmint shooting though. I didn't mind that, because it was destroying pests. But I didn't like shooting at duck with the shotgun. And besides it kicked my shoulder and made too much noise."

He smiled. "I see. I am beginning to look forward even more to joining you in New Orleans. So there is hunting there, eh? And you are interested in rifles and guns? Did you know that I was a connoisseur of guns? I have a very fine collection, including ancient weapons that have become collector's pieces. Come, we will test your knowledge. We will see just how much you know. And perhaps one day I will take you hunting on the slopes. There are wild boars up there that give good sport, and an occasional deer."

I followed him as he walked across the room. "How do you find this rifle, Uncle?"

"A good weapon in its class. For dangerous game—very good. But unfortunately, there is no dangerous game here except the boars, and the Wetherby is a little heavy for pig-shooting."

"You used a heavy rifle on pigeons," I said accusingly. "I watched from my window."

He turned as he opened a door I hadn't noticed before, among the shelves of books at the back of the big room.

"I heard that you didn't like that."

I colored. "I admired your markmanship, Uncle Maurice—but not the way it was done."

He laughed abruptly. "Yes, I know. The wheat. At least you are honest about it. Gabrielle informed me that you did not like what I did. Why, may I ask?"

"It seemed cruel and unfair to me," I said. "And you shot so well that it was obviously not necessary."

He shook his head. "They were drugged. They would have felt little pain. And I considered it necessary. For the survival of the vultures, and another reason. You know how I dislike—being with people. Do you expect me to take a shotgun and follow the pigeons? With the people of the village gaping at me? No, I prefer the pigeons to come to me, so that I can both feed the vultures and practice my shooting."

"Is it necessary to kill the pigeons at all? I mean, other food can be found for the vultures, surely?"

His brow drew together in a frown and his brown eyes studied me coldly. "Yes, other food can be found for them. Very well, I will consider that. And no doubt I could find another sport. Would that please you, Denise?"

"Why, yes. It would, truly, Uncle Maurice," I said. But with that cold look in Uncle Maurice's eyes I was not so sure about it all. I was, in fact, beginning to wish I'd said nothing.

"Well now," he said, his eyes acquiring a more pleasant gleam, "that's settled! You have decided me. You won't see the vultures outside my window tomorrow, or perhaps for many days. I promise you that. Now come and look at my collection, and point out the weapons you have seen before."

Light flooded that other room suddenly, and I was looking past him at a veritable arsenal of weapons arranged around the walls. As he had said, they ranged from ancient arquebuses and flintlock pistols to the most modern automatic weapons. Most of them I'd never seen before, others only in TV shows or motion pictures back home.

I walked around beside him, while he took an occasional weapon from its pegs and handled it with an easy familiarity as he explained its history and the way it worked.

"Do you recognize this one?"

"Yes. Eliot Ness has one on television. It's a Thompson sub-machine gun. And this . . . isn't this a British Sten? You have enough weapons to start a revolution, Uncle Maurice.

It's a wonder the French Government allows a private person to keep them, even in a collection such as this."

He laughed and put the sub-machine gun back on its pegs. "When I returned to France the Government had called in all the arms of the Maquis. But there were, of course, caches of arms in the Châtaigneraie that only we leaders knew about. I took my choice of them for this collection before I informed Paris of their whereabouts. Nobody asked any questions, Denise, and France owed me this small pleasure possibly."

I could not deny that.

"All the same, Uncle Maurice, in the wrong hands they can be dangerous. Wouldn't it have been better to take the bolts and hand them in? They do in America."

"No," he said curtly, "it would not. I am a perfectionist, Denise. A weapon with parts missing is not a perfect example of the craft at all. I feel I am entitled to my war souvenirs. Many of these weapons are German, or Vichy French, and their owners died in the giving. In my eyes that gives them a peculiar value."

I shivered and turned away, and he laughed. His left hand gripped my arm with an unexpected strength, as we walked toward the door so that I could feel the strong fingers digging deeply into my flesh, and winced.

"War is not a matter of table manners and niceties, Denise," he said in an odd voice.

A timid knock at the outer door cut across his voice, and he looked irritated at the interruption.

"Who is there?" he demanded.

"Louise, M'sieur," a faint and nervous voice replied.

"I ordered nothing."

But then I remembered, and I said quickly: "I did, Uncle Maurice. I ordered coffee for us both. They were baking in the village as I drove through, and I bought some hot cakes I thought . . ."

The pressure of his fingers relaxed abruptly. "Fresh cakes?" he said. "I have a weakness for such things. You are a thoughtful girl, and I thank you. Gabrielle thinks sweets are a weakness. She is no pastry cook, and neither is Marie Labrousse, so perhaps that is why." He raised his voice. "Come in, Louise."

He closed the armory door behind him and locked it. He was putting the key ring back in his pocket as Louise entered with her tray.

"Violette Cloete is famous in these parts for her pastries," he murmured appreciatively.

I smiled. "Or pot-au-feu. Grandfather was always talking

70

about the great iron pots on the back of the stoves. I saw, and smelled *pot-au-feu* twice at Vaison. Once in the cottage of your tenants the Bourgets, and again at the farm. Mademoiselle Bourget's *pot-au-feu* smelled delicious."

Momentarily his eyes looked at me uncertainly. "Oh yes, the soup, of course." He shook his head. "Such a mess is not to my taste."

"At the Bourgets' it smelled delicious."

"A matter of opinion," he said absently, his eyes on the cakes. "I have smelled it at the farm. The Bourgets are dirty and eat like swine. Give me an honest beef goulash cooked in a clean pot. Not a gruel of stale and putrid leavings. You will find no *pot-au-feu* at the Château-les-Vautours, Denise."

"But, Uncle, surely the *pot-au-feu* at the farm that Grandfather was always talking about was not like that?" I protested. "Why, it was never allowed to stop simmering. How could it become—putrid? You were practically reared on it, like Grandfather. He said it was delicious."

He looked up at me quickly. "Oh yes, of course. But then, Denise, our parents were good healthy farm folk, and clean. The women were fine cooks. I liked it then, naturally. It was our staple food. Perhaps that is why I have such distaste for it now . . . . One tires of even the best dish with constant repetition. And, tastes change."

He moved to place my chair with his usual courtesy. He changed the subject abruptly as Louise left us and closed the door.

"I have been thinking about the inquiries you are going to make for me at your embassy. Could you do it by telephone? You see, Denise, we are very busy in the fields at the moment and it would not be convenient for Albert to drive you to Paris. We cannot spare one man, especially Albert."

"But, Uncle Maurice, I could drive myself." I was suddenly thrilled by the idea of driving that beautiful car to Paris. "I could take two days and stop overnight at—"

"No." Uncle Maurice interrupted brusquely, but then his voice softened. "No, Denise, I do not like the thought of you driving all that way alone. If the car should break down in some isolated spot . . ." He shrugged. "There is a telephone in the village at the Cloetes'—the people who run the inn."

I sat silent for a moment, disappointed. "I guess I could do it by 'phone, the preliminaries anyway. It's just that these things are so much easier to do in person."

"I am sure your embassy will be more than obliging when they hear the facts, Denise."

"Yes, I guess it will be all right."

"Good. That's settled," he sat back comfortably in his

71

chair. "But you must be sure that no one overhears your talk. Do not let anyone in the village suspect that I am thinking of leaving here. They are so loyal, these peasants, Denise. So loyal and concerned for their master that they become possessive, jealous even. When I first brought them here from Vaison . . ."

He talked on quietly, eating his cakes fastidiously. Listening, sipping my own coffee and nibbling Violette Cloete's delicious pastry, I answered him carefully.

A strange man, my uncle, I decided. Something of a gourmet, though his tastes were not exactly what I expected to find in a Gérard and a Frenchman. He could be hard, or courteous, kind or intolerant. And he was certainly overindulgent to Gabrielle and Albert. He had done more than enough for France, and for Gabrielle and Albert. He would doubtless leave them all well off enough. And the way Gabrielle had talked to him—almost as though she had some hold over him, and that it was something that Albert Bernard shared. Moreover, what could the conversation I had overheard mean? My uncle's voice had had steel in it when he had ordered Gabrielle out of the room. Steel and—fear?

The Gérards had always been gentle, kind people. Perhaps it was his experience in the Maquis that had made Maurice Gérard different. Uncle Maurice, it seemed, was not much like Henri Gérard, my grandfather, or the way he had led me to expect all Gérards must be.

Listening to his quiet voice, while I though about these things, I lost my appetite for Madame Cloete's cakes . . . .

CHAPTER SIX

I WOKE UP SWEATING, full of some nameless fear born of a forgotten dream. I sat up in bed startled, and drew up the covers protectively. I felt suddenly very small and helpless in the great four-poster bed.

I looked first at my door, with my heart pounding heavily, but the chair that I propped there each night was still undisturbed. Around me the chateau was silent, and bright moonlight filled the room through the open windows. The drapes swayed slightly in a night breeze that held the chill of high places and was cooling my hot skin rapidly, already

72

making the perspiration on my forehead and upper lip feel pleasantly cold.

Slowly I became aware that my mouth was dry and that my head ached slightly, and I remembered the wine that Uncle Maurice had pressed on me at dinner. Perhaps it was my hangover that had wakened me. My thirst and the headache, and no doubt also the bright moonlight shining directly on my face from a full moon riding a clear sky above the mountains.

I lay back slowly again, remembering dinner last night. Or possibly tonight. I had no inclination to grope for my watch to find out, and the ornate gilded clock that stood on an old-fashioned armoire was in deep shadow along the opposite wall.

It had been a strange meal, now that I thought about it. Gabrielle herself had served it, explaining that Marie Labrousse and the girls had left early. I had never seen my uncle so jovial, or Gabrielle as friendly. The dishes had been good, so good that I knew Marie Labrousse must have prepared them for us before she left. Gabrielle brought in first one bottle of an excellent sparkling Burgundy, and then another.

To my surprise, Uncle Maurice asked Gabrielle to sit with us over a glass of wine. She seemed in a strangely exalted mood. She told stories about some of the villagers that made my uncle to laugh heartily, though I felt my cheeks warm, for some of them were almost lewd. And occasionally they exchanged glances that puzzled me, for it was as though they were indeed lovers and somewhere beyond tonight's dinner a tryst waited.

But though my uncle pressed wine upon us both impartially, I noticed that he drank only sparingly himself. And toward the end of the dinner his strange eyes studied us as though we were specimens he had experimented on with his bottles of choice Burgundy.

Not that it seemed to make much difference to Gabrielle, for when she at last stood up and began to gather the dishes, her hands were steady enough. I supposed the constitution that went with that ageing but muscular body must be stronger than mine. For I had grown drowsy and was reluctant to leave the table because I was no longer quite sure of the coordination of mind and legs.

When at last I did stand and excuse myself, Uncle Maurice stood courteously with me. We had lingered longer over dinner than ever before, and I had drunk more Burgundy than I ever had at one time in my life.

My uncle walked to the door with me and bade me good-night. I started to climb the stairs. Behind him I heard the clatter of Gabrielle's dishes, and her laughter.

"She should sleep well tonight," her coarse voice drifted through the open door. "She has had a little too much wine."

"Yes," my uncle said, "she should sleep soundly enough."

"The fox has not lost his cunning, eh?" Gabrielle said. "Yet so have I had too much wine. And the wine you sent in for Albert, the heavy wine that you know he has a weakness for. No doubt that great fool also has had more than he should. Could you be thinking by any chance that if someone gets hurt through carelessness it will be one of us? Because if you do . . ."

"Quiet, fool!" he said angrily.

The door closed abruptly then as I stumbled and clung to the stair rail.

I had been glad to undress and fall into the great bed. But I had remembered to place the chair propped against the door, the back jammed beneath the handle.

I stared at it now, then I winced at the bright moonlight streaming through my window. The way my head throbbed was certainly unpleasant.

I needed some aspirin and a drink of cold water. And that great, bright moon was just too much. I took my time transferring thought to action, for I quickly discovered that my head ached far worse in a vertical position than in a horizontal, and when I bent in search of my slippers I almost groaned aloud. Uncle Maurice's Burgundy was certainly potent!

In the end I did without slippers, and drew my robe on over the flimsy nightdress and stood up. I was not thinking clearly yet, I decided disgustedly, for I should have flicked on the bedside light before I got out of bed. Now I had to either crawl across the bed again to put it on, or walk around the bed to reach it. I chose the latter course as the least painful for my throbbing head. I groped for the switch and pushed it.

Nothing happened.

I muttered one of Grandfather's favorite French expletives. I could hear the faint but steady thumping of Albert's diesel engines that drove the generator. But either the power had been switched off, or, which seemed far more likely, the globe of my bedside lamp had burned out.

I groped my way into the bathroom, for its small, high window made it darker in there than the bedroom. But I found my aspirin and a glass. I dissolved the tablets and drank a long ice-cold water chaser greedily.

One thing was certain, I thought as I came back into the

bedroom. The next time Uncle Maurice produced his choice Burgundy I would be more wary. Much more wary.

Outside my window the moonlight made the vineyards a pale reproduction of the day, full of dark shadows. Somewhere unseen a night-bird called with a lonely, melancholy sound. And as though in answer, thin and distant in the village, a dog began to howl eerily, and another and another took up the chorus so that they sounded like the wolves Uncle Maurice had told me still lived in the remote forest.

I shuddered. The Châtaigneraie had indeed become a strange place. Deserted farms, wolves, vultures, and the memories of old war horrors. It was not at all the friendly, healthy place that Grandfather had pictured for me. I doubted now that it had ever been. Why in these very rooms around me long ago men and women had died by violence, slaughtered during the Revolution.

In my imagination I saw fierce faces staring up at my window from beneath cockaded hats, gleaming, bloodied weapons waving below. I could almost hear the screams of women around me, the fierce shouting, the rattle of shots.

"Death to the aristocrats!"

How many had died here then, and since, in other wars? From my window I could see the piles of stones and remnants of wall of the older, fortified wing. I shivered. Now I was really cold, and my thinking was way out if I meant to sleep again tonight.

And then as I turned away, I saw movement suddenly in the vineyards on my left near where the wall turned. A dark figure crossed an open space and vanished behind the intruding corner of the wall beyond Uncle Maurice's window. I stared, trembling, at the open space. Something else moved there stealthily. Again a dark figure moved across to pass out of sight beyond the wall. A larger figure than the first, and somehow even more menacing, for the moonlight glinted on something in its hand.

I watched, frozen behind my curtains. Nothing else moved, but somewhere a door opened softly downstairs. A side door, I decided. Somewhere beyond the library. The pounding of my heart held me still in terror. I dared not turn my head, but I could imagine those figures in the chateau now. Perhaps creeping stealthily toward my uncle's room.

Or mine!

I fought an impulse to scream. Nothing else moved in the vineyard. Nothing moved on the slopes. Whoever they were—they were now inside the chateau, I was sure of it.

I remembered the conversation I had overheard between

my uncle and Gabrielle. It returned to me in fragments that made more disturbing sense suddenly.

"He watched them camp under the crag near the waterfall . . ."

"Take us with you . . ."

"If they are what you think—they may expect us to come to them. Have you thought of that? I'll take a look at them tonight. There's a moon . . ."

I stood there, confused by my thoughts, my imagination conjuring up unknown dangers to my uncle and myself, for I cared little enough what might happen to Gabrielle or Albert. Yet why should anyone threaten danger to us at the Château-les-Vautours? No more were coming. I had seen only two figures, unless others had passed before I noticed them.

"We are as good as ever we were! Take us with you tonight and we'll prove it to you . . . ."

Gabrielle had said that. And my uncle had replied: "Very well."

I could never ask about that without admitting that I had listened. But I *had* listened. If there were trespassers up in the forest, perhaps the figures I had just seen were my uncle returning with Gabrielle and Albert after reconnoitering in the moonlight.

Tomorrow perhaps they would complain to the gendarmes in Aurillac.

I tested the back of the chair beneath the doorknob, and it seemed secure. I listened, holding my breath.

Yes, someone was moving about downstairs. More than one person. Footsteps sounded, and the distant mutter of voices, quickly subdued. It was my uncle, I decided, and probably Gabrielle and Albert. But my fear prompted me to be sure, so I eased the chair away silently and opened the door and peered out, listening.

Something metallic bumped against a chair in the direction of the library. All sound stilled at once for a long moment. Then I heard another door opening eerily. I stilled, horrified, remembering my uncle's collection of weapons. Whoever was down there was going into the armory!

But in another moment I felt like laughing at myself for my foolishness. And why not? With wolves and bears in the forest, not to mention those mysterious, unknown men camped at the waterfall, was my uncle likely to walk unarmed through the night? That *was* my uncle down there, returning the weapons they'd carried to their proper places.

I let my breath sigh out quietly in relief. They were coming from the armory again now. I heard the door close and then the library door. Their footsteps moved cautiously in the passage downstairs that led from the great reception room, then in the reception room itself. They did not speak, but I could hear Gabrielle and Albert walking on toward the servants' quarters. Then the stairs creaked beneath my uncle's weight faintly as he came up.

I leaned against the doorway, holding the door partially open still, and closed my eyes weakly in relief. My uncle climbed silently, for I could not hear him, but he should be at the top of the stairs now, and turning toward his own room. I would wait until he closed his door before I closed mine; otherwise he might hear.

He seemed a long while getting to his own room. I stood just within my own doorway concentrating every sense in the effort of listening, but could hear absolutely nothing. I began to feel a warning tingle of apprehension. Why was Uncle Maurice taking so long to reach his room and open his door?

Could I be mistaken? Could that be someone else I had heard climbing the stairs so stealthily? Someone coming toward me in the darkness?

And as I froze in sudden horror at the thought, the bedside light just behind me flooded my bedroom with its light, throwing my shadow against the opposite wall of the passage outside, and showing me a dark and menacing figure standing within three feet of me out there.

I was staring horrified at the most hideous face I had ever seen!

A face of dead white flesh, crossed by hideous whorls and ridges of red scarring, looking back at me with only the gleaming eyes and thin-lipped mouth human! A skeletal face with only a thin layer of flesh and tortured, hardened skin covering the bony structures below the eyes. It seemed to leap at me, and a hand caught my throat, forcing me back against the wall.

"Quiet, you little fool!" a harsh voice hissed.

A scream had started involuntarily in my throat; it rose high and shrill for an instant before those terrible fingers subdued it. I tore at them frantically, choking, forced backward to my knees, fighting to breathe.

Somewhere vaguely I heard running footsteps coming in answer to my scream. A voice shouted something fiercely in a language that I did not recognize.

"No!" someone cried in French. "Don't! Have you gone mad?"

Other hands joined mine suddenly, tearing at those steel fingers. Someone else caught him, dragging him backward

77

into the passage. I fell like a rag doll dropped carelessly, gasping for breath, feeling the carpet rough against my face, fighting nausea and the same plunge into the darkness of unconsciousness into which I had fallen at Vaison.

"Let me go," a voice muttered thickly. "It is over, there is no need to hold me. She was standing at the door. The light shone on me, and she saw me and started to scream."

It was my uncle's voice, thickened by spent emotion. I tried to say something, but no sound came, and I was being turned over roughly upon my back, still fighting for the breath that whistled in my bruised and swelling throat.

The face of Gabrielle Bremen stared down at me malevolently. She grinned. "So now you have seen what a burned face looks like, eh? And you did not like what you saw, and were foolish enough to show it, and scream, and throw him into a rage? He does not like anyone to look at him in horror. Or scream. I suppose you know that now, eh?"

"I'm . . . sorry," I tried to whisper. I forced myself to turn my head and look at Uncle Maurice again. "It was just . . . seeing you so . . . suddenly there."

I don't think any of them understood what I was trying to say, for the sounds came out as a strangled croaking even to my own ears.

Albert said: "Come, I will walk to your room with you."

My uncle looked at him. "I must find out why she put the light on my face."

"Leave her to Gabrielle and me," Albert said soothingly. "As for the light—perhaps we woke her coming in. The lights were off, remember? No doubt she switched on her own light earlier, then heard us downstairs. When I switched on the lights again just now she was at the door, perhaps."

I tried to tell them that Albert was right.

Gabrielle watched me and grinned. "She croaks like a raven. You have left your mark on her throat."

"It was an unfortunate mistake," Albert said mildly. "I will take him to his room now. We will look after her."

But my uncle shook off Albert's hands.

"Why were you at the door, Denise? Why did you switch on the light so suddenly in there?"

I drew away from them, farther against the wall. In the struggle my robe had twisted up behind my back. A button lay on the floor near me. I became aware that my breasts and body showed clearly through the thin nightdress. I straightened the robe, drawing it about me with shaking hands.

"She is modest, the little one," Gabrielle murmured, with mock sympathy.

"It was as Albert said," I managed to enunciate. "I heard something . . . and looked out. The light just came on . . ."

"Albert put the words into her mouth for her," Gabrielle said. "You are a fool if you believe them."

"Why did you scream?" my uncle asked. Above the horrible scarring on his face his eyes seemed over-large.

"I don't . . . know. It was just . . . seeing you so suddenly for the first time without the mask. That, and the sudden light on your . . . face. I did not know it was you. I thought . . ."

I cut that off, but they were all three staring at me intently.

"You thought what?" Uncle Maurice asked. "That I was someone else?"

My voice was coming back.

"Something woke me, I'm not sure what. I got up for a glass of water and some aspirin. I saw someone coming through the vineyard when I went to draw the drapes. Then I heard the door downstairs open and someone came in. I thought it must be . . . some intruder. I meant to call you then, but began to think it might be someone from the chateau who'd been out late and returned . . ."

"At this hour?"

"But you *were* outside. That's why you're dressed, isn't it? I didn't know what time it was. I never looked." But I turned my head painfully and saw the clock. Two-thirty. I added quickly, "Because I thought it might be you, I waited, Uncle. Then I . . . heard you come upstairs, and I didn't want you to think I was spying on you, so I waited for you to go into your room and close your door before I closed mine. Only I'd forgotten the light that I switched on when I got out of bed. And the light came on, and—I saw you."

My uncle looked at Albert inquiringly. The big man nodded as if to say: I believe her.

My uncle looked at me slowly again.

"Perhaps this might have been avoided when you first came, if I had allowed you to see me as I am."

"And why not?" Gabrielle said. "With Albert and me the way you look has become commonplace. One grows used to such things."

My uncle touched with the tips of his fingers the ridges of his ghoul's face. I watched him, my eyes wide, but with, I hoped, my fear hidden. For fear is a stimulant to people like Gabrielle Bremen—when they see it in others.

Gabrielle's lips writhed. "Do not let her fool you."

But my uncle, unexpectedly, seemed to take control again. "You see skeletons where there are only shadows, Gabrielle," he said. "What happened is between Denise and myself, and we will discuss it alone without your help." He looked at Albert deliberately. "I hurt her, and already I regret it. Go to bed, and I will make my peace with her. As she says, it is something that could not happen again."

Albert seemed to consider both sides of the question in his slow way, his almost colorless eyes holding my uncle's for what seemed a long time to me, before he said: "As you say, M'sieur. We will leave you with Mademoiselle now. The night is almost gone. Coming, Gabrielle?"

For a moment she seemed to poise as though about to attack me. But Albert moved with an unexpected speed and, catching her elbow, propelled her quickly out of the room. They disappeared along the passage, with Gabrielle still protesting in a low voice.

I became aware of my uncle watching me, and that he had drawn up the collar of his jacket, throwing his scarred face into shadow.

"I would give a great deal that this hadn't happened, Denise," he said in a low voice.

"So would I, Uncle Maurice," I said with feeling.

His fingers moved, touching his face. "About this, I am not as other men. When I am aroused about it, I do not know what I do. It is a psychosis, you understand? I am not responsible. I cannot stand to be stared at, or loathed for the way I look, or pitied. A woman's horror at the way I look, a scream, and . . ."

He gestured, and put his hands up to cover his eyes, and bowed his head. Pity touched me, so that I wanted to comfort him. I reached out a hand to touch him, and remembered what he had said about pity and withdrew it hastily.

"I understand perfectly now, Uncle Maurice," I said in as calm a voice as I could muster. "And I swear to you that I will never hurt you again that way, now that I know and understand."

He looked at me again, and nodded. "I believe you," he muttered. "I *must* believe you, Denise. Wait." He moved to the door and stared toward the stairs, listening. He turned his head. "They have gone to their rooms. There are things here you do not understand, that I must make clear to you. I will be back in a moment. . . ."

He moved out into the passage. Silently. I could not hear him walking away, though I knew he was out there walking toward the stairs. Alone, I began to tremble suddenly. Tears of self-pity flowed. I shook all over. My throat felt like a boil about to burst. It took effort not to jam the chair beneath the handle of the door to bar it against his return. I wanted to run hysterically from the room and the chateau, out of the

Châtaigneraie, out of Auvergne, out of France! Yet I could not have run a yard for the way I shook.

I groped to the bed, and sank down upon its edge with my face in my hands, sobbing, the tears running into my hands copiously and down my wrists, and dripping upon my Paris nightgown to leave dark spots.

"You must not cry, Denise."

I had not heard him come in, but he was standing there staring at me. He had put the mask on, and above it his eyes were my uncle's eyes again as I knew them.

"I . . . can't help it," I sobbed. I groped for a handkerchief in the pocket of my robe and dabbed at my eyes hastily, turning my face away from him. "You will not need the mask again with me, Uncle Maurice, unless you choose to wear it."

His eyes frowned briefly above it. "With you, I will choose to wear it always, Denise," he said. "When we are together. It has become a habit that gives me confidence to enjoy your company. But you must be prepared now for what you will see if you ever come upon me unexpectedly without it. You understand?"

I nodded.

He thrust something into my hands and drew the chair near me and sat down. "This is my way of saying that I am sorry that I gave you so much pain and fear. I meant to give it to you as a gift when the papers were arranged. But take it now as a peace offering—and I will find you another gift when we are ready to leave this place forever."

I stared from the rather battered leather case that he had given me to his eyes above the mask. "You do not need to give me a gift, Uncle Maurice. It was all my fault. I . . ."

"It is yours, Denise. Open it."

I turned it around curiously in my hands. It looked like a very old jewel case. It had been fine leather once, and there was a protruding catch. I pressed the catch and the top of the case flew open, and I gasped incredulously.

I was staring at a magnificent ruby necklace, the large pendant jewel gleaming in the light of the bedside lamp in its rich gold setting, five other smaller rubies set in the same old-fashioned gold settings on either side.

"But, Uncle," I gasped, "these are rubies, aren't they? You just can't give this away!"

He said calmly, "They are Burmese rubies, which I believe are the finest in the world. They were brought to France from Indo-China before the war by a Government official for his mistress. Partisans killed her. . . . But their history is not important. They are yours, if you will accept them from me as

81

a peace offering, and forget that sometimes I . . . am overwhelmed by the impulses that I cannot control. Rubies are for your coloring. On you they will be beautiful. Will you accept them on my condition that tomorrow you will forget tonight, and never speak of it again?"

I stared at him. "Will I . . ."

I had never seen anything as beautiful in my life, or had the opportunity to own anything so valuable. I moved impulsively to kiss him in thanks, but he stiffened and drew away from me.

"Is it agreed?"

"You have my word, Uncle Maurice," I said fervently.

"Then put them on, and see for yourself how they become you. And then sit down quietly and listen to what I have to say about the things tonight that you do not understand."

I hardly heard the last part as my fingers fumbled eagerly with the catch, and I put the gleaming necklace around my neck and ran to the mirror. I peered into it.

"Will you switch on the other light, I cannot see," I cried impatiently.

He laughed softly. "How impetuous you are, girl!"

But light flooded the room, showing me the gleaming, lovely jewels and within the golden triangle that held them, the bruising on my throat already turning blue and swollen. Above them my pale face stared back at me, the pallor through my tan showing a slightly jaundiced tinge, my eyes shadowed, my hair awry from the struggle. I had never looked worse!

"I look shocking," I muttered. "But I have never seen anything as beautiful as the necklace, Uncle Maurice."

He nodded, studying me as I walked back and sat on the bed. "In a few days the bruises will be gone. But you must wear something high about your throat so that Louise and the other servants from the village will not notice. They gossip easily in the village."

"I will wear a scarf, or high-necked sweaters then."

"Good girl." He stood up abruptly, and went to the door to listen; he switched out the light and came back again. "They have gone to their rooms," he said quietly. His brown eyes swept over me, so that I felt them on the curves of my body rather than on the ruby necklace, and it was an odd, embarrassing feeling, so that I drew the robe closer, and he looked away and smiled.

"Even as you are, you are a very beautiful young woman, Denise," he said in the same quiet voice. "Jewels and fine clothes could do little for you otherwise. One day, when all this is behind us, it will give me great pleasure to buy such things for you in America. But that is our secret, and it must be kept that way. Now listen and I will try to explain the things that you don't understand, but which I believe you are intelligent enough to have discovered in part tonight."

I stared at him. "You mean the way Albert and Gabrielle acted? I can understand your indulgence to Albert perhaps, but not to Gabrielle." I shivered involuntarily. "Uncle Maurice, I can't understand why you allow that horrible woman to remain near you."

"I do, because I must."

"Then she . . . they, have some hold over you? I suspected that. But what did Gabrielle mean she . . . she wanted to do to me? I was . . . terrified."

He laughed softly. "Why, she and Albert would have sent you back to America at once, Denise. Tomorrow, if they could," he said calmly. "They have been against your coming here all along."

"But why?" I demanded. Send me back to America? I would have agreed wholeheartedly at the time if they had put it into words. I had expected something far worse, though I could not have said what. I had known horror, and the evil in Gabrielle's eyes and Albert's calm but reluctant determination had seemed to indicate something far worse. Yet I could believe it now, because I remembered the conversation I had overheard in the library. . . .

He shrugged. "They are jealous people. They dislike change. They are suspicious that you may take from them the benefits they enjoy here. The peasants of the Châtaigneraie are a rural people who resent change. They have not changed much themselves in two hundred years. Life has been hard for them for generations. They have it easy here at the Château-les-Vautours, and they don't want to change that." He looked at me intently. "That is my problem, Denise, and I mean to change it. I mean to escape—leave them, with something to live on, of course, and go to America—with your help."

"To escape . . . the hold they have upon you?"

He nodded, watching me.

"But," I muttered, "I don't see how they could stop you. After what you have done for them, and for France . . ."

"It is true that I won a name as one of the leaders of the Resistance," he said slowly. "But there was a time when I, like many others, was uncertain. France was divided. There were two Frances, you understand, Vichy, and the France of De Gaulle. Pétain and Laval kept urging us to collaborate with the Germans, De Gaulle urged us to take up arms against them." He shrugged. "Who was one to believe? Who knew then what was best for France?"

"My grandfather knew," I said. "De Gaulle."

"But your grandfather was not in France, Denise. Neither was De Gaulle. For us who were here it was a different matter."

"All the same," I said, remembering the things Grandfather had told me about Uncle Maurice, "I cannot believe that you deviated toward Vichy for long. Or did anything disloyal to France." I said it firmly, because I believed it, and was surprised when he smiled sardonically.

"To which France, Denise?"

"There is only one France, neither Pétain's or De Gaulle's. To France, Uncle Maurice."

He nodded, frowning. "You have a certain understanding. Very well, judge then. In the Châtaigneraie we were close to Vichy, and therefore we were of Vichy, no matter what private doubts some of us had. After the fall of France there was only one band of Maquis in the Châtaigneraie, led by a very resolute man whom I will not name even to you. He came to me at Vaison asking me to form a partisan band from the village. Two of his people were with him—one was Gabrielle. I told him it was impossible, for the villagers would have no part of it. They were for Vichy. They would betray me at once."

I stared at him appalled. "The people of Vaison?"

He nodded. "It is as simple as that, Denise. They preferred to stay alive under Vichy, eating occasionally and with their sons and daughters unharmed, to starving and dying in the hills. Then he asked me to join him personally. It was not an easy decision to make. If I said that I would at that time, I knew that I would be risking betrayal by my people, and death for a cause in which I had neither confidence nor belief at that time. Yet if I said no, they had guns in their hands. They would have been fools to leave alive behind them one who had refused to join them and might betray them."

"But you would never do that!"

"Hear me out," he said, frowning. "Although I did not then know it, they had already asked someone in the village. Cloete, the elder brother of Henri. When he said no, they left him lying outside the mill where they had met him by arrangement."

"How horrible!" I exclaimed.

"It was war," he shrugged. "But I did not understand their necessity then. Or even know about it. I asked for a little time while I tested the feeling of some of the villagers whom I felt I could trust. I asked them to return the next night at the same time. And because they thought me an important man who would come their way with or without the villagers, they agreed."

"And they came back?"

"Yes," he said. "They came back. But the Germans came first to investigate the death of poor Cloete, suspecting that the partisan leader had caused it. They came to me. They said they would take me to Gestapo headquarters for questioning and punishment as a suspected member of the band. Someone in the village the night before had seen the partisans walking towards the farm it seemed, and had reported it. So . . ."

"Yes?" I said, staring at him unbelievingly.

"They were not alone, Denise. A French officer of Vichy was with them. He also threatened me, and demanded that I tell the truth. Cloete was dead, and we were a small community. Cloete was one of us. The partisans were not—they were strangers. I told the truth, Denise. I obeyed the French officer's order, and told the exact truth. No more, no less. They set a trap, and the partisans walked into it at the farm the next night. They died there, except for Gabrielle Bremen who got away in the darkness and confusion. She fled north and joined another band. Albert led it, and became her lover. In the Châtaigneraie there were no Maquis after that until I formed my own band more than a year later. Albert's band had moved far to the north. There were many such small bands in France. Each worked alone. It was not until the British and De Gaulle started to drop arms and advisers that we became co-ordinated in any way. I never saw Gabrielle again until after the war. But I met Albert, in a prison . . ."

"I know," I muttered. "In Germany. He told me that."

He said curtly, "That's all. That is why I . . . am indulgent to Gabrielle and Albert. They know. And such things are not forgotten in France. I won a name as a leader of the Maquis, I was decorated after the war, I won respect throughout France. All these things would be taken away from me if that was known. My life could be taken with them, or perhaps not now, after . . . the other things. But I would certainly be disgraced. I would probably go to prison. It could cost me the wealth—which I hope to leave to you one day."

"I don't know what to say," I mumbled, confused. "It all happened so long ago. Afterward you fought well for France. You have done so much since."

He stood up abruptly. "Judge me, if you will, Denise. For I have put these things in your hands now. You know as much as they do. I am as much in your power as theirs, remember?"

"I would never speak a word to harm you," I said, dismayed by the thought. He nodded, as though he had expected no less.

"See how much I trust you," he said, "to speak of this to you. But you must also trust me, Denise. Well, we will see. Good night, Denise. Try to sleep. I will instruct them not to wake you early in the morning."

"Good night, Uncle Maurice," I muttered.

I watched him close the door gently. The necklace felt strange and heavy around my bruised throat.

CHAPTER SEVEN

I WOKE UP TO AN impatient hammering on my door, starting up in fear that like the last wisps of fog still clung to my mind from last night.

"Who's there?" I called.

"Gabrielle. I have brought your tray."

I slid out of bed and groped for slippers and robe. The pain in my throat that had woken me up during the night was gone, but the marks of Uncle Maurice's fingers still showed plainly against the white skin.

I fumbled with the chair, dragging it aside, and Gabrielle came in, glancing at it contemptuously. "So now you bar your door against us?"

I fought the stirring of anger. I had decided before I fell asleep that I would no longer antagonize Gabrielle, for fear that I would endanger Uncle Maurice. So I forced a smile and took the tray from her and put in on the bedside table.

"You are a woman, Gabrielle. When you were my age wouldn't what happened last night make you find some way of keeping your door closed?"

"I was never as soft, or as silly as you," she snorted. "I am sure of that. Of what use would a chair be against anyone determined who wanted to get in here?"

"Perhaps. But knowing it was there helped me to sleep."

"Pah!" she muttered. "How foolish can a young girl be! But maybe there is a scheming brain inside that pretty head

86

of yours. So you got around him, last night, eh? And now suddenly we're all friends?"

"I'd like it to be that way," I said. "And I'm prepared to try. Are you?"

She looked at me suspiciously. "You are, eh? Why? What went on in here last night after we left you?"

I shrugged. "What could there be between Uncle Maurice and me? He said he was sorry that he'd hurt me. I said that I was sorry that my foolishness had upset him. We agreed to forget it. That's all."

"He bribed you," she said, with a suspicious glint in her black eyes. "You like pretty things, eh? Dresses? Jewels, perhaps?"

"Jewels?" I laughed. "What girl doesn't! You talked once about when you were younger. Don't tell me you didn't like pretty things."

"It was a time of war. A hard time. Still, even war had its compensations." She nodded, studying me intently. "But a woman who can be bribed cannot be trusted. Perhaps he gave you a gift, eh? And now you hope for more. Is that why you are trying to appease me?"

I am not long on patience. "I give up!" I said angrily. "All I'm trying to do is make my stay here a little more pleasant for both of us. You seem to resent me being here, though I've done nothing to make you dislike me. But have it your way. If that's what it has to be—keep away from me. At least the mutual inconvenience should not be for very long."

She gave me a strange, thoughtful look. "You have decided not to stay then? You intend to go back to America?"

"People are more friendly there."

"So? And when will you leave, eh?"

It took effort to answer with any civility, for that was going too far. But I remembered what Uncle Maurice had said, and compressed my lips.

"The way you make me feel unwelcome here, I should book my passage tomorrow. And perhaps I will!"

She nodded, a look of satisfaction coming into her mean eyes. She laughed. "Giving poor Gabrielle the blame, of course. Ah well. I have broad shoulders, and could bear it. You have a certain spirit. Perhaps under different circumstances we could have got along together. I shall try to be nice to you until you leave here, now that I know that you do not intend to stay with us for good. Now don't start thinking how insolent I am, and how I don't seem to know a servant's place. For neither you nor anyone else could ever teach me that. So eat your lunch, and I will let a little light and air in here."

She strode across the room and drew back the curtains. Bright sunlight flooded in, reminding me of that first day when she had done the same thing, and I had watched the slaughter of the pigeons.

"If my uncle is practicing shooting today, you needn't bother with that, thank you, Gabrielle," I said hurriedly.

She laughed. "And there too you have won a victory, eh? Do you see the vultures? The pigeons are below on the lawns, more of them than I have seen for a long time, for Labrousse fed them well this morning—on a different grain it seems. Can't you hear them below?"

She watched me as I stared toward the window, suddenly hearing the busy cooing of pigeons below.

"They are not afraid?" I asked, surprised.

"They never were afraid," she said contemptuously. "At least—not until it was too late for fear."

My curiosity drew me warily to the window. The lawns below were covered with pigeons, the white ones spreading their tails and between picking, pursuing the female of their choice. They were eating greedily and without ill-effect. I glanced up involuntarily, seeking the vultures. No dark specks floated above the chateau, or sat replete in the trees or on the stone wall.

"Where are the vultures?" I asked, surprised.

"I thought that would please you. They are not here. They have fed elsewhere, and fed well no doubt. Up in the forest. Look up there at the edge of the forest and you will see them."

I stared across the vineyards. Villagers worked in a different field, and I saw Albert with them, and Labrousse. Beyond, at the edge of the forest I could make out an irregular line of black dots on the branches, motionless. I shivered, and looked away.

"Someone fed them up there?"

"Someone fed them. Your uncle and Albert went up there this morning. No doubt they shot a pig, or perhaps a deer or a wolf. Slit the skin here and there to make feeding easier, and by night nothing is left save the bones and a little flesh that the wolves will scatter and devour at their leisure no doubt. Wolves have a taste for bone marrow." Her eyes gleamed. "Or perhaps they killed two wolves and dragged one of the bodies into the caves for them to feed on tomorrow, eh, Mademoiselle? And so the vultures still eat, and Mademoiselle's sensitive nature is not offended. I can remember a time when the master was not so considerate."

She grinned and left me feeling the better for our parting. I nibbled the food and drank coffee. Outside the day sparkled like champagne. In the fields some of the villagers were singing as they worked. I showered and dressed. In relief I thought about Etienne Métier at Vaison. This morning even a man who lived the extraordinary life of a special agent for the French Government seemed a nice, normal person compared to the people of Château-les-Vautours. I thought of Etienne almost with affection.

I had long since forgiven poor Pierre Bourget, and of Madeleine I had only pleasant memories. I would have liked to drive to Vaison again today, but the day was already partly spent and I had to go to the village to telephone the consulate for Uncle Maurice. But my thoughts fled to Vaison in relief. They were mostly, I admitted secretly, thoughts of Etienne Métier's friendly eyes and handsome, tanned face.

I remembered how he had pleaded for me to sit for him, and I hoped that he would come to the village of Tocsin, even though I doubted that my uncle would allow him to remain or even see me.

But after I had dressed in a high-necked sweater and skirt, I took the rubies from my locked traveling bag and put them on and admired them again. They were certainly lovely. Diamonds might be a girl's best friend, but I decided I'd settle for rubies like these any time. In the daylight they glowed softly, with a rich, dark red against the gold. Even over my white high-necked sweater they looked magnificent, and I took them off only reluctantly.

I could not doubt Uncle Maurice's generosity in giving them to me. I was locking them away again in my traveling case when I heard singing someplace, coupled with the sound of an approaching truck. Some man with an unusually pleasant tenor voice was singing above the uncertain engine sound.

"*Tiens voilà du boudin . . .*" he sang. "Here's the blood sausage, the blood sausage, the blood sausage, for the Alsations, the Swiss and the Lorrainers. . . ."

I walked to the window and stared out. An ancient truck was climbing the road from the gates toward the chateau, turning now into the gravel drive. I watched it pass beneath my window on its way to the kitchen door. It was piled high with fruit and vegetables, bags of grain and flour, and what were obviously the swatched shapes of hams and sides of bacon. In the back the singer stood bareheaded, the sleeves of his worn shirt rolled to the elbows to reveal the brown arms.

89

Etienne Métier!

I felt an unexpected, quite unaccountable elation at seeing him again. His funny song I felt was intended to attract my attention. I leaned out the window and waved, and his eyes that had been searching the windows as he passed saw me at once, and a smile changed his face, making it almost boyish.

"Good morning, Mademoiselle," he called up in a clear voice. "I hope you are enjoying your vacation? Is it not a glorious morning? What light to paint a portrait, eh? And these mountains and vineyards, and this place . . ."

I found myself laughing as I had not laughed before in the Château-les-Vautours. Almost as though I were back in New Orleans, and that was my date in an old car wanting to take me to a dance, and trying to find the courage to ask my grandfather.

It was a long time since I had taken such care with my make-up. I ran downstairs, hearing Gabrielle's unpleasant voice in the kitchen accusing the Marceaus of some neglect.

My uncle was coming from the library, for I heard him cough and close the door carefully behind him. His feet sounded on the stairs as I reached the reception room and looked round quickly.

Gabrielle's voice came to me from the kitchen, belligerently. "And since when, Marceau, have you been allowed to bring strangers to the chateau, eh? The place for our tenants at Vaison is home on their fields and at work. Not loafing around up here."

"He told me what a delightful housekeeper M'sieur Gerard had, Madame Bremen," Etienne's voice said, laughing. "He sings your praises day and night after he has been to the chateau. Isn't that right, Jacques? And such a fine cook too, he says. Oh, I, Etienne Métier, know quite a lot about you, Madame Gabrielle Bremen, believe me. Why he drives poor jealous Madame Marceau to the brink of insanity the way he talks about you. And a woman who can do that to Jacques; Jacques who has the cold blood of fish in his veins as you might expect in someone with fish's eyes; why Madame, such a woman I had to see for myself. Right, Jacques?"

"He is mad, as all his kind are mad," Jacques' voice growled uneasily. "Take no notice of the fellow, Madame Gabrielle."

"You see?" Etienne laughed. "You see how skillfully he hides his affection for you? But do not be disappointed, Madame Bremen—it is only because poor Marie is outside listening. If you two were alone in here I'll bet he'd sing a different song."

"Fool," Gabrielle grunted. "Though you are right about

90

his fish's looks and blood. Who'd have him, indeed? . . . Labrousse should not have let you past the gates. . . . Why did you bring him, Marceau?"

"He pestered me, Madame Gabrielle. He—"

"This is the artist, eh? Métier? Young man, you do not look much like an artist to me. Or act like one. Or sing like one."

"*Tiens voilà du boudin, voilà du boudin, voilà du boudin. . .*" I could almost see his eyes half-closed quizzically in there. "Dear Madame Gabrielle, you intrigue me almost as much as you do poor Jacques. There is no doubt you have a wit. Why should I not sing of blood sausage, when we brought you strings of it? Why not indeed?"

"Where did you learn to sing that song, eh, artist? Not in any studio, I'll swear. Where then?"

He laughed. "Where then?" he mocked her. "She is clever also, eh? Madame, don't you know what song that is?"

"Of course I know it," Gabrielle snorted. "I asked where *you* learned it, since you are supposed to be an artist, not a fighting man, M'sieur."

"Perhaps Madame has heard of Dien Bien Phu then, and also of the Third Regiment of the Foreign Legion that fought there against the Viet-Minh and Ho Chi Minh? That was my regiment. That was our song."

"In Indo-China? Vietnam?" she asked incredulously.

"But of course, Madame. Where else?"

"And what are you, who have been a soldier in the Legion, doing wasting your time painting, and working on a farm, eh?"

"If you had been in Dien Bien Phu, you would not ask that one, Gabrielle," Etienne's voice said, feelingly. "Anything would be better than Dien Bien Phu and fighting the Viet-Minh."

"Pah!" Gabrielle said disgustedly. "You are as weak as the rest of your kind. I have been in worse places than that. Many times. Now get out of my kitchen and make room. There is work to do."

"Oh, I can take a hint," Etienne laughed. "I will sit in the sun outside and wait for poor Jacques."

"And send that fool Marie in while you're about it. Does she think she can sit on her fat buttocks out there while I do all the work?"

"I wouldn't be surprised. But I'll tell her." He started to whistle cheerfully, and the sound went outside, stopped briefly as he reached the truck, and then pursued its musical way around toward the front of the chateau.

"That is the artist? The nephew of the Bourgets'?"

I had forgotten Uncle Maurice, but he had been standing silently just behind me. I jumped, startled. "Why yes, Uncle. Etienne Métier is his name."

"An artist, eh? It is easy to say. Every rogue in France claims to be either an artist, a writer, or sculptor. It is an easy way of living off the charity of others. Or concealing one's real aims." His voice had a curious edge of suspicion.

I said: "Oh but M'sieur Métier is an artist, Uncle Maurice. I have seen his work, and it is very good."

"At Vaison? It is easy to claim the work of another."

"But this was his own work," I said indignantly. "He was working on one picture when I was there. A landscape with figures working among the wheat."

"You saw him painting it?"

I stared at him. "Why are you so suspicious of M'sieur Métier, Uncle Maurice?"

"Did you see him painting, Denise?" he demanded, frowning at me.

"No, I didn't actually see him painting. He was working in the fields with his uncle and aunt. But I saw a half-finished painting, another only recently dry. He asked permission to paint my portrait."

He sighed and looked away. "You know why I am suspicious. It has become second nature down the years. I have a horror that one day all France will know about me. . . ."

His voice died, and I said impulsively: "I'm sorry, Uncle. But there is no danger of that, unless it comes from Gabrielle or Albert. What danger could come to you from M'sieur Métier?"

He glanced at me. "I have told you, I do not always think clearly about these things, or need a reason to suspect strangers."

But a thought had occurred to me, and I hardly heard him. "Uncle, if you are suspicious of M'sieur Métier—why not allow him to paint my portrait? He said that he would paint me here, or in Tocsin. It would not be any inconvenience. If he painted me, then you would quickly discover that he is not only really an artist—but also happens to be a very good one."

"I am something of a connoisseur of the arts," he muttered, studying me. "I would know in a moment, you understand that?"

I smiled. "And I know that if he does, you may have quite a valuable painting one day. I'm sure of that."

"Valuable? There are no longer good, really good French painters," he said gloomily. "Picasso is Spanish. Braque and

Léger but follow Picasso. Jacques Villon, the semi-abstractionist, Caillard the realist, the primitives? I care for none of them. And as you know, I do not like strangers coming to the chateau."

"He could paint me in the village."

He studied me for a long moment. "Are you interested in this young man, Denise? Has he as you Americans say . . . made the pass?"

I flushed crimson. "Really, Uncle Maurice! I've met M'sieur Métier only once, and then only for a few minutes and as your tenant. I have no interest in him whatever. But it would be fun to have my portrait painted."

He nodded slowly. "Very well. Tell him you may sit for him. I will pay him well for the portrait, if I consider it good."

I smiled, feeling the hot color fading from my cheeks. "He will want to thank you, no doubt. Like most artists, he does not appear to have much money. He works in the fields beside the Bourgets at Vaison, and at the mill. He appears to be working for the Marceaus today."

"No thanks are necessary, Denise," he said. "I must speak to Marceau. You tell him." He started to turn away, and stopped, frowning. He came back to stare at me intently. "If he paints you, Denise," he said in a low voice, "you will not wear the necklace I gave you. That is important. And you will keep your throat covered. Understand?"

I shrugged. I could understand the latter, for I had no intention of allowing anyone to paint the marks of bruising on my throat. But I *had* thought of wearing the rubies at once when he said he would permit Etienne to paint me. Yet he was right, of course; to wear the rubies I must show my throat.

"Whatever you say, Uncle Maurice."

His eyes smiled at me briefly. He nodded. "We are beginning to understand one another now, eh, Denise? You will find that you will not be the loser for that. And perhaps one day soon there will be no need for any more of this suspicion, eh?"

"I am sure of that, Uncle Maurice," I said with confidence. I smiled at him, and tried not to hurry toward the front doors.

Outside, the sunlight was glaring, and I blinked impatiently while my eyes adjusted to the brilliance, seeking Etienne. I discovered him where I would have least expected him, for he had crossed the lawn and sat on the grass beneath the trees in deep shadow, his dark head bent over something white on his knee.

As I walked closer, my footsteps silent on the grass, I saw that he was sketching rapidly.

He glanced up at me and grinned, and went on with what he was doing as though he had seen or heard me the moment I left the front of the chateau.

"Are you sketching the chateau, M'sieur?" I asked indignantly. "My uncle will be most annoyed if he sees you."

"Most annoyed," he agreed. "That's why I came over here where he can't see me from the kitchen." He put his head on one side and stared at the page of the pad, and then nodded. "Not bad at all," he said. He stood up and caught my arm. "Now, that leaves only the south side windows. Come on. Your uncle will be coming back from the kitchen very soon. He will look for us then, being human—at least, in part human. He may even step outside the front door looking for us. By then we will be turning the corner on our way back with the sketches of the four sides of the chateau complete. But we will have to hurry, eh, Denise?"

It would have taken force to detach my arm from his hand, as I was hurried toward the corner of the house across the lawns.

"You're making me a party to something I don't understand," I protested. "I have no wish to annoy my uncle."

"I can understand that, Denise," he said grimly. "I would sooner annoy the devil himself. But if we hurry, there's no immediate danger. So come on. Hurry."

"No. I want no part of this. I . . ."

We went around the corner almost running. The rose gardens were on this side of the chateau, set among lawns and shrubs. Most of the wing on this side, I knew from my tour of the chateau with Uncle Maurice, was unused. I breathed easier as he released his grip on my arm.

"Give me five minutes," he said. "That's all I need. Stay near the corner. Or better still, wait until I signal you and then walk back toward the front door as though you're looking for me. That should clear you with dear Uncle Maurice, shouldn't it?"

"He doesn't mind where *I* go. It's *you*."

"Exactly," he said. "Now don't waste time, there's a good girl. When I wave to you, back you go. You haven't seen me. Right?"

"No, it isn't right," I said indignantly. "Whatever you're up to, M'sieur, I don't like it. I want no part of it."

But he was already gone across the lawns, walking with long, swinging strides. I watched him turn to study the chateau, walk back a few steps, and then squat and begin sketching rapidly again.

I watched him, simmering silently and impatiently. Etienne Métier was a most exasperating young man.

He glanced down at his watch and waved his hand at me with a shooing motion, as though I were some chicken that had intruded curiously into his studio in the farmhouse at Vaison. To the devil with him! I'd go inside right now, and let him do his own explaining to Uncle Maurice if he caught him with his sketchbook and pencil.

I walked angrily back around the corner, and stared in surprise. Uncle Maurice was doing exactly what Etienne had expected him to do. He had evidently come back from the kitchen to the front door in search of us, and now he came slowly down the steps and stared around. He saw me approaching almost at once, and waited there frowning at me, a grim figure with black velvet covering his face beneath the eyes.

"Where is he?" he demanded as I came up, his eyes fierce.

I shrugged. "M'sieur Métier? I don't know, Uncle. I thought he might have walked around the chateau. After all, he's an artist and the chateau is a beautiful and historic building."

His scowl deepened. "He isn't there?"

"I can't see him," I replied ambiguously. "But perhaps he merely walked back toward the kitchen as I came out. You didn't see him there?"

"No," he muttered. "I did not see him there. But he could have been walking back as I came from talking to Marceau."

"And while I came outside looking for him here," I said, smiling. "Why, of course. No doubt that is where he is right now, at the kitchen, or in the truck waiting for the others. Shall we walk around there together? You decided you'd talk to him yourself, Uncle?"

He hesitated momentarily, and I realized suddenly that this was the first time I had ever encountered my uncle outside the chateau. But he merely nodded, and we started walking briskly around the gravel path, passing the library window up there and the window of Uncle's room, and then my own room high up on the far corner before we turned toward the kitchen and the servants' quarters.

"He doesn't seem to be here," my uncle muttered angrily.

"Someone's in the truck," I said quickly, hoping my voice did not sound too anxious, for I expected the figure in the front seat to be Marie Marceau since it could not possibly be Etienne. That oaf I was sure was still around on the south side of the chateau making his sketches.

"There are *two* men in the truck," my uncle grunted. He stopped abruptly, staring, and I with him. "Who else did that idiot Marceau bring with him?"

"I saw nobody else except Madame Marceau. . . ."

But he was walking grimly toward the truck now, and I followed him, hurrying to keep up as I watched the front door of the truck open, and Etienne slide down, smiling at us both cheerfully.

"Good morning, Mademoiselle, M'sieur," he greeted us. His eyes met mine briefly, reassuringly. To get there so fast I knew that he must have had to run along the southern wall of the chateau, and most likely scramble over the ruined wing almost under the noses of Gabrielle and the people in the kitchen. But he looked so calm and breathed so easily that that seemed incredible.

I stared at him dumbly until my uncle spoke curtly: "You are Métier?"

"Yes, sir! Etienne Métier, at M'sieur's service."

My uncle stared past him to the truck. "And this one?"

"Pierre Bourget, M'sieur. My uncle and your tenant. Pierre, where are your manners? Say good-day to M'sieur and Mademoiselle Gérard."

"Good day, Mademoiselle, M'sieur."

I watched the familiar gesture as Pierre Bourget took off his cap and bent his head humbly. My uncle scowled at him.

"What are you doing here, Bourget?" he demanded.

"I helped with the loading, M'sieur."

"How many men does it take to load and unload a truck? Let Marceau do his own work in future, Bourget. And you also, Métier. There is no welcome for strangers at the Château-les-Vautours."

"It is my fault, M'sieur," Etienne said quickly. "Since Pierre is your tenant at Vaison, I thought you should meet. You haven't met M'sieur Gérard before, have you, Pierre?"

"M'sieur's face is covered," Pierre mumbled. "How could one say?"

My uncle stared back at Pierre with sudden intensity, and I could see Pierre's hands on the cap starting to tremble.

"Does this man think he has met me before somewhere?" he asked in an angry voice.

"M'sieur," Etienne said calmly: "As I said, I just thought that as landlord and tenant you should meet. It was meant civilly enough. My uncle Pierre has improved the farm greatly, and I have helped him. A landlord should know what his tenants do. But if the thought offends you . . ."

96

My uncle glanced at him, then back at Pierre. "Was it long ago you thought we might have met?"

"Long ago, M'sieur. But . . . I cannot tell."

"It was during the war, perhaps?" My uncle moved closer, past Etienne who stepped aside, warily.

"Perhaps, M'sieur," Pierre muttered in a frightened voice. "My memory is . . . not what it was. I . . ."

"None of us are what we were, Bourget," my uncle said in the same odd voice. He put his head and shoulders into the cabin of the truck and I watched unbelievingly as his left hand came up and slipped off the mask. He thrust his face toward Pierre, who cringed away with his eyes staring and his hands moving up involuntarily toward his own face. My uncle stood there bent forward, the square of velvet folded in a triangle in his left hand. His right arm moved abruptly, and Pierre cried out sharply, for the steel claw had caught his right hand at the wrist, closing upon it like a vice.

Pierre mumbled something unintelligible, staring at my uncle's face and shaking his head slowly. He had withdrawn to the far side of the cabin, held there only by my uncle's claw gripping his wrist.

"If I had met you, I would remember you, Bourget," my uncle said. He released the man's wrist and his fingers brought up the triangle of velvet, the claw joined his fingers in fastening the knot again with an astonishing dexterity before he turned slowly and looked at Etienne contemptuously, the mask back precisely in place.

Etienne said in a cold voice: "I told you the fault was mine, M'sieur. It was not necessary to hurt him, or frighten him if he is frightened of such scars."

"So you are an artist, eh?" my uncle said, as though Etienne's words had no importance whatever. "And you wish to paint a portrait of my niece?"

Etienne nodded slowly, as though considering.

"So Mademoiselle Gérard mentioned that? Yes, it is true. I am an artist, and I wish to paint her portrait."

"Very well," my uncle said curtly. "You shall paint her. You have a commission, Métier. Name your fee."

I watched color come into Etienne's face. "Mademoiselle Gérard has great beauty, M'sieur. I like to paint what is beautiful. I had no thought of a fee when I made the offer. I meant the painting to be a gift to her, to remind her of France when she returns to her own country. That was all."

"It is I who will make the gift—not you. You will paint my niece as a commission, or not at all."

Etienne shrugged. "Then I will paint her as a commission, M'sieur. One thousand francs is a fair figure."

My uncle nodded. "I see you do not value your art very highly. Very well. M'sieur Cloete at the inn will provide you with a room to work in. His wife no doubt will see that you restrict your efforts to painting. There is no need for you to come here again. You can make all your arrangements with Madame Cloete. Come with me, Denise. Good day, Métier . . . Bourget."

"Good day, M'sieur, Mademoiselle," Etienne murmured.

I turned away slowly to follow my uncle, relieved that it was over. A thousand francs was about two hundred American dollars. I could feel Etienne's eyes following me as I walked away. My uncle walked silently without looking back.

I was glad I would see Etienne again. But what on earth had he been up to today? Sketching the chateau without my uncle knowing and bringing Pierre Bourget with him. I shuddered at the thought of that disturbing scene.

Who could forget my uncle's scarred, tortured face? I knew that I never would.

CHAPTER EIGHT

AFTER THE UNPLEASANT scene of the morning, my uncle regained his good spirits. Over a delicious salad lunch and a dry white wine he became almost gay. He talked hopefully of what American surgeons might do for his scars, and gave me innumerable instructions on how to conduct my conversation with the embassy. He even seemed pleased that Etienne Métier was to paint my portrait.

"Who knows," he exclaimed cheerfully, "I might even buy some more of his work if it is as good as you claim, Denise. And I will know, you understand, as soon as I see this portrait, whether he is a charlatan or a genius."

I finished the last of a refreshing cup of coffee and smiled back. "Well, I don't know that he's quite in the genius class, Uncle Maurice. But I'm sure he's not a fraud."

"We'll see." Uncle Maurice stood up and came around the table to hold my chair. "If you are going to make that call you had better do it now. I know these officials—their working day seems to finish after lunch."

I stood up and brushed flakes of bread from my skirt. "I'll go right away." Impulsively I put my hand on his arm and this time he did not flinch away. "And I'm sure I'll have some good news for you."

His rare smile came and went behind the mask. "It's a bit far to walk, Denise, you had better take the car."

He handed me the keys and stood watching until I had backed the Mercedes out of the garage and started down the drive.

Tocsin was quiet in the afternoon sun. The men must have been working in the fields still or sleeping off the effects of the lunchtime wine. But my knock at the door of the house adjoining the inn was answered quickly. A plump, smiling woman opened the door and stood gazing at me curiously.

"Madame Cloete?"

"Yes, Mademoiselle?" She had the same high color as her husband and evidently the same preference for the local wine I could smell on her breath.

"I am from the chateau, Madame. Did a young man call here this morning? He was to arrange for a room to paint . . ."

"Ah, of course. M'sieur Métier. And you are the subject of the portrait. Please, Mam'selle, come in. Would you care for a glass of wine?"

"Thank you, no. I've just finished lunch." I allowed myself to be led inside. "Did M'sieur Métier make a definite arrangement with you?"

She plumped herself down in a curved, thickly padded rocking chair, her work-worn hands clasped across her stomach.

"Yes Mam'selle, it is all arranged. Tomorrow at ten he will be here and expecting you. He said the morning light would be best as our rooms lose the light in the afternoon." Madame Cloete put a hand to her mouth to smother a yawn. "Mademoiselle is looking forward to the occasion?"

"Oh yes," I laughed. "This is the first time anyone has wanted to paint me."

She looked at me shrewdly between half-closed lids. "And such a handsome young man, isn't he?"

I felt a surge of color come to my face and changed the subject hurriedly.

"M'sieur Gérard has told me you have a telephone here."

"Yes, Mam'selle. You wish to call someone?"

"Yes. I have to call a . . . a friend in Paris."

"Paris, eh?" Her eyes gleamed with curiosity then slitted as she yawned again. She heaved herself from the comfortable chair and beckoned me to follow. Down the short, dim passage she stood back and opened a door.

"Here it is, Mam'selle." The room was scarcely bigger than a closet. It contained only a table and a hard chair and on the table was a telephone which must have been an antique.

"You turn this handle until the bell rings, Mam'selle, and when the girl answers you give her your number. You know the number you want?"

"Well, no, I don't. . . ."

"No matter. This is connected to the exchange in Aurillac. The girl will find it for you."

I sat down at the table and took a pad and pencil from my bag. Madame Cloete hesitated in the doorway.

"There is something else Mam'selle requires?"

"No thank you, Madame," I replied firmly.

"All right." She seemed disappointed. "I shall wait in the front room."

I waited for her footsteps to fade before I lifted the receiver and gave the handle a brisk turn.

After about ten minutes of confusion and staccato French voices, I finally got through to the American Embassy. An Under Secretary questioned me closely about my uncle's reasons for wanting to enter the United States.

"There should be no great difficulties," he said at last. "I will mail the papers immediately. Your uncle must fill them in himself before a notary. And since your uncle is a wealthy man, Miss Gérard, it shouldn't be too much of a problem to find a photographer willing to go to the chateau to take the photographs for the visa."

I thanked him and hung up, and started back down the passage. Madame Cloete was sitting in the rocking chair, an empty wine glass beside her. Her eyes were closed and her mouth slightly open. Resonant snores shook her well-padded frame and set the chair gently in motion. I stiffled a giggle and a longing for a camera of my own at this moment and tiptoed out, closing the door gently behind me. I would pay her for the call tomorrow.

The sun was already low as I drove through the gates and the chateau glowed in a warm mellow light. looking more beautiful than I had ever seen it. The villagers were returning from the fields, silhouetted against the brilliant sky. To my surprise my uncle was closeted in his library with strict orders not to be disturbed. Gabrielle gave me his apologies; some urgent business which could not wait until morning. Even more surprising, Gabrielle was pleasant, even gay, and totally incurious about my visit to the village. Uncle Maurice must have told her about Etienne Métier and the portrait.

I dined alone by candlelight at the huge table, waited on by a silent Gabrielle, and after coffee I went up to my room. I lay propped up on pillows in the soft bed, reading desultorily. But the print kept blurring, and in its place rose the tanned face of Etienne Métier.

The muted sounds from the kitchen ceased and the chateau was silent. I switched out the lamp and slid deeper into the bed.

Tomorrow. I would see Etienne tomorrow—

I was roused from sleep by Gabrielle's heavy knock at my door.

"Mademoiselle! Are you awake, Mademoiselle?"

"Yes, Gabrielle. What is it?" I stretched and yawned, reaching for my robe.

"M'sieur Gérard wishes you to join him at breakfast. In thirty minutes, Mademoiselle."

"Okay." I slid out of bed and made for the bathroom.

Thirty minutes later I found Uncle Maurice at his breakfast—fresh warm croissants and hot chocolate.

"Well, Denise," he said, his eyes smiling behind the mask. "Did you sleep well?"

"Just fine." I warmed my hands around a mug of chocolate. "Like a log."

"Good. I am sorry I could not dine with you last night and hear your news. Did it go well?"

"No trouble at all, like you said, Uncle Maurice. They are going to send the papers for you to fill out. They should be in the mail now."

"Excellent. Now what exactly did they ask you?"

Uncle Maurice questioned me minutely about the telephone conversation and when he had finished there was nothing left of breakfast but a few bread crumbs. And it was almost ten—Etienne Métier would be waiting.

I pushed my chair back. "Uncle Maurice, may I take the car to go to the village? The first sitting was arranged for this morning and I'll be late if I walk."

"Ah yes, the artist awaits. Very well, here are the keys. And I wonder if you would make another call for me. To Alphonse Rouzier—here, I will write it down for you." He took a notebook from his coat, and wrote a few words, painfully and clumsily with his left hand. "This is his number in Paris—he is my broker. You will tell him that one parcel is on its way and that there will be one last consignment after that. A very large one. Can you remember that?"

"Yes, Uncle Maurice." I glanced surreptitiously at my watch. Five after ten already. "Is that all?"

"Just one other thing, Denise." He bent down and produced a parcel from under the table. It was about the size of a shoebox, wrapped in heavy paper and sealed with wax. He handed the parcel to me and I was surprised by its weight. "This is to go by special mail, Denise. It is stamped and ready, and a messenger will call for it at the inn at half past one. You have just to hand it to him."

"Yes, Uncle Maurice. Good-by. I'll be back this afternoon."

I parked the Mercedes near the inn alongside the ancient truck I had last seen when the Marceaus had come to the chateau. Unaccountably, my heart seemed to beat faster as I almost ran toward the house. This is ridiculous, I told myself firmly, and slowed to a more dignified walk. What did Etienne Métier mean to me? He was just a man. An attractive man, but . . . I remembered the look in his gray eyes that time at the farm when he had asked me to sit for him. Nonsense, I must have been imagining things.

My hand barely touched the door before it flew open as though someone had been standing right behind it.

"Denise!" Etienne Métier drew me inside swiftly and closed the door. "I was beginning to think your uncle had changed his mind."

"No," I smiled at him, flattered by his impatience. "We were just a bit late with breakfast and then my uncle asked me to—"

"No matter," he interrupted, starting down the passage. "You are here, so let's get started."

He threw open a door and sunlight flooded the passage. As I walked in I saw an easel set up with a blank canvas, and a box with tubes of paint and brushes—

"Good morning, Mademoiselle Gérard."

The strange voice made me start. A man was standing in the far corner of the room, screened from both the windows and the door by the easel. I glanced apprehensively at Etienne Métier, who was standing with his back against the door. The strange man was gray-haired with a neat moustache and the erect bearing of one connected with the gendarmerie or the army.

"Who are you?" I asked, confused. "I mean, what—"

Etienne's hand caught my arm firmly, guiding me toward the older man.

"Denise, I would like you to meet my commanding officer, Colonel Guiet."

The colonel bowed slightly and gestured at me to a chair. But I remained standing, glaring at Etienne Métier.

"Just what is going on, M'sieur Métier?" I demanded indignantly. "Is this why you were so impatient for me to come? I don't believe you want to paint me at all."

"That's not true, Denise," he replied gently, urging me toward the chair. "I am going to paint you and I'm going to start today. But," he shrugged, "business before pleasure. Colonel, if you could explain."

The colonel bowed slightly. "Sit down please, Mademoiselle Gérard. We have reason to believe now that Franz Gebauer is somewhere in the vicinity of Tocsin village. We believe that he has been living in the Châtaigneraie secretly for many years. We believe also that you can help us find him if you will, by answering a few questions."

I shrugged and sat down, and looked at Colonel Guiet. "I can't understand how I can help you. What do you want to know?"

"Captain Métier has informed me that you mentioned meeting two young men on the road to Tocsin on the same day that Pierre Bourget attacked you at Vaison?"

I frowned. "Yes, I met two young men. Hitchhikers. They asked me the way to Tocsin. They were looking for someone there. A friend of the father of one of them, they said. They showed me his photo, and asked if I knew him, or had seen him in Tocsin or at the chateau."

Colonel Guiet looked at Etienne angrily. "You did not tell me this, Captain!"

"I did not know it," Etienne said, flushing. "She neglected to mention that to me. What she said was merely something that she mentioned in passing as unimportant. It only became important after I had received the report on the two Israelis."

I said indignantly: "I mentioned it to you because I thought they might be engaged in the same search. I thought you'd want to know more about them. When you did not ask, I felt sure they were your men and you did not wish to speak of them."

"My mistake, then," Etienne muttered, obviously embarrassed as he looked at the colonel.

The colonel made an impatient sound. "Nothing is too trivial for attention, Captain. Mademoiselle, are these the two men you met?"

They were in a single photo, sitting at a table drinking what looked like beer in long glasses. They wore shirts and shorts, and their caps were upside down on the table. I could not mistake those dark, intent faces.

"Why yes, they are. We talked for a little while after they stopped my car. I'm sure they're the same men. They spoke French with an accent that sounded . . . well, German, I thought."

"They are Israeli," Colonel Guiet said quietly. "But you are right about the accent, Mademoiselle. They were both born in Germany. Did you hear names? Did they address each other by name perhaps?"

I nodded, studying the photo again. "Yes, they did. This one was called . . . Jules. This Jossi, I think."

"Jossi and Jules Haurat," Colonel Guiet said, frowning thoughtfully. "There is no doubt in my mind about her identification, Captain. These are the men." He looked back at me. "They asked you the way to Tocsin, you said?"

"Yes, they did. They said they'd come in through the mountains from Mont Dore. They were not sure where they were. But they did not seem to me to be the kind of men who'd get lost easily."

"You are right, Mademoiselle," Guiet said. "They are not. Nor are they the kind of men to get lost on the way to Tocsin along a good road."

"But they may not have gone to Tocsin at all," I thought aloud. "They could have turned toward Vaison, or gone back over the Massif. I told them I might see them in the village when I got back later. I asked Cloete the innkeeper about them, and he said they hadn't come in to Tocsin, so they must have turned aside into one of the other roads before they reached the village."

"They did not reach Vaison, or any of the villages across the Massif," Colonel Guiet replied.

"So perhaps they found Gebauer, or Gebauer found them," Etienne's voice was grim.

Colonel Guiet nodded. He had brought out another photo and was studying it. He said: "In which case, Mademoiselle, the two young men you met, who happened to be Israeli agents, are either dead, or at this moment on their way out of France with Franz Gebauer in the same manner their people took Adolph Eichmann out of South America for trial and execution in Israel."

"In which case your purpose is served just the same," I said. "So why worry?"

"*If* they have Gebauer. *If* Gebauer did not kill them," Etienne muttered. "And if they do have him, how is that going to sound for France in the world's press, Denise? As propaganda? How will the outside world consider the

104

fact that Gebauer was able to live free in France for twenty-one years? This is not South America. This is *France*. Gebauer is one of the worst of war criminals. Almost as important in the public mind as Eichmann to be caught and punished for his infamous crimes."

"I see."

"Is this the same man you saw in the photo the Israeli showed you, Mademoiselle?"

I took it slowly from the colonel and examined it. I shivered. It was the same man, the face perhaps a little older, but even more evil for that in its darkly handsome way. I returned it hurriedly.

"It is the same man, Colonel," I said in a low voice. "Is that . . ."

"S. S. *Haupsturmfuehrer* Franz Gebauer," Colonel Guiet muttered. "At one time Assistant Commandant at Treblinka. Later given command of a camp on the River Spree below Berlin."

He put the photo carefully back into his pocket. "You have not seen a man in the Châtaigneraie resembling that photo, Mademoiselle? Much older naturally, for it was taken more than twenty years ago. Not long before Hitler died and Gebauer made his carefully planned disappearance. His hair could be gray, or white now. His face more deeply lined."

"No," I said with certainty. "I have not seen that man."

Colonel Guiet nodded slowly. "Your uncle, M'sieur Gérard, plans to go to America, Mademoiselle. Is this a sudden decision? Made in the last few days perhaps?"

"No, not really," I replied. "It is something my grand-father discussed by letter with me many—" I broke off and stared at the two men suspiciously. "How do you know my uncle is thinking of leaving France?"

"Just routine, Mam'selle," Colonel Guiet gestured. "We have been keeping tabs on everyone in this district for months now."

"But—I arranged it all by telephone." I was bewildered. "Nobody knew about that call but my uncle and myself."

"Your embassy is always very co-operative in the matter of apprehending war criminals, Mademoiselle. We have a useful arrangement with them. Now tell me, was your uncle's decision a sudden one?"

"No, I told you. He had spoken of it several times in letters. But why? Is there any reason why my uncle should not leave France, Colonel Guiet?"

"No," he said quietly. "I know of no reason why Maurice Gérard should not leave France, Mademoiselle. Yet I am

105

curious. You say it was considered for a long time, yet is it not true that the *decision* has only just been reached—since you arrived in France at your uncle's invitation?"

"I don't see why you need to ask me such questions, Colonel, since you already seem to have all the answers," I said angrily. "Put that way—yes. The final decision has only been reached since I arrived."

"It is your wish then, that he return with you?"

"And why not? He is the last of the Gérards, my only remaining relative on my father's side of the family. Yes, it is my wish. And if he delayed making the final decision, that is understandable. He is disfigured, and very sensitive about such things. And there is the problem of photographs to overcome. It took some persuasion from me to convince him to take the final step at last."

"Ah, yes," Colonel Guiet murmured. "A problem indeed." He turned his head and looked at Etienne. "Captain, does Duval still have his studio at Aurillac?"

"Yes, of course," Etienne said. He looked at me quickly, too quickly I thought. "Paul Duval is the answer to that problem, Denise. He is an excellent photographer. He is most discreet, and was himself once an active leader of the Maquis. He would understand how your uncle feels about these things, for he lost a leg during the war and his face is also scarred. I am sure Paul would go to the chateau to take the photographs for your uncle's visa. Or he is easily found in Aurillac; everyone knows Paul."

"Thank you," I said. "Paul Duval—I'll remember the name. That's all that you wanted to ask me, then?"

"And you have our thanks for being most co-operative, Mademoiselle," the colonel smiled, standing up. "I am sorry for interrupting your painting session, Mam'selle. But now I will leave you to it."

He crossed to the window, vaulted over the low sill and disappeared round the corner where the truck was parked. I stared after him, half astonished, half furious.

"Well!" I breathed, turning to glare angrily at Etienne Métier. "If you have quite finished your private inquisition M'sieur, I shall leave."

I picked up my bag and the parcel and marched to the door. I twisted the knob viciously—nothing happened. The door was locked. I swung around.

Etienne was leaning nonchalantly against the wall, tossing in one hand a heavy, old-fashioned key.

"How dare you, M'sieur! Open that door at once or I'll scream the place down."

"Please, Denise," he grinned placatingly. "I'm terribly sorr

106

about it, but I was under orders. There was nothing I could do—"

"Right now you can unlock that door," I snapped.

He stood his ground and spoke softly. "You are so lovely when you are angry, Denise. When we are married I shall keep you angry most of the time. I will be the proudest husband in France."

"What?" I cried indignantly, feeling the color rush into my cheeks hotly.

"It is the truth," he gazed at me steadily. "I intend to marry you one day, Denise; you might as well become accustomed to the idea. It occurred to me the moment I saw you in my bed at Vaison, and has never left my mind since. I swear it."

"Then it had better occur to you that I will surely say no!" I said. "In the unlikely event of your ever asking me nicely, that is. And it was not *your* bed at all, it was Madeleine's bed. And luckily for you I was unconscious at the time; otherwise, if you looked at me in the way what you just said seems to me to mean, you would certainly have had your face slapped, M'sieur."

"Because I looked at you with admiration?" He sounded astonished.

"Because you are bad-mannered and arrogant, and presumptuous," I said. "And right now I would like you to open that door so I can go. After this—this outrage I'm afraid you'll have to find another model."

"Ah," he said, as though suddenly enlightened. "I see it now. It is because of the questions the colonel asked about your uncle. You are not really angry with me at all. It is the poor colonel who has enraged you."

"You," I cried, "are a fool!"

He tilted his head back and laughed heartily. "Oh I know my faults, Denise. I know them very well. As you say, I am bad-mannered and arrogant, and . . .? What was that other? Yes, of course, presumptuous. And I am also certainly a fool, as any man who falls in love. But none of us is perfect, and you will learn in time to love me for my faults as well as for my qualities. I must have some good points, mustn't I? I have learned to love you for your faults, Denise. You are as hot-tempered as any French girl, and as spoiled as any American girl. And, as I informed the colonel, you are also impulsive and incapable of scheming, and I would not have you any other way at all. Certainly not."

"You," I said, "are the . . . the most insufferable. . . ! Oh!"

107

"Scoundrel?" he suggested in English. "No, not that. Villain? No, that . . . these are words no longer used much, eh? Perhaps stinker? No, that is English, isn't it? Smug, but that is not a noun?" He shook his head, looking comical as he considered, with his dark brows bent, his lips half-smiling. "Your American words elude me. But of one thing I am certain, Denise. If I had the art to paint you as you look now, so full at the same time of rage and beauty, they would surely hang it in the Louvre one day."

I will never know just how it happened then, but laughter came bubbling uncontrollably from my throat, and I found myself in his arms.

And he was saying gently, almost unbelievingly, as though a miracle had happened: "But it was true what I said, Denise. I do love you. Each time I look at your lips I wonder if they will remain closed against my kiss, or welcome me. . . ."

Afterward I sat for him for nearly two hours while he made preliminary sketches. And I knew this portrait would be good.

I was twenty-one and completely in love for the first time in my life. I knew that love was shining from my eyes as it was from his.

Etienne would not show me his sketches. "You must wait for the finished portrait. Oh, my Denise, it will be the best thing I have ever done."

He held me close for a moment and then kissed me gently.

"And now, my love, I must go."

"Must you go right away?" I pressed my face against his chest.

He turned away and started to gather up his equipment. "Colonel Guiet has been hiding in the truck all this time and I have to get him to the main road by half after one."

"Damn your colonel!"

He laughed at the spark that came into my eyes at the mention of Colonel Guiet.

"Wait here until the truck leaves, Denise. And I'll see you here the day after tomorrow. After lunch. I must go to Paris tomorrow but I'll be back in time."

He slipped out, leaving me standing in a daze. I heard the truck grind its way out of the village, but I did not leave the room until Madame Cloete's voice roused me from my stupor.

"Mademoiselle Gérard, are you there? A messenger is here to collect a parcel from M'sieur Gérard."

Still in a dream I handed over the parcel and then made the telephone call to Paris for Uncle Maurice.

I drove slowly back to the chateau with Etienne's last whispered words running through my head.

"Remember, darling, whatever happens, I love you. I will be watching over you. I will never be far away now that we have found each other. . . ."

CHAPTER NINE

TIME PASSED SLOWLY, but for once quite pleasantly at the chateau. Gabrielle seemed content with only an occasional vindictive remark. Her eyes told me plainly that in her mind she already had my bags packed for America. My uncle was now obsessed with the application, to which he seemed to be giving great thought and extraordinary care.

On the day of my next sitting, Uncle Maurice decided to drive to Vaison to see Marceau. The day was well chosen, for both Albert and Labrousse were occupied in the fields, each with a number of villagers to supervise. It seemed natural enough for me to offer to drive him there.

Gabrielle contented herself with a derogatory sniff, and some remark about me that I pretended not to hear. We detoured through Aurillac and Duval's studio, for I had suggested Duval to my uncle with the recommendation coming from the embassy, since I could not say that it came from Etienne. Duval proved to be a pleasant fellow, and he must certainly have proved tactful because except for a brief moodiness as we drove out of Aurillac, my uncle recovered quickly from the ordeal. He even seemed quite interested in the village of Vaison as we drove through it, though he refused to stop.

I could not see Etienne, but perhaps he was still on his way back from Paris. Madeleine and Pierre were working in the fields and turned to stare at us. And I saw the old mill, its stone walls somber even in the bright sunlight, and shivered as I remembered.

But Etienne would be in Tocsin this afternoon, I knew. He would be there waiting for me in Cloete's house, he would allow nothing to change that. Nothing.

I was glad that my uncle stayed for only a few words with the Marceaus. I did not like that surly couple with their mean ways. He decided to take the wheel for the return trip when we left, and drove expertly and at high speed, as though he had become impatient of my slower and more careful driving. He took the direct route from Vaison to Tocsin, avoiding the highway. It was rough, but it cut a lot of time on the return trip, enough time that our visit to Aurillac and Duval's studio would never be noticed.

We were back at the chateau for lunch, and afterward I hurried up to my room to change and make up my face.

When I was done, I stood for a minute gazing out the window. Again, no vultures hovered above the chateau today. Albert or Labrousse must have fed them in the forest in the morning while I drove my uncle to Vaison.

But as I looked for their humped shapes at the edge of the forest, I noticed also that the people of the village were gone from the fields, and when I looked toward the village itself, the great gates of the Château-les-Vautours were closed. I stared back at the forest again, frowning, and almost at once I saw the vultures. I stared at them with disgust. They were not sitting replete upon their branches as I had expected. They were circling above the trees at a point near the crest of the mountain. I watched them fascinated, reminded of my first day at the chateau, for they were flying in steadily decreasing circles as I had seen them do that day before they fell on the drugged and slaughtered pigeons.

They lost height slowly, converging upon one point, finally vanishing behind the trees. I stared at the forest and wondered on what they were feeding now.

I shuddered and pulled myself together. I had better get down to the village or Etienne would be wondering where I was. I picked up a handbag and ran gaily downstairs.

I expected Gabrielle to be in the kitchen, but she was not there. Neither were Marie Labrousse or Albert. The servants' quarters were empty.

Perhaps it was Gabrielle's afternoon off. I supposed she must have one. Though what she would do with an afternoon off puzzled me, unless she rested in her room. I couldn't imagine Gabrielle visiting friends in the village for a friendly chat.

I remembered the descending vultures suddenly. Perhaps she was up there with Albert feeding those horrible birds. That would be more like Gabrielle. I went out through

110

the kitchen door and stared around. Yes, the truck was gone, the garage locked, and the Mercedes inside. Gabrielle kept one key and my uncle the other so if I wanted to go to the village I'd have to walk.

I glanced up at my uncle's window, where I knew he was closeted with the application papers, wondering if I should disturb him. I decided against it. It was a fine afternoon for walking and it would not take long.

I walked softly on the grass until I came to the end of the drive. Ahead the road led down through the fields to the gates and the Labrousses' house. If the Labrousses were out also on this fine afternoon, I was out of luck, for the gates were sure to be locked as well as closed and the stone wall with its spiked top was too high for me to climb.

Still it was pleasant walking. The vines on either side of the road were green and pleasant to look at, the small green grapes were starting to swell with promise. The air was full of the sound of bees, gathering honey for the square, white-washed boxes that Pierre Labrousse tended high up on the slope. I thought of Etienne and was content.

The gates were locked, the great padlock and chain sagging heavily in place. I made my way through the Labrousses' garden and rapped on the door, hearing the slow shuffle of feet in response.

"I am coming," Marie's voice muttered beyond the door. "Have you forgotten your way inside? What is the matter with you today, Pierre. I—" The door opened and she stared at me, startled. "Mademoiselle! What are you doing here?" Her eyes looked beyond me toward the chateau quickly, with fear in them. I stared at her, surprised. Her eyes were reddened as though she had been crying, her face pale. Her usual friendly air was gone.

"I have an appointment in the village, Marie. That's all. Is something wrong?"

"Wrong, Mam'selle?" Her eyes came back to me, studying me anxiously.

"Haven't you been crying?"

"Why should I cry?" Her fingers went up to her eyes quickly, and fell away. "I have been asleep. Perhaps that has reddened my eyes, Mam'selle. It is a day for sleeping, and Pierre away with the others, driving them off somewhere in the forest in the truck. I know not where. . . ."

"With Gabrielle and Albert? So that's where they went?"

She looked at me evasively. "I do not know where they went. Does the master know you are going to walk to the village?"

111

I laughed at her. "Really, Marie. The chateau is not a prison. I do not have to account for every movement. To my uncle or anyone else. Would you mind opening the gates? I want to go through."

She looked at me doubtfully for a long moment. "Where are you going?"

I fought a rush of anger. "If it's of interest to you, Marie—I have an appointment with an artist. It is something my uncle arranged. So will you please open the gates."

"Yes, Mademoiselle," she muttered. "At once then."

She reached up to a hook inside the door and took down a great bunch of keys that might have been the pride of some medieval jailer. She came out blinking into the sunlight and glanced at me. "You will not be away long?"

"An hour or so perhaps. Why?" I asked, still seething inwardly.

"Because of the wolves, Mademoiselle," she said in a low voice. "It is not safe to walk alone here, by day or night. Louise and the other girls from the village are all terrified if they must do that at dusk. It is the time the wolves prowl down from the forest."

"Nonsense," I said. "I am not afraid of wolves or anything else in daylight, Marie. And I have no intention of walking around alone at night."

"It is bad luck to say such things. I will watch for you coming back. If it is late and Pierre is home he will walk to the chateau with you—if he does not bring the truck down. And if I do not hear you there is a bell here. . . ."

She showed me the bell, and the rope that dangled from it. It looked as though if rung sturdily it might serve as a tocsin for both the village and the chateau. I nodded curt thanks and walked quickly down the winding road to the village. The buzz of male voices came from the inn, and I remembered that the villagers had returned early from the fields above the chateau. I turned away from the inn itself toward the house where the Cloetes lived.

Madame Cloete opened the door and stared at me in surprise.

"Yes, Mademoiselle?"

"Good afternoon, Madame. I have come for my second sitting."

She frowned. "He is not here, Mademoiselle Gérard."

"He is not?" The disappointment I felt was quite out of proportion.

She shook her head, "Alas no, Mam'selle. It is not the

way the young man planned it, I am sure. It is the fault of Henri Cloete, that fool husband of mine."

"Perhaps he will come later. If I could wait here . . . ?"

"But of course, Mademoiselle. Come in. It is a great pity," she murmured sympathetically. "Henri spoke of talking to you on the day you came here. And the young man started asking questions about the two men you met on the road. Tocsin is a small place you understand, and such things interest us because there is little else to speak of here. They were sharing a bottle of wine, as men do, in the inn you understand, and there were others listening. And the baker mentioned that he had seen two such men while cutting wood for his ovens off the road to the Massif. . . . A glass of wine perhaps, Mademoiselle? . . . It is possible the M'sieur Métier may return at any moment, for he has been much longer than any of us expected. Still, artists are strange people, are they not? One is never quite sure what they will do."

The room was comfortable, almost bourgeois. Over the empty fireplace a soldier in uniform looked down at me from a hand-carved frame, a stern-faced replica of Henri Cloete posed stiffly.

"I have some Burgundy, if Mam'selle cares for red wine?"

"I like Burgundy, Madame, thank you."

"A fine wine," she said. She was fussing, standing to polish a spotless glass until it gleamed. I walked over to the photo and looked at it closer, then saw the glass-covered box with the medal and ribbon inside displayed like an offering beneath the photo.

I said, surprised: "Your husband won a *Croix de guerre*, Madame Cloete?"

"The brother of my husband, Mam'selle. His only brother, Jean. Are they not as alike as two peas from the same pod? It is a common mistake people make when they see the photo for the first time. Oh, my husband had courage all right. He fought with the Maquis, but there nobody noticed courage, for as Henri says, courage was a common thing."

I nodded. "This was in the fighting before the capitulation, of course. What a shame. And afterward, he was killed? War is cruel."

"Indeed it is." She brought the wine. "May we never know war again, Mam'selle."

"I'll drink to that," I smiled.

She nodded, and sipped with me, and looked at the photo. "Poor Jean. He was such a handsome young man too. Did you read the citation? He destroyed two German tanks,

113

no less. On a narrow mountain road. Those behind could not get past, and in the meantime his battalion was able to escape to better ground. He was killed of course. The decoration was posthumous. The President himself pinned the medal on Madame Cloete's breast and kissed her. What consolation for a mother. Though if it had been me, I would sooner have my son."

I stared at her, frowning. "But . . .? Madame, may I read the citation? You did say that your husband had only one brother?"

"Only one. They were very close. Jean was the elder by a year. The leader. Henri's grief was pitiful. . . ."

She talked on, but I did not hear. I was reading the faded citation intently. It was there. The decoration was posthumous. Corporal Jean Cloete had paid the supreme sacrifice that his friends might live. He had died as the second tank exploded.

I put it back slowly. Why had my uncle lied to me about Jean Cloete? He had not been killed by French partisans at all near the old mill at Vaison. He had been killed fighting as a soldier for France, months before the capitulation. Before there *were* any partisans in the Châtaigneraie, or the need for partisans existed. I shivered suddenly, remembering my uncle's tension that night, the story I had believed that had come so easily when it was needed.

But if Jean Cloete had died like that, then the whole story fell apart at once. My uncle had lied. If Gabrielle and Albert had some hold on him from which he sought to escape with my help to America, it was not because he had given information to the Germans that had caused the death of a French partisan leader. It was not that at all.

I turned, my wine forgotten in my hand. Madame Cloete was still talking. I answered perfunctorily, not sure what she had said.

"Your brother-in-law was a hero, Madame."

She laughed. "You misunderstood me, Mam'selle. I was no longer speaking of Henri's brother Jean, but of your friend the artist. What a curiosity he has. You should have heard the sharp way he questioned poor Achilles. I am speaking of the baker, of course. He had Achilles floundering as though he stood before a judge, no less. But Achilles stuck to his story. He insisted that he had watched the two young men climb the wall of the estate and go into the forest above the vineyards. So what? It is of no importance where young men go. There are so many of them footloose in France these days."

I murmured something. "Madame, where did M'sieur Métier go?"

She shrugged. "Where else but to look for those young men? A foolish thing, they must be long gone and all he'll find up there is the woods, empty."

"Of course," I muttered. I drained the wine in confusion and put down the glass. "Madame, I must be walking back."

"You won't wait for him then?" She raised her eyebrows in disappointment.

"If you would be so kind as to tell him that I called and that I'll get in touch with him tomorrow."

"Certainly. If he had spoken to Henri about it, Henri would have saved him time. Henri knows the Massif better than most men. He lived up there like a hunted animal with your uncle's band of Maquis during the war. He knows every inch of it. He was devoted to your uncle, though these days he shakes his head sadly when he speaks of M'sieur, saying that since the war he is a different man. That he has become as a stranger."

"The war, and his injury, " I murmured sickly.

"Yes, of course. We women understand these things. But men don't. Henri cannot understand the change in him. Or his coldness now. It is a pity though that the artist did not ask my husband for advice. For I heard him say afterward that there was only one place that they would find suitable for a camp. It is a waterfall high up there, with deep limestone caves near it. Only they had to be careful, because of the bottomless cavern. . . ."

A waterfall. Only part of my mind had listened to Gabrielle as she had talked about two strangers in a conversation that I hadn't understood. The two Israelis were the strangers. My mind saw the vultures circling up there. I was full of fear and sickness and confusion. The sickness was for myself but the fear suddenly for Etienne.

I became aware that I was walking back along the village street, with Madame Cloete staring after me in astonishment from her door, the wineglass still held in her plump hand. I waved and she waved back, but it was halfhearted, and I knew that I must have offended her by my precipitate departure. I had walked halfway to the gates before my mind started to clear. I had to see what was up there in the forest. I had to!

I left the road sharply and plunged in among the scattered trees that grew on the slope below the gates. I found myself running, glad that I wore sensible shoes with low heels. When I ran out of breath I slowed. On regaining it, I plunged on again as desperately.

115

I had forgotten the wolves in the forest. I had forgotten everything except that Etienne was in danger up there, and I must warn him. But first I had to find a way in over the great stone wall that loomed above me and seemed without end. The village and the chateau dropped behind out of sight, but the wall went on and on.

CHAPTER TEN

THE WALL DIPPED abruptly ahead, giving me hope, but rose again as steeply a few yards farther on. I stopped, staring ahead. I ran and knelt on wet ground peering at the base of the wall where rank weeds grew. The dampness was a seepage, the water moved downhill away from the wall. I tore at the long weeds. I felt the sting of nettles but barely noticed the way my hands burned and itched.

It was there, a small opening in the wall to allow the runoff from rain and storms to get away. A little water ran across the moss-covered stone coming from the same rank growth of weeds at the other side. But it was a way through—if I was slim enough.

My head went through, and in, and then my shoulders. The moss helped for it was slippery with damp, but I had to lie flat and kick my way through. Then I was stuck fast and could not move either way and my mind saw the water rising very slowly to drown me by slow inches.

Finally my hands caught the other side of the wall and it was easier. I wriggled and pulled myself out and lay panting on wet grass above marshy ground. It seemed to take me a long time to stop trembling, and when I did I was already staggering high above where I had crossed under the wall, as though some sense greater than reason or conscious thought carried me on desperately.

It was dark under the forest trees, and I remembered the wolves again. I sought some weapon as I trudged uphill in thinning air that had me gasping. I found the root of a tree that was short and solid and fitted my hand at the small end. It was not much of a weapon, but it gave me confidence. To reassure myself, I remembered that Grandfather had told me once that the wolves of the Châtaigneraie were afraid of humans, and would never attack by day.

I came to a small valley with a stream of running water, and fell on my knees there, bathing my hot face in water that felt like newly melted ice. I rested for a little while, trying to think above the pounding of my heart and my exhausted breathing, with the icy water dripping from me, and my clothes looking as though I'd fallen in a ploughed field on a wet day.

The rocks about me were of limestone. And this was a creek. Perhaps if I followed it on up the mountain I would find the waterfall I sought, as the Israelis must have found it before me, and the limestone caves in which Cloete thought they had camped.

But as I moved to get up, I heard a faint scuffing sound somewhere near. I groped for the piece of wood and gripped it, turning my head very slowly toward the sound. At first I saw nothing, for it was dark beneath the forest trees, then something moved slightly no more than thirty feet away in deep shadow beneath the low branches of a fir tree. It looked like a big dog with a rough gray-brown coat, but its eyes shone redly from the shadows where it stood watching me unblinkingly.

I cried out fiercely and jumped up, and all in the one movement threw the piece of wood at it. The wood fell short, but the beast turned away silently and ran off, and at the same time I saw two of its fellows run with it in shared fear.

I found myself laughing. At least one member of the Gérard family was truthful. Grandfather! The wolves *were* afraid of humans, and no more to be feared by day than the dogs they resembled if one did not show fear of them. I recovered my piece of wood and my courage. I climbed, following the stream. Once I saw a clear footprint, and knew that a man had made it, and because of its freshness concluded it must be Etienne.

I struggled on faster, resisting an impulse to call for him, and hearing somewhere distantly above me now the sound of falling water.

I came on it suddenly, bursting through a screen of undergrowth, and stifled a startled cry at a great flapping of wings and the slow rise of those cursed vultures all around me. Only the leader remained, that great bird that Gabrielle had pointed out to me, his beak and bald head soiled with the blood of the great strip of meat upon which he had been feasting, one claw gripping it firmly until he took a last disdainful peck and, holding a portion in his beak, flapped up heavily. I threw the root at him as he rose, and had the brief satisfaction of seeing the wood hit him

117

quite heavily so that he dropped the meat from his beak and fluttered frantically as though in fear of me.

The others had settled on the surrounding trees, but the leader fled higher, disappearing still in flight toward the mountaintop. As I stepped out onto crisp grass, one by one as though at an order the lesser vultures followed him. Pieces of meat that looked like veal were strewn about, some already starting to decay. I saw no bones, and the smell sickened me. I recovered my piece of wood and crossed the open space quickly to stare at the waterfall. It was not much of a fall, a thin stream of water as clear as crystal that fell about fifty feet from a narrow cleft in rock above it.

But this was the place, I was sure of that. Someone had made a small fire near the entrance to the dark mouth of a cave beside the fall.

I went that way nervously, gripping the wood. "Etienne," I called softly. "Etienne."

Nothing moved around me. No birds sang, for this was a place of carrion birds. I shivered and crept nearer to the small cave, seeing another beyond the waterfall on the other side of the stream that looked larger, deeper, and must hold the bottomless cavern of Violette Cloete's telling.

It was light in the small cave, and dry. I could see it would be a good camping place. It went in far back, becoming darker in there, but still dry and clean-looking.

But if anyone had camped in here they had left no traces that I could see, except perhaps . . .

I stopped abruptly, staring down at a dark stain on the cream-colored stone. I shivered, studying it doubtfully. It looked like blood. It took effort on my part to touch it with the tip of one finger gingerly, for it was far back in the cave where it was difficult to see clearly. It felt, I supposed, about the way blood long dried *might* feel. Rather like a coat of thin reddish-black paint that the stone had absorbed.

I came out hurriedly, and stared about. I raised my voice higher. *"Etienne!"*

I jumped as the cave caught the sound, and it echoed faintly behind me. But nothing moved, nobody answered. I shuddered as I glanced at one of those pieces of dirty meat, fouled by the vultures' feeding and the earth upon which it lay. But I told myself firmly that it was merely the meat of a pig or deer that my uncle or the others had shot up here to feed those accursed birds. And I remembered what Gabrielle had said about storing the meat in one of the caves. That could account for the blood, if

118

it was blood in there. But why were there no bones? Hadn't she talked about making cuts in the carcass, and . . .

I shuddered. This was no place to think about things like that, and already the sun was creeping down into the west. I wanted to be far from this place before dark. Very far.

I started to wade across the creek, walking on stones where I could, for it was not deep and the water was icy. But despite my care a shoe filled with water and squished as I moved. On the other side I emptied it and shook it out and felt better. I approached the second cave warily. It was much larger than the first. Quite light for the first few yards, then branching off into two tunnels, one to the left and one to the right, both seeming to have no end. I took the left branch and stopped quickly. I had chosen the branch that held the bottomless pit! It yawned just in front of me, unmistakable.

It sloped left, a descending tunnel, very steep, yet with stalactites hanging from the roof like icicles, and their counterparts thrusting up from the ground where the slope allowed them to grow and the slow drip had built them over the centuries.

I stared down appalled. Suppose I'd fallen in there, coming upon it suddenly? But I forced myself to smile. I had not been in any danger. The stalagmites thrusting up must have stopped me from the final fall into the darkness that lay just beyond the lip of the cavern below me. The stalagmites were thick enough and numerous enough to catch a human body.

I started to turn away, and stopped. Something *was* caught down there. Something small and dark caught between the bases of two of the stalagmites not far down. I peered down intently, feeling cold suddenly, for it had the shape of a boot with the sole toward me. I thought of Etienne with a rush of terrible anxiety. I started to reach for the first of those spearlike stalagmites, easing myself from it to the next, with my weight braced against it and my heart pounding wildly.

Bent forward, I stared down. It *was* a boot. I could see its shape clearly now. My fear prompted me to turn back, but anxiety drove me to reach carefully for the next stalagmite and cling to it, steadying myself before I could look again.

I bent forward, peering around the column of limestone, and saw it clearly. A boot from which a sock protruded, badly stained, and beyond the sock something . . . a pale and whitish something, that ended in . . .

119

I screamed shrilly in horror, and turned away, scrambling frantically to get out of there back to the clean sunlight. The caves below and around me caught the sound and threw it back at my ears in shrill and terrified sound. I fell, and hurt my knees but did not notice. I caught at the stalagmites desperately with bleeding fingers. I reached the top and started to run toward the light. I could not yet understand what I had seen, but there had been a foot in that boot, a human leg in the bloodstained sock, a leg that from the knee joint up to the hip had been stripped of flesh, leaving just the bare white bone.

I ran frantically toward the entrance and out into the sunlight. Slipping into deep holes but caring nothing for the water now, I crossed the stream and started across the grass past those horrible strips of meat. Only suddenly a figure barred my way, bursting from the leaves and undergrowth ahead. I screamed again, seeing Albert's face full of rage and his big hands reaching for me, and behind Albert, Gabrielle, holding a weapon in either hand.

I turned away, but was too slow, and my piece of wood lay forgotten in the great cave. His hands caught me easily and threw me down, and I felt his breath on my face and one of his knees pinning me while he gripped my arms and held me still.

"She came from the pit! Kill her!"

Across Albert's broad shoulder, Gabrielle's face stared at me, twisted by hate and fury.

"No," Albert said. His eyes stared at my face without expression, his brows drawn in slightly as though he were considering something. I found his expression more frightening than Gabrielle's fury.

"Kill her! Or move aside!" Gabrielle gritted. She put down one weapon; the other she held in her hands looked like some kind of sub-machine gun. Its short, ugly barrel moved over Albert's shoulder and pointed between my frightened eyes.

"No," Albert said again. He reached out his left hand almost casually and pushed the weapon aside and held it there.

"You fool!" Gabrielle spat like an angry cat. "What makes her different from the others? Kill her now, I say. *Kill her.*" She was trying with all her strength to bring the barrel back into line with my body, but Albert held it easily with his hand.

He shook it, and almost threw her off her feet, and momentarily, looking into her obsidian eyes over his shoulder I saw the impulse form there to kill him as well as me.

120

"Look out!" I screamed.

She released the weapon he held by the barrel and was leaping for the other. She had her hands on it when he sprang up like a great cat, turning the weapon he held on her.

Terror held me where I was, and weakness that made me tremble as I watched. Her eyes widened in shock as she whirled with the other weapon in her hands and saw him. She froze abruptly, half turned toward us.

"Put it down, woman," Albert said quietly. "Down."

Her black eyes flickered like a snake's as she sought an opening. She started to talk very softly. "What has come over you? Has she turned your head as she has his, with her pretty face and silly ways? I told you how it would be, didn't I? When she first came, I said to you—"

"Put it down, Gabrielle. Don't make me kill you."

"She is too dangerous to let live," Gabrielle said. But a tone of uncertainty was creeping into her voice. I saw to my amazement that she had started to cry, that large tears were running silently down her face. I remembered suddenly that Uncle Maurice had said she and Albert were once lovers. "Would you kill me? Gabrielle? If you want to play with her a little before you kill her, why should I care now? Take her, if you want. But kill her quickly then, and throw her down with the others."

Albert smiled at her. "And have you shoot me the moment I turned my back?" He shook his head. "I know you too well, Gabrielle. Put it down."

"No! I swear it! . . . Why are we quarreling?"

"Because you want to kill her, and we are at cross-purposes. I will count three. One . . . two . . ."

He meant to kill her. I could see it in the way he tensed over the weapon.

"Wait!" she cried. She moved, putting down the weapon. I could see her hands trembling. She turned away with her shoulders shaking and he walked over and scooped up the weapon that now appeared to me to be a twin to the one he held.

"She is nothing to me, as you are nothing to me now," he said grimly. He turned and looked down at me. "But she has things to tell us, and there is not much time to learn them. Kill her now and we learn nothing. How did she know the Israelis were here? She went straight to the cave. You saw her as well as I did. But there is something else. I followed her when she went to the village. There was another man there besides the artist. He looked more like a man from the Sûreté."

They were both looking down at me now. Gabrielle said in a bitter voice: "If this is true . . ."

"Tear a strip from her skirt and tie her hands. It will be dark soon now. We will take her down there and find out. You were very good at such things once. Let's see if you have lost your cunning."

She nodded and bent quickly. Her great hands caught the tough material of my skirt and tore it from me. She ripped off the hem and rolled me over brutally and put her knee into my back while she pulled my wrists together and tied them cruelly tight.

"Get up," she ordered. I tried, but could not, and she caught my arms and jerked me upright. "He will kill her," she said to Albert. "Would it not be better if we did it here and went into the mountains without him?"

"In the Mercedes we might reach Spain," Albert grunted. "Without him. If we are quick. On the Massif he would have no chance at all once they know we're there."

"My uncle will kill you for this," I muttered sickly.

"Her uncle!" Gabrielle exclaimed. She laughed, and held out her hand for one of the weapons.

Albert shook his head. "In the Mercedes perhaps," he said. "But not here. With luck we could be in Spain by morning."

"The three of us?" Gabrielle pushed me toward the bushes.

Following with the weapons, Albert said: "Without him. Or her. If they are here, it is because of Gebauer, not because of us. Do you think the Israelis would have come for us? We are better without him now. In time we will find someplace. Keep her moving."

The branches struck my face. Behind me Gabrielle drove me forward with blows. We were closer to the vineyards than I had expected. We burst unexpectedly from the forest and the first field lay ahead. In the west the sun was setting, and already there were deepening blue shadows among the mountains.

It was easier walking between the vines. But Gabrielle gripped my arm, her strong fingers biting deeply into my flesh.

She started talking to me softly. "How did you know about the Israelis, little one? Did your lover tell you? The man Albert spoke of just now? It is easy to talk now. Later it will not be. But you will talk. You will tell me whatever I want you to. You will see. A soldering iron will make you eager to answer whatever Gabrielle asks. I will tie you in a chair down there, and you can make as much noise as you like. Nobody will hear you. And I do not mind."

"What . . . do you want to know?"

Her fingers twisted my arm viciously and I almost fell. "How did you know about the Israelis?"

"I met them on the road the day I drove to Vaison. They asked me the way to the chateau. They . . ."

Her fingers gouged viciously. "Go on! Speak up so that Albert can hear. You met them on the road? You are lying of course, for what I am doing to you now is nothing. But go on."

"It is the truth. They showed me a photo. They asked me if I had seen the man in it."

"And you said?"

"I did not recognize him."

"But you know who he is, eh?"

"Yes. Franz . . . Gebauer."

"How did you know?"

I stayed silent, and she twisted too viciously so that I stumbled and fell, and Albert's deep voice said angrily: "Get her up. You are wasting time."

She dragged me up and fastened her fingers in the neck of my sweater and twisted that. I kicked back at her shins with my heavy shoes.

"If she . . . chokes me, Albert . . ." I managed to gasp, "how can I . . . walk?"

"Stop it," he said roughly. "You will have your chance later, woman. Keep her moving, and ask no questions now. You delay us."

She thrust me forward. "You will pay for that," she said, limping now. "I owe you plenty, girl. And I am not one to forget a debt, as you will discover!"

I couldn't think of a better expletive than Grandfather's, so I added vindictively: "Boche!"

She laughed. "I have heard that name before. Of course I am German. *And* Albert. *And* the man you thought your uncle, you stupid little fool. Not that knowing that is going to do you any good."

"What did you do . . . with Maurice Gérard, my uncle?" I demanded.

"Gebauer ordered his execution, of course. He was shot quietly, and disposed of. Gebauer had himself sent to a different prison as Maurice Gérard. The records showed Gérard's facial scarring, and that was enough. We added the amputation of an arm for gangrene while Gérard was held at the prison. Gebauer had lost his arm, and he was burned in a bunker. He had a good mind in those days,

123

before living in this place softened him. We all did. Albert took the name of another man we ordered shot, and I the name of a woman. With Maurice Gérard there to identify us as two of his people, there was no trouble. The occupying forces released us after checking. Nobody contradicted that, because those who knew were dead. How he laughed afterward, when he came back to Vaison with his decorations."

"You should have controlled him better," I muttered, remembering with horror. "He killed that woman at the mill at Vaison then. And the two girls. You fool! That is going to kill him now, and you with him. What do you think made them suspect you in the first place? They—"

She hit me with a swinging blow that knocked me down. I fell sprawling among the vines with my head singing, and she fell with me. Albert stumbled over us both, and cursed as he dropped one of the weapons, and got up to kick us both to our feet.

I was thrust forward again. But anger was overcoming my fear, and I'd have my say now if they killed me for it.

"They'll find the two Israelis up there," I cried. "They know where they are for the same reason I knew. Your friends the vultures gave you away. And they'll find you now, wherever you go. For they know you're here, and who you are. If not the French, then the Israelis. If you go to Spain or anywhere else they'll find you and drag you back for trial and execution—"

The collar of my sweater twisted, cutting off both voice and breath. This time Albert had me, half-carrying me with one big hand. Choking, with the world around me darkening, I felt myself dragged along. The chateau loomed above me. Gabrielle was opening the kitchen door, and the kitchen was in darkness. She stood aside and Albert dragged me in.

The lights came on suddenly and I saw the man I had known as Uncle Maurice standing in front of the open door. On the table near him was his heavy rifle.

"We found her coming from the cave," Albert said.

Gebauer—I had gotten used to his real name—smiled sardonically as he took in my disheveled appearance.

"So you went for a stroll in the forest, Denise. Perhaps you have been too thorough in researching our local history."

"She knows everything," Gabrielle snapped. "I told you it was dangerous bringing her here. The word may be out now."

"He was using me to escape to America," I shouted, wrenching myself away from Gabrielle. "He wanted to get

124

clear of you just as you two plan to leave him now."

Gebauer's hand moved toward the rifle. "She's lying, of course," he said, a shade too quickly for it to sound convincing. "But I'm afraid she must die."

Gabrielle swore as she rushed to grab the rifle and Albert raised his gun. All their attention was focused on Gebauer, so that they failed to see the shadows which suddenly appeared at the door.

"Drop it, Gerhardt!" Colonel Guiet's cold voice ordered. "Don't move, any of you! We've men outside, and you can't get away."

Albert whirled and the weapon in his hands came up and fired a burst of shots so close to my head that I felt the heat. Across the room Gebauer bolted, and screamed. And somebody else dived at me and threw me down and sprawled over me, someone heavy enough to drive most of the remaining senses from me. I think I screamed too, but I doubt that anyone heard, for almost in one movement Albert leaped out into the yard and there were fierce shouts and a lot of shots out there, and then a wild struggle of some sort, and yells and more shots. And two men who seemed to appear from nowhere leaped on Gabrielle as she swooped on the second weapon and tried to point it at me.

I lay still on the floor, because the man who was holding me so tightly was Etienne, and I could feel the scared thumping of his heart against mine, which was beating even faster and harder.

Hands reached to help me sit up then, hands that were not Etienne's, which had seemed content just to hold me where I was. And across the room I heard Colonel Guiet ask anxiously: "Is she hurt?"

"Her hands are tied," Etienne muttered. "But I don't think she is hurt." He shook me, and then hugged me. He demanded: "In God's name, what were you doing up there in the forest, you little fool?"

"Looking for you," I said. "I found out my uncle wasn't really my uncle, and I remembered something Gabrielle said about the waterfall and Madame Cloete said you'd gone up there looking for the Israelis, and—"

He hugged me so tightly then that I couldn't say any more at the time. But I heard Colonel Guiet say quite callously: "Well, at least Gebauer should live to be executed even though Gerhardt managed to put three bullets into him."

And someone else came in from outside and said in the same coldly impersonal tone: "I'm sorry, Colonel, but we

125

just killed Gerhardt up in the vineyard. He would have reached the forest otherwise."

And Colonel Guiet tut-tutted, and said: "Well, two out of three will have to do."

The two men who held Gabrielle were twisting her arms together so that another man could put handcuffs on her, and Gabrielle was giving far more than she was getting, with feet and teeth and what sounded like extremely bad language in German.

Colonel Guiet came over and looked at me, and shook his head. "Untie her hands, Captain. Mademoiselle, you have more courage than good sense, and you certainly made the arrests harder for us. What were you doing up there? I presume they caught you peeking in the cave where Captain Métier had already discovered the bodies of the two Israeli agents?"

"I was looking for Captain Métier," I muttered. "As I just told him. I thought they'd caught him up there. I saw the vultures, and . . ."

He nodded when I stopped and couldn't go on. "A pity you took such an unnecessary risk."

"I didn't think it unnecessary," I said angrily. "I happen to be in love with Captain Métier."

Etienne's arm tightened around me, and Colonel Guiet momentarily looked almost human. "Excuse me, then. So it is a case of love, eh? Well, well. I see. Then perhaps I should make Captain Métier responsible for bringing you to my office in Paris to clear up a few small matters?"

"An excellent idea, Colonel," Etienne agreed quickly.

"What small matters need clearing up?" I asked suspiciously.

"A matter of a parcel you gave to a messenger in Tocsin and the telephone call to a certain Monsieur Rouzier. The box contained stolen jewels, jewels taken from their victims by the Nazis during the war."

"Errands which she handled quite innocently on behalf of a man she thought her uncle, and without knowing anything about their contents, Colonel," Etienne said quickly.

Colonel Guiet gave him a slightly bitter look, but nodded. "But of course, Captain." He looked at me. "I don't suppose that Gebauer . . . I mean the man you thought your uncle, gave you any small item of jewelry? As a gift perhaps?"

Mentally, I watched my rubies vanishing. I said with a tinge of bitterness: "Yes, he did. A necklace." I put my fingers up and touched my throat, remembering. I looked past Colonel Guiet at the man on the floor. They had torn open his shirt and were putting dressings on his wounds.

His eyes were closed, and he seemed asleep, except that he was breathing hard through his open mouth. His scarred face, maskless, looked contorted and horrible. I shivered, and said: "I'll get them for you, Colonel."

"There is no need, Mademoiselle," he said. "I already have them." He brought the case out of his pocket and opened it. "This is the necklace?"

The rubies gleamed in the light as he moved them, and I could almost feel them about my throat again. I nodded silently.

"You note, of course, Colonel," Etienne said, "that Mademoiselle freely admitted receiving the gift? And that she also offered to find and bring it down to you?"

"I note that," the Colonel said, frowning sourly at Etienne.

Etienne smiled and said pleasantly: "Mademoiselle has been completely honest with us, Colonel, at all times."

"Oh quite," the Colonel agreed.

"And there is a possibility that the rubies were purchased by Gebauer and not stolen at all, and therefore the gift itself was quite legitimately made. The matter will need some deep inquiry, I think."

"Which you, of course, are prepared to make, Captain?"

"But certainly, my Colonel," Etienne said, giving my hand a secret squeeze. "No doubt also it will be difficult to decide what is the stolen property of Gebauer, and what the property of M'sieur Gérard and his heir."

"Ha!" the Colonel snorted. "Well, we'll see. In the meantime, Métier, get the girl out of this morgue and take her down to the village. Or better still to Aurillac, since your people live there. Oh, and ask Duval for the plates, since the photos helped make the identification possible."

"A matter also in which Mademoiselle helped us greatly, since she persuaded him to go there," Etienne was pressing the point. "As she helped me decoy Gebauer to the truck so that Pierre Bourget could attempt an identification, which unfortunately proved impossible because of Gebauer's scarred face."

I said then: "There is one other thing, Colonel. I gave a message to M'sieur Rouzier to the effect that my . . . that Gebauer would make one last consignment, a large one. Rouzier asked me if someone else might continue to send the consignments, because he thought there must be still a lot more to come."

He nodded and thanked me, and Etienne helped me upstairs and helped with my packing. It was quite dark when we left for Aurillac, driving the Mercedes.

We stopped several times on the way, because Etienne wanted to kiss me and the road was narrow. And we argued whether we wanted to bring up our children in France or America, and in the end New Orleans won because it is neither quite one nor the other and I knew secretly that Etienne would love New Orleans. As I knew my grandfather had, despite his protestations.

These were the important things we spoke of, though we talked of inconsequential things also. Like the way we intended to shoot the vultures if by some quirk of fate the French courts gave us the chateau.